If You Stay

If You Stay

The Beautifully Broken Series
(Book One)

COURTNEY COLE

FOREVER

NEW YORK   BOSTON

Copyright © 2013 by Courtney Cole
Cover design by Sarah Hansen
Excerpt from *If You Leave* copyright © 2013 by Courtney Cole

Forever
Hachette Book Group
237 Park Avenue, New York, NY 10017
www.hachettebookgroup.com
www.twitter.com/foreverromance

Printed in the United States of America

First print on demand edition: April 2013

Forever is an imprint of Grand Central Publishing.
The Forever name and logo are trademarks of Hachette Book Group, Inc.

The publisher is not responsible for websites (or their content) that are not owned by the publisher.

The Hachette Speakers Bureau provides a wide range of authors for speaking events. To find out more, go to www.hachettespeakersbureau.com or call (866) 376-6591.

ISBN 978-1-4555-7828-3

To anyone who has ever found comfort in oblivion.

Acknowledgments

I always have so many people to thank, and not nearly enough space to do it. But I'll try.

I'm not going to name the person who inspired Pax, because he wouldn't want me to. But I *am* going to thank him. I want to thank him for being strong and for doing what is best for him and for recognizing it himself. I will love him forever.

M. Leighton, thank you for always being there for me, no matter the time or place. You are truly the best friend a girl could ever have and I am so very thankful for you. I love you.

Autumn from Autumn Review. I love you, I love you. Thank you for talking me down from ledges and speaking rationally to me when I am practically having panic attacks. Thank you for being such a good ear and such a good friend. Your input and advice is always spot-on. I'm lucky to have you.

Fisher Amelie. I love you. You have had one rough year, but you have still managed to come out on the other side as the same gentle spirit that you always were. I admire that about you. I am thankful that you are who you are and that you are in my life.

Kelly Simmon! You are awesomely amazing. I am blessed to have found you and blessed that you wanted to take me on. Best. Publicist. Ever.

My grandparents are no longer here, but I'd still like to thank them. They are responsible, in large part, for the person that I am today. They led by example—and what an example it was.

My kids. Thank you for being you. For making me laugh and cry and showing me what the purest love actually is. I will love you forever and ever and ever.

My husband. I don't even know what to say. You are truly my better half. You support me, let me cry on you, make me laugh. I would be lost without you. If only you would learn to cook, you would be perfect. Haha. Seriously, I love you more than I can say and am more thankful for you than words can express. *Love never fails.* We've proven that a hundred times already and I can't wait to prove it a hundred more with you.

Thank you to everyone at Hachette. Thank you for bringing me on board and for picking IF YOU STAY out of the masses. I can't even describe how exciting it has been.

And...My readers!!! Thank you so, so much for reading my work. Thank you for your emails, your Facebook posts, your tweets. I am so grateful for you. It is because of you that I do what I do.

If You Stay

Chapter 1

Pax."

I can't be sure that the girl said my name. Her voice is muffled and unintelligible and hard to understand, mostly because my dick is in her mouth.

Slumping against the black leather seat of my car, I push the girl's head down further, wordlessly urging her to bury more of me in her throat.

"Don't talk," I tell her. "Just suck."

I close my eyes and listen. I can hear the spit pooling in her mouth and sliding out the corners. Her cheek makes a soft sound as it grazes my open zipper. She moans periodically, although I don't understand it. She's not getting anything out of this. My hand is on her head, pushing, pushing. Guiding her movements and her speed. I grip the hair at the base of her neck, winding it in my fingers; pulling it, releasing it, then pulling it again.

She moans again.

I still don't know why.

I still don't care.

I'm high as fuck.

And I don't know her name.

Everything is a fog, except this moment. I tune out the crashing sounds of Lake Michigan to our right, and the sounds of the cars on the highway a few miles away. I block out the glowing lights from town. I tune out the roaring quiet and the occasional thought that someone might happen by and see us. No one is out here on the beach, not at 11:00 pm. Not that I would care anyway.

Right now, all I'm focused on is this blow job.

I already know that I'm not ready to come, but I don't tell her because I don't want her to stop yet, either. I let her go for a few minutes more before I push her away.

"Take a break," I tell her as I settle back into my seat.

I don't bother to put myself away, I just sigh loud and long as I relax in the breeze. The girl turns her attention to the visor mirror, trying to straighten her mess of a face.

"Wait," I instruct. "Hold on for a minute."

She looks at me in confusion, her lipstick smeared. I smile.

"I know you want some of this," I tell her, grabbing a little bottle from my jacket pocket. I dump a few coke pebbles onto a little mirror on my console and crush them with a razor, dragging the powder into two straight lines.

I offer her the little straw and now she's the one smiling with her distorted clown mouth.

She snorts at her line, coughs, then snorts it again.

Settling back into her seat, she tilts her face to the car roof as she lets the drug take effect. Her eyes are empty as she thrusts the straw at me and I hesitate for only a second.

I've hit it hard today and I've done more than I usually do.

Of everything.

But for some reason, the need to disappear into the black is strong today, stronger than usual. And it's on days like this that I hit the hard stuff. I grab the straw and do my line, breathing in the powder that never fails to take me away. Even when I can count on nothing else, I can always count on this.

The familiar burn immediately numbs my throat. The emptiness spreads throughout the rest of my body, dulling my senses, speeding up my heart. I can feel the blood pulsing through it, hard and pounding, carrying oxygen to my numb fingers.

I fucking love this shit.

I love the way it dulls everything but my attention. I love how it heightens my awareness while still turning everything else black and numb.

This is where I am comfortable. Drifting here into this nothingness, this obscurity.

Coke makes it easy to exist in the emptiness.

I run my fingers through the traces of the remaining powder and slide it along the skin of my erection before grabbing the girl by the back of the neck. I shove her head back down and she opens her mouth willingly. This is most definitely not against her will. She wants to be here.

Especially now that I have fed her habit.

Especially now that she can lick her habit from my dick. If she moans now I'll believe it because she's getting something out of it, too.

"Finish," I tell her. I stroke her back while she moves and I can't feel my fingers.

Her head bobs for a few more minutes and then without warning, I come in her mouth. Her eyes widen and she starts to pull away as my ejaculate seeps from the edges of her lips, but I hold her fast by the back of the neck until my dick stops throbbing.

"Swallow," I tell her politely.

Her blank eyes widen, but she swallows obediently.

I smile.

She gags, but she doesn't heave.

"Thank you," I say, still polite. And then I lean past her and shove open the passenger side door. It creaks as it swings wide, evidence that cars were still made from iron back in 1968. I pull out my wallet and hand her a dog-eared twenty.

"Get yourself something to eat," I tell her. "You're too skinny."

She's got the look that girls on nose candy get. The way-too-thin look. That's one downfall of the stuff. It's good for drifting away into oblivion, but it's hell on your appetite. If you don't make yourself eat, you'll waste away and start looking like shit.

This girl doesn't look like shit. Yet. She's not ugly. But she's not pretty either. She mostly looks hardened. Mousy brown hair, pale blue eyes. Bland, stick-thin body. I can take her or leave her.

And I'm leaving her.

She glares at me as she wipes her mouth.

"My car is in town. Aren't you at least going to take me back to it?"

I look at her and note how there are three of her that blur into one, then back into three, before I shake the blurriness from my head and try to focus again.

Nope. Still three of her.

"Can't," I tell her, dropping my head heavily against the headrest. "I'm too fucked up to drive. It's not that far, anyway. It's not my fault that you wore five-inch stripper shoes. Just take them off. It'll make it easier to walk."

"You're a fucking asshole, Pax Tate," she spits angrily. "You know that?"

She grabs her purse from the floor and slams my car door as hard as she can. My car, Danger, shakes from her efforts.

Yes, I named my car. A 1968 Dodge Charger in pristine condition deserves a name.

And no, I don't care that this coked up little bitch thinks I'm an asshole. I *am* an asshole. I'm not going to deny it.

As if to prove that point, I can't even think of her name right now even though it only took me one second to recall the name of my car. I might remember the girl's in the morning or I might not. That doesn't matter to me at this point. She'll come back. She always does.

I've got what she wants.

I strip off my jacket and lay it on the passenger seat, zipping my pants back up as I watch her stomp away. Then I open my own door, dangling one black boot over the doorsill, letting the cool breeze rustle over my flushed, overheated body.

The landscape up and down the coast is jagged and rolling and wild. It is so vast that it makes me feel small. The night is inky black and there are barely any stars. It's the kind of night where a guy can just disappear into the dark. My kind of night.

I rest my head against the seat and allow the car to spin around me. It feels as though the seat is the anchor that is holding me to the ground. Without it, I might drift off into space and no one will ever see me again.

It's not a bad notion.

But the car is spinning too fast. Even in this state, I know it's too fast. I'm not going to worry about it, though. I simply pull out my vial and take something to slow things down. My vial is like a magician's hat. It's got a little bit of everything in it. Everything I need; fast or slow, white or blue, capsule, pill or rock. I've got it.

I wash the pill down with a gulp of whiskey. I don't even feel the burn as it slides down my throat. I consider it for a minute, the speed that things are turning and blurring around me. I decide I should take another pill, maybe even two. I put them in my mouth and take another slog of Jack before I toss the bottle onto the passenger side floor. I realize that I don't know if I put the cap back on or not.

Then I realize that I don't care.

The drug-induced fog blurs my vision and all of the blacks and grays swirl together and I close my eyes against it. I still feel like I'm moving, like the car is spinning round and round.

The night swallows me and I am propelled into the darkness, far above the clouds and into the night sky, sailing through the stars, past the moon. Reaching out, I touch it with a finger.

I laugh.

Or I think I laugh.

It's hard to say at this point. I don't know what's real or not real. And that's just the way I like it.

Chapter 2

Mila

I love the night.

I love everything about it.

I love how the blackness hides things that I might not want to see, yet at the same time exposes things that I wouldn't see in the light of day. I love the stars and the moon and the velvety wetness against my skin. I love how Lake Michigan turns black in the dark and shimmers like shattered onyx glass in the moonlight.

It always feels a little bit dangerous. Maybe that's why I like it, too.

I grip my camera as I step over the soft, damp sand of the beach. The breeze is always cool here, but it's just because the air is cold as it blows in from the lake. The water is always frigid, summer or winter, like God dumped a big glass of ice water into it. I wrap my sweater more tightly around me before I look through the lens again.

The moon is full tonight and it hangs just at the edge of the horizon, right where the water meets the sky. It's got a reddish tint to it, something that we don't get to see very often. The sailors call it a Blood Moon and I can see why. It's ethereal and beautiful; haunting, actually. It's why I'm here tonight.

I start snapping pictures; kneeling, standing, then kneeling again.

When a large wisp of fog floats partially in front of the moon, I gasp. I've never seen a more perfect picture. It will make an amazing painting. And the framed print will look good, too. Either way works for me since I've got customers for both.

I take at least a hundred pictures before I'm finally satisfied with the light, the luminosity and the angle. As I tuck my camera into its bag, I take a huge breath of the fresh, crisp lake air and enjoy my walk back along the beach. I love the way my bare feet sink into the thick silvery sand and I take care not to trip over random pieces of jagged driftwood.

It's a good night to let my thoughts drift. The air is so still and the silence is enormous. Even the seagulls have gone to sleep, so there is no one here to bother me. Complete and perfect solitude.

As the breeze blows my hair away from my face, I absently think of my to-do list in my studio and what I need to order tomorrow when I re-stock my supplies. I also wonder if I remembered to lock my house, although it won't be a huge issue if I didn't.

In a larger city, I'd have to be more careful about that, and definitely more careful about walking alone at night. But here in Angel Bay, I'm as safe as I'm going to get. We have a crime rate here that belongs in a 1950's Mayberry kind of town. The most crime we see is jaywalking during peak tourist season.

As I climb over a dune and into the parking lot where I left my car, I'm surprised to find a black, glistening muscle car facing the lake. It hadn't been here when I arrived earlier.

I sigh. My solitude has been interrupted. But honestly, it doesn't matter. I'm leaving anyway.

Slipping my shoes back on, I pad across the pavement toward my car, but as I do, I notice that the other car's door is standing wide open. I can hear the dinging sound from here. Apparently, the keys are still in the ignition.

That's strange and I pause, staring at the lonely car.

I'm uncertain, because it's dark and I'm alone. But the insistent buzzing ding of the open car door pulls me to it. I can only hope that the owner isn't a mass murderer. I curl my fingers around the cell phone in my pocket, as if it could actually shield me from danger. Regardless of the ridiculousness of that thought, I keep the phone planted firmly in my palm.

As I draw closer, I see a black battered boot dangling through the doorsill of the car. It isn't moving.

Normally, I wouldn't think anything of it. I'd think that the person attached to the black boot was just asleep. But something seems wrong here. Something tangibly ominous seems to hang about like a cloud. Not many people could sleep with that annoying buzz coming from the open door.

I creep up on the car and gaze inside, covering my mouth with my hand as I do. There is an overpowering stench of vomit and I immediately see the reason. The guy in the driver's seat has passed out in a large pool of orangey-red puke. His mouth is slack, hanging open, and sticky tendrils of vomit stretch from his chin to his chest. I shudder. It's definitely not this guy's finest hour.

He's very, very still, but I know he's breathing because he's making strange gurgling noises. The tiny snorts vibrate through the cartilage of his nose, muffled by the vomit bubbling around his mouth.

That can't be good.

I gag from the smell and shake his shoulder. His head lolls loosely around and hangs to his chest. I shake him again, but he doesn't come to, his head just jerks limply from side to side, like a doll with a broken neck.

Holy crap.

I feel more panicky by the minute, my heart thrumming like a hummingbird trapped inside my ribcage. I'm not sure what to do. He could've just passed out from drinking too much. In fact, I see a bottle of whiskey on the floorboard that could attest to that. But there's something wrong. Something that I can't put my finger on, but my gut is screaming at me now.

So I do the first thing that I think of.

I pull out my phone and call 9-1-1.

They answer on the second ring and ask what my emergency is. I stare at the young guy.

"I'm not sure," I say uncertainly. "But my name is Mila Hill and I'm down on Goose Beach in the parking lot. There's a guy here, passed out in his car. I can't wake him up. I think something's wrong with him."

"Is he breathing?" the woman on the phone asks calmly. I check again, then tell her yes.

"That's good," she tells me. "Do you feel comfortable waiting there until help arrives?"

"Yes," I tell her. "I'll wait with him."

Knowing that help is on the way calms me down.

I move a couple steps away and watch the unconscious man.

He still isn't moving, except for the slow, ragged rise and fall of his chest. I swallow hard as I glance over the rest of him. He's got tattoos on his toned bicep and a jagged scar in the shape of an

X at the base of his thumb. I know this, because his arm is now dangling outside of the car. Vomit runs down his forearm and drips onto the pavement. I cringe and move back to him, lifting his hand and placing it on his stomach.

His stomach is hard and flat. And covered in vomit. If he weren't lying in that vomit, he'd be handsome. That much is certain, even in the dark. He looks to be in his mid to late twenties. He's wearing black jeans, a black t-shirt and has brownish-blonde hair. He's got day old stubble and I find myself really wishing that he'd open his eyes.

"Wake up," I tell him. I don't know him, but I definitely want him to be okay. I've seen friends pass out from drinking before. This isn't that. This is far worse. The strange gurgling coming from his nose is proof of that.

I glance at his car again. I've seen it around town, but I don't know him. I've never bumped into him before...until now. And this isn't a great first impression.

I am trying to wake him again when I hear a woman's angry voice.

"Pax, you fucking asshole. I'm not walking into town, so you're going to take me. I fucking mean it."

I startle, then straighten up to come face-to-face with the owner of the less-than-pleasant words.

She's as startled as I am.

I've seen her before. She's a rough-around-the-edges woman who hangs out all day in a bar on Main Street. Since my shop is only a few blocks away, I've seen her walking around. Right now, she's wearing a tight-tight mini skirt and a shirt that is so low cut, I can practically see her navel. She's covered in old, faded tattoos and her make-up is smeared. Classy.

"Who the fuck are you?" she demands as she stomps up to the

car. Her brown hair is tousled and tangled. She looks harsh. And then she starts screaming when she sees the guy in the car.

"Pax!" she screams, as she rushes to him. "Oh my god. Wake up. Wake up! I shouldn't have left you. Holy fuck, holy fuck."

"What's wrong with him?" I ask her quickly. "I called 9-1-1 because I couldn't wake him."

She yanks her face away from his.

"You called the police?" she snaps. "Why would you do that?"

I'm incredulous. Clearly, her way of thinking is much different than my own. Her priorities are definitely in a different place.

"Because he needs help," I tell her. "Obviously. An ambulance is on the way."

She starts to glare at me again, but the guy in the car, Pax, starts gurgling again. And then he abruptly stops. He is still, his chin buried in his chest which is no longer moving.

The woman and I look at each other.

"He's not breathing!" she cries as she grabs him. "Pax! Wake up!!"

She's shaking him so hard now that his teeth are rattling. I grab her arm.

"That's not going to help," I tell her urgently.

Holy crap. She's right though, he's not breathing. My mind is buzzing as I try to figure out what to do and before I can decide on a plan of action, my body is moving with a mind of its own.

I shove the woman out of the way and pull on Pax's arm with all of my might. He only comes partway out of the car, dangling half in, half out. He slumps over, his head almost grazing the concrete. His legs are firmly tangled beneath the steering wheel and we are now both covered in his smelly vomit.

"Help me," I bark at the motionless woman. She snaps out of her hysteria and between the two of us, we drag the man out of the car and onto the sandy pavement. I kneel beside him and feel for a heartbeat. He's got one, but it's faint and thready. And since he's not breathing, I know it won't last long.

Shit.

I try to remember the details of CPR, fail and then just do the best I can. I pinch his nose closed, tilt his head back and breathe into his mouth. He tastes like ashes, Jack Daniels and vomit. I fight the urge to gag, fail, and dry heave to the side. Then I square my shoulders and give him a couple more breaths.

I gag again as I pause and listen at his chest.

Nothing.

He's still not breathing.

"Do something," the woman hisses.

I tune her out and breathe into Pax's mouth again.

And again.

And again.

Nothing.

What the hell do I do now? I am past being repulsed at the taste in his mouth. I'm only focused on trying to keep his lungs filled with oxygen, trying to make him take his own breaths. But it's not working.

He's not breathing.

I am frantic and on the verge of hysteria myself, when I give him two last futile breaths. And then I have to lunge out of the way as he chokes, then coughs, then vomits in a geyser-like fountain of orange puke.

I quickly shove him onto his side so he doesn't choke on it.

By this point, he and I are both completely covered in his vomit. It isn't pleasant, but at least he's breathing now. It's ragged and slow, but he's breathing. His eyes are still closed, but I can see them moving now, rapidly, behind his eyelids.

And then he starts convulsing.

Oh my God. I don't know what to do.

"What do we do?" I cry out to the girl behind me.

I don't even look at her, I am just focused on the orange foam coming from this guy's mouth. It billows out and upward, soaking into his nostrils and smearing everywhere as he flails. Bits of it fly off of him in orange flecks and land on my sweater.

I grab his arm and hold it down. He's strong, even in this state and it takes all of my weight to keep him immobile. I practically lie across his chest, his arm folded beneath me. After a moment, his convulsions stop and he's limp. But he's still breathing. I can hear the rattle of his chest. It seems like every breath he takes is an effort.

I am on the verge of crying, simply from not knowing what to do, when I see red and blue lights flashing against his car.

I exhale a breath of relief. Help has arrived.

Thank God.

"Run over and bring them here," I tell the girl. I turn, only to find her gone.

What the hell?

I peer into the darkness and see her running away, up and over the nearest sand dune. Apparently, she doesn't want to be here when the authorities arrive.

Interesting.

It takes the paramedics only a minute or so to leap from their ambulance and begin administering help to the prone man in front of me.

I'm not sure what to do, so I shrink back to the periphery and limply wait. I watch as they shove a breathing tube down his throat. And then I watch as they do chest compressions, which can only mean one thing.

His heart stopped.

At that realization, mine feels like it stops as well.

I don't know why. I don't even know him. But being thrown into this intense situation makes me feel connected to him. It's a stupid notion, but I can't help feeling it. Even though the only thing I really know about him is his name.

Pax.

I can hear the sickening sound of his bones cracking and bending while the paramedics thrust hard against his chest, trying to force his heart into beating again. It makes me cringe and I look away, trying to tune it out. It's at this moment, while my eyes are squeezed shut, that a police officer approaches me and asks me some questions.

Do I know him?

What was I doing here?

How did I find him?

Was he alone?

DoyouknowhowlonghewashereDoyouknowwhathetookDoyouknowhowmuchhedrank?

The cop's monotone runs together and I answer as best as I can.

By the time he is done, the EMTs are loading Pax into the ambulance. They run to the front and jump in, their tires squealing as they lurch from the parking lot and onto the road leading to town. Their siren and lights are on.

That's got to be a good thing.

That means he is still alive.

Right?

I'm frozen in place and shaky as I stare at the car, as I watch the policeman search through it. He puts some items into plastic baggies and shakes his head.

"I don't know why I bother. His dad will get him off, just like he did last time."

The cop is muttering and I'm not sure if he's talking to me or to himself. So I ask.

He smiles grimly. "Either of us, I guess. The situation is just frustrating. Here's a kid who could have the world on a string, but he seems to be dead set on fucking himself up. Pardon my language, miss. But he needs to land himself in jail or rehab, in order to straighten himself out. But he comes from money and his father is some big shot attorney in Chicago, so he always gets a pass. One of these times, though, someone's gonna take him away in a body bag. He's just lucky that you found him in time tonight or today would have been the day."

Lucky.

I picture the orange foam that erupted from his mouth as Pax had convulsed on the rough pavement in front of me and I'm not so sure that I'd use that word. Whatever he is, *lucky* doesn't seem to be it.

I'm shaken now as I head to my car and drop onto the seat. I am covered in vomit and my mouth tastes like an ashtray from the seediest bar in the world. I grab a bottle of water and gulp at it, swishing it around inside my mouth and then spitting it out on the ground.

What the hell just happened? I had come here to get some shots of the beautiful, tranquil full moon and had ended up saving someone's life.

Unless he dies.

And in that case, then I guess I ended up doing nothing at all...except acquiring a horrible taste of someone else's vomit in my mouth and seeing images that I am sure will haunt my dreams for some time to come.

I take another shaky drink of water and turn the key in my ignition.

I hope he doesn't die.

I really do.

Chapter 3

Pax

I feel the light threatening to seep into my closed eyelids, so I squeeze them tighter. I'm not quite ready to wake up yet. *Fuck you, world. You can wait.*

Stubbornly refusing to open my eyes, I reach for my vial, which should be next to me on the nightstand along with a pack of smokes, a lighter and razor blade.

My fingers grope awkwardly, but the bed stand isn't where it should be.

Muttering under my breath, I decide that if my fucking housekeeper keeps moving shit, I'm going to fire her.

But as my consciousness returns, bit by bit, I realize that *I'm* not where I should be, either. The bed beneath me is hard and small and it crinkles like plastic when I move.

What the fuck?

I open my eyes to find that I'm in what seems to be a hospital room. I have an IV needle taped to my hand and I'm wearing a thin hospital gown. There is a blanket folded over my feet and there are plastic guardrails on the bed.

What.

The.

Fuck.

I gaze around quickly and find that I'm alone. The walls are bare and white, but for a dry-erase board that has *Your nurse today is Susan* scrawled across it and a clock that is ticking away the time. *Tick, tick, tick.* The noise is annoying. Its black hands tell me that it is 3:07.

How long have I been here? I see a plastic sack with my name written on it in black marker propped in a nearby chair and my boots sitting on the floor below it.

That's it.

I'm alone in a hospital room and I have no memory of how I got here.

It's disorienting.

I focus, trying to remain calm as I attempt to recall the last place I remember being.

A swirly, foggy memory emerges; a crashing sound, a moonlit night. Sand. Stars.

The beach. I was at the beach with that bar whore, Jill. She's always willing to do anything for a few snorts of coke. And since I was in the mood for a blow job, I called her up. I don't really remember much else, though.

I have a few hazy memories of Jill walking away. I think she was yelling.

And that's it.

And now I'm here.

Fffuuuuccccckkkk.

I groan. As I do, a nurse bustles through the door in faded blue scrubs, wearing a tired expression and a stethoscope wrapped around her neck. She must be Susan. And Susan's eyes glimmer for a moment when she sees me conscious.

"Mr. Tate," she says with interest. "You're awake."

"And you're a genius," I sigh tiredly, resting back against the pillows. I should feel ashamed of being a dick to her but I don't. I only feel tired and sore. I tug on my IV. The tape pulls at the hair on my arm. "Can you take this thing out? It stings."

Susan's tired eyes house amusement now, a notion that pisses me off.

"Do you find something funny?" I snap.

She shakes her head now, rolling her eyes.

"Nope. There's nothing funny about a twenty-four year old kid who tries to off himself. I find it interesting that you would complain about the sting of an IV that is feeding you, but you didn't care much about the sting in your nose when you overdosed."

I stare at her as harshly as I can, although it's hard to make an impact when I'm wearing a see-through hospital gown tied in the back.

"I didn't try to off myself," I growl. "Fuck that. If I wanted to kill myself, I would have done it a long time ago. Only pussies kill themselves. And I'm not a fucking pussy. Who are you to judge me? You don't know me."

I'm pissed off now, at her judgmental face and her misconceptions. Some bitch in worn out cotton scrubs making fifteen bucks an hour seriously thinks she can tell me what's what?

"Please don't swear at me, Mr. Tate," the bitchy nurse says pleasantly as she pokes at the button on my IV machine. "I'm only here to help. I'm not judging you. I've actually seen far worse. I'll call your doctor and tell him that you're awake. And in the meantime, your father left something for you."

She walks to the little particle-board dresser that sits across from the bed and picks up a folded piece of paper, bringing it to me. When she hands it to me and her dry fingers brush mine, her eyes change from annoyance to sympathy. Neither sentiment is welcome.

I grab the paper, crunching it in my hand.

"How long have I been here?" I ask.

I'm calmer now, more polite. She's right. She's here to help, or at least, she's paid to take care of me. It's probably to my benefit not to piss her off. The fate of my painkillers rests in her hands.

The nurse glances at the whiteboard. "Looks like four days."

"Four days?" I'm astounded. "I've been out of it for four days? What the hell?"

She stares at me, a stern expression settling over her plain features.

"You were in really bad shape, Mr. Tate. Very bad. You should consider yourself lucky. Your heart stopped twice and CPR was performed. You've been heavily sedated to allow your system to return to normal after all of the stresses of the overdose. You might notice some tracheal tenderness and some soreness around your ribcage. You had a breathing tube and several of your ribs were cracked during CPR efforts."

I stare at her dumbly.

"I died?"

She nods. "Apparently. But you're not dead now. You've been given a gift, Mr. Tate. You should think on that. I'm going to go call your doctor."

She turns on her heel and leaves, her white tennis shoes squeaking on the floor.

I'm completely stunned.

I fucking died.

And now that she has brought it to my attention, my ribs do hurt. Fucking A. I groan as pain shoots through my midsection.

And then I remember the crumpled up note in my hand. I look at it, at the bold, scrawling handwriting.

My father's handwriting.

Pax,

I almost couldn't help you this time. I called in my last favor. The next time you mess up, you'll be serving time.

Pull yourself together. If you need help, ask for it.

I think you should move to Chicago, so you can be nearer to me. I'll help you in any way that I can. Just because you have money, doesn't mean that you don't need emotional support. You can't do everything alone.

Think on it.

And stay out of trouble.

—Dad

I fight the urge to laugh because I know it would hurt my banged-up ribs. What the fuck ever. The idea that my dad thinks he can offer me emotional support is too hilarious to take seriously. I don't even think he has any emotions, not anymore. Not since mom died. She took the human side of Paul Tate with her.

I toss the note in the trashcan, but it bounces off the rim and lands on the floor. Shit.

I consider the notion of trying to get up and get it, but decide against it. I'm too sore and it's just not that important. House-keeping can pick it up later.

However, before I can think any more on it, the tip of a shoe appears next to it. My gaze flickers upward and finds a girl standing there. She's staring at me with clear, green eyes and she's holding a vase of flowers.

And she's fucking beautiful.

My gut immediately tightens in response. Holy shit.

She's small, with long dark hair draped over one shoulder and clear green eyes framed in thick black lashes. Her skin is bright and glowing. And why am I noticing her skin when she's got such a great rack? I fight to keep my eyes away from her full, perky tits and focused on her face.

She smiles a wide, white smile. A gorgeous kind of smile.

"Hi," she says softly. "I didn't know you'd be awake."

There is gentle familiarity in her voice, as if she knows me.

I'm confused. How fucked up had I been? Do I know this girl? My instincts say no. She's not the kind of girl I tend to hang around. I usually keep the needy ones around, the ones who are willing to do whatever I want, just because I can give them what they need.

This girl is not one of them. That much is blatantly apparent. She reeks of sunshine and wholesomeness. It's foreign to me. And fascinating.

I cock my head.

"I'm sorry. Do I know you?"

The beautiful girl blushes now, a faint pink tint along the delicate curve of her cheek. I immediately have the urge to run my fingers along the color, although I don't know why.

"No," she answers and she seems embarrassed. "I know that this is probably weird. But I'm the one who found you on the beach. I came the other day to make sure that you were okay. And then I wanted to bring you some flowers because your room seemed a little bare. I'm an artist, so I love color. And now I seem like a stalker, don't I?"

She's rambling. And it's cute as hell. I smile. And as I do, I feel like the Big Bad Wolf and she's little Red Riding Hood. *My, what big teeth I have.*

I smile wider, especially when I realize that she's even wearing a dark red shirt. And it's stretched tightly across her perfect rack.

"It's okay," I assure her. "I like stalkers."

Her head snaps up and her eyes meet mine, her gaze startled. I have to laugh again. Something about her seems so innocent. She'd truly be startled if she could hear my thoughts about her smoking hot body.

"Thank you for the flowers," I tell her, chuckling. "They're nice. You're right. The room can definitely use some color. You can set them over there if you'd like."

I motion toward my empty dresser. She moves in that direction, stopping to pick up the crumpled note from my father.

"Is this trash?" she asks innocently. I nod and she drops it in the wastebasket.

"Thanks," I tell her. "That's just where it belongs."

She looks puzzled, but she doesn't question my words. Instead, she places the flowers on the dresser, then sits in the chair next to me. And stares at me.

I stare back.

"What?" I ask her. "Why are you looking at me like that?"

She smiles. "I'm just happy to see your eyes open. I know this is going to sound stupid, but you were in a bad way on Goose Beach. And I haven't been able to get those images out of my head. So it's nice to see you wide awake and perfectly fine. I'll have something to replace those bad images with now."

Well, the idea that I'm perfectly fine is debatable. But I'm a little puzzled. She seems genuinely concerned, truly troubled. And she doesn't even know me, so why should she care?

So I ask her that.

And she's the one who's puzzled now.

"Why wouldn't I be?" she asks, and then she pulls on her full lip with her teeth. My gut clenches again as I catch a glimpse of her pink tongue. "Anyone would be concerned. And it was the first time that I'd ever tried CPR. I don't even know if I did it right. And it was the first time I'd ever seen someone overdose. I wasn't sure exactly what was wrong when I first found you. But you didn't seem like you were just drunk. I'm glad I called the ambulance."

I stare at her now.

"You called the ambulance?" Interesting. I wonder what the hell happened to Jill? She probably left me to die, the fucking whore. You get what you pay for, I guess. A few snorts of coke apparently don't buy much.

Beautiful Girl nods. "Yes, I did. The girl who you were with wasn't too happy about that. But I thought you needed it. And it turns out that you did."

Ah, so Jill *was* there.

"There was a girl with me?" I raise an eyebrow, probing to find out what happened with Jill.

Beautiful Girl shakes her head. "Not at first. She came while I was trying to decide what to do. She was mad at you for something- until she saw the condition you were in. And then she got hysterical. She left when the paramedics arrived."

That sounds about right.

"Well, thank you for calling help," I tell her slowly, eyeing her, taking her all in. "I'm Pax, by the way."

She smiles. "I know. Stalker, remember?"

I smile back. "Well, you have me at a disadvantage. Because I don't know *you*."

And that's a damn shame.

She holds out her hand and I take it. Hers is small and soft, almost fragile.

"My name is Mila Hill. It's very nice to meet you."

And it is.

I know I should tell her to run far, far from me, but of course I don't. She's like a ray of sunshine in this bleak hospital room and I soak her up. She's got good, healthy energy and I like the way it feels to talk with her.

She's like a breath of fresh air.

I may be the Big Bad Wolf, but even wolves need to breathe.

Chapter 4

Mila

I stare at the man in the bed, at this tattooed, hard man.

Pax Tate is beautifully sexy in a very masculine way. There's not an ounce of fat on him, he's muscled and strong. I can see that from here. He's got an air of strength about him, like nothing is too much for him to handle, although his recent overdose contradicts that notion. I feel like there's a certain sadness to him, probably because his eyes hint at things that I don't yet know about him, troubled things. His body is hard, his face is hard, his eyes are hard. Like stone.

And even still, I am pulled inexplicably to him.

I can't explain it. It's not logical.

Maybe it is the vulnerable look hiding in his glittering hazel eyes; the eyes that almost seem warm, but contain too much past hurt to quite allow that, so they appear hard instead. Maybe it is the devil-may-care attitude that exudes from him. Or perhaps it is the jaded look on his face, the expression that tells me that he is simply waiting for me to show that I am only here because I want something from him, which isn't true, and part of me wants to prove it.

I don't know why I'm here, actually.

I don't have a good reason.

I reach over and graze his hand with mine, right in the spot where his thumb forms a V with his index finger. There is jagged scar there in the shape of an X and I remember seeing it the other night.

"How did that happen?" I ask Pax curiously, as I finger it. It's clearly old, but it's apparent that it was a really deep cut. The scar hasn't faded much, but the edges have that fuzzy look that old scars get. He looks unconcerned as he shrugs.

"I don't know," he tells me casually. "I don't remember getting it. There are a lot of things in life that I don't remember. It's all part of it, I guess."

"All part of what?" I ask. I feel like he is baiting me, challenging me. But challenging me to what? It almost feels like I've been invited to play a game, but the rules aren't going to be explained.

"Part of what happens when you fuck your life away," he tells me, his voice harsh now, cold. I feel the urge to shiver from it, but I don't. Instead, I simply pull my hand away from his. His eyes meet mine. He notices my retreat.

"Why do you think you've fucked your life away?"

I have to make myself say the word. It feels so foreign in my mouth because it's not something that I normally say. Pax smirks, almost as if he knows that, as if it sounds so out of place on my lips that it is funny. I fight the urge to scowl.

"I don't think it," Pax answers tiredly. "I know it." He settles back into the pillow of his hospital bed, wincing slightly as he moves, his face set determinedly as he tries not to show the pain. I remember the crack that his ribs had made on the beach when the paramedics were saving him and I wince too. It has to hurt him.

"How many ribs are broken?" I ask. "I'll never forget the sound."

Pax looks at me now, startled. "You saw it?"

I nod. "I don't know why I stayed. I didn't know what to do, so I just stood there. I watched them work on you and load you into the ambulance. And then I stripped off my shirt and sweater before I drove home—because you puked all over me and I smelled like something died. I drove home in my bra."

Pax chuckles now, amused by this. As he laughs, his eyes do warm up; they flicker with something other than the jaded boredom that seems to normally live there. For some reason, that makes my stomach flutter. *Maybe there's warmth in there after all.* Or maybe he's just amused.

"It sounds like I owe you a sweater, then," he says, his lip twitching. I notice how he doesn't apologize for puking on me, but then, for some reason that doesn't surprise me. Pax Tate doesn't seem like someone who apologizes.

It's my turn to shrug.

"It doesn't matter. I've got more."

I pretend to be nonchalant, although in reality, that's the last thing I am. I'm a planner, which is contrary to my artistic side. I carefully plot things out, I plan my life. Although, I certainly didn't plan for this detour. I would never have expected that I'd be sitting in this hospital room with a stranger.

My thoughts must be showing on my face, because Pax notices. Apparently, he doesn't miss much.

"You don't like hospitals much, do you?" he asks gently.

The kind tone in his voice seems both foreign and familiar to him, as though he can easily change in a moment's notice from apathetic to genuine. The idea that I stirred him into feeling something strikes a chord deep down in me and I shake my head.

"No. My parents died a few years back. I'll never look at hospitals the same."

Pax is interested now and he cocks his head again, examining me. I can't help but notice his strong jaw and the way his brow furrows as he thinks. His natural good looks combined with his rebellious and dangerous attitude make him gut-wrenchingly sexy.

"They died at the same time?"

He asks this strange question, rather than offering his condolences as normal people do. I find his honest curiosity refreshing, so I nod.

"Yes. They died in a car crash. It was a foggy morning and they were driving on a little two-lane highway along the coast. A semi swerved into their lane and hit them. They died at the scene."

I don't know why I just told him that. I don't like to talk about it, but normally I don't have to. Our community is fairly small and anyone who lived here during that time knows about it.

"If they died at the scene, why do you have an aversion to hospitals?" Pax asks, his gaze thoughtful. And still genuinely interested.

I think back to that morning, how I was in a Humanities class in college. I was tired and blurry-eyed from lack of sleep the night before. The Dean himself had come to the classroom and pulled me into the hall. His face was twisted and awkward as he told me there had been an accident.

I don't know any specifics, he had said. *But you should go.*

So I did. I rushed to the hospital and when I arrived, I somehow knew as I walked through the doors that something was very, very wrong. No one would meet my eyes, not the doctors or nurses passing in the halls and not my old neighbor Matilda, who had somehow managed to beat me to the hospital.

She had wordlessly led me to an empty room; a chapel, I think, where she quietly told me that I wouldn't find my parents there, that they'd been taken to the morgue. She had been so matter of fact. And then she had caught me when I had collapsed to the floor. I still remember my fingers releasing the leather handle of my purse, and how it had hit the ground, spilling all of its contents onto the blue carpet. My lipstick had rolled to Matilda's feet and she had picked it up and handed it to me, her face white and solemn.

I gulp now.

And then I realize that I had just spoken all of this aloud.

Pax is staring at me intently, the expression on his handsome face unreadable as he processes the details of the most painful day of my life.

"I'm sorry," he says quietly. "That must have been horrible for you. I didn't mean to dredge up old memories."

His words are simple, his voice is not. He is a complex person, which seems to be all I can figure out. He's difficult to read, but his complicated and seemingly contradictory nature is intriguing. I feel my belly twinge as I stare back at him, as the gold in his eyes seems to swirl into green.

"It was a long time ago," I answer simply. "I've put it to bed."

"Have you?" he replies, his eyebrow raised. "You must be talented. Sometimes, the past doesn't want to sleep."

"That's true," I admit. "You're right. Sometimes, at the least opportune times, the past is an insomniac, alive and well."

He nods as if he understands and I wonder if he actually does. But he doesn't say anything more and I let it go.

In fact, I stand up, picking my purse up off of another hospital floor.

"I've taken up enough of your time," I tell him politely. "Thank you so much for humoring me and letting me see that you are doing okay. You're going to be just fine, Pax."

I don't know if I'm trying to convince him or me. He looks like he isn't sure either, but he smiles and holds out his hand. It is slender and strong and I take it. He shakes it, like we're businessmen.

"It was nice to meet you, Mila. Thank you for saving my life."

His voice is husky. I gulp and stare into his eyes and I can't tell if he really means it. Somehow, it seems that he doesn't really want saving.

But I smile anyway and I turn around and walk away. When I am partway down the hall, I turn and glance back into his room. He is still watching me, his eyes intent and fierce.

I swallow hard and turn back around, putting one foot in front of the other. Before I know it, I'm in my car. And I still don't know what the heck happened.

Chapter 5

Pax

A week in the hospital is one fucking week too long. That much is certain.

I slowly curl up out of my pillows and sit perched on the edge of my bed. I wince a bit as the movement disturbs a cracked rib and I try to take shallow breaths so that it doesn't hurt. The chest compressions from the paramedics did a number on my ribcage. I know they were trying to save my life, but shit. Did they have to crack four ribs?

Fuckers.

As I wait for the pain to settle and for my eyes to adjust to the light of day, I stare out the windows at the large lake that looms in front of me.

Lake Michigan is huge and vast and gray, and my loft-style home is perched above it on the edge of a bluff. Each room facing the lake has floor to ceiling windows so I have a good view no matter where I'm at. And I never worry about who might be walking on the beach below and might see me walking naked through my house. It's my private beach. If anyone is trespassing, they deserve to see my ball-sack.

I reach for the vial on my nightstand, wincing again.

Running my thumb around the metal rim of the lid, I absently let my mind wander as I try to clear the blur of sleep from my head. And then I give up on that and dump a little white pill into my hand, something to help me with that process because I'm too impatient to wait.

I'm slacking off the other stuff for a while, though. Regardless of what my father thinks, I don't need to take it. I'm not a fucking addict. And since it's not fun to get my stomach pumped and my ribs pummeled, I think I'll refrain from that particular activity for a while.

I knock the pill back with a swig of water from my nightstand, ignoring the fact that I wish it was beer. It's only 11:00 a.m. and I've decided that I'm not going to drink until 5:00 p.m. on any given day and I'm not going to have any of that "It's 5:00 somewhere" bullshit. I'm not a fucking pussy. Regardless of popular opinion, I can restrain myself when I want to.

I stumble from my bed, stretch as carefully as I can and make my way into the bathroom, stepping down into my shower.

My shower is one of my favorite things about this house. It's a huge tiled expanse, completely ensconced in stone and has four shower heads hitting me from all different directions. It was custom made to fit my tall body because I hate having to duck down to get clean. There's room for a party in here, if I wanted. And I have had many a party in this very shower with groups of willing women.

The memories of those bare, wet breasts and long thighs all crowded into this very shower makes me instantly hard and I slather soap in my palms before I take things into my own hands.

As I do, Mila's face appears in my head. It's unexpected and sudden, but I focus on it, on her soft voice and full tits as I take care of business. I close my eyes and pretend that my hand is hers. I picture her soft skin, sliding against mine. I picture slamming her against the wet shower wall and fucking her until she screams my name, all while her legs are wrapped around my waist.

It doesn't take long until I am finished.

With a satisfied sigh, I wash myself and grab a thick towel, drying off gently. And I'm still thinking about Mila Hill. What the fuck?

On the one hand, I suppose it's normal. She did save my life, after all. And for the life of me, I can't remember if I thanked her. Normally, I wouldn't give a shit, but there is something about her that makes me think about things that I normally wouldn't. Something soft and sweet, something real and genuine.

And now I'm acting like a fucking pussy.

I grab a pair of jeans and a t-shirt and pull them on.

I'm going to put this to rest right now. I'll simply ask around and find out where she works, tell her thank you and get on with my life. She definitely isn't the kind of person that I should invest time in. There's no way that my lifestyle or my personality would ever please her, not in the long run. And I'm not in the business of changing myself for anyone.

As I jam the key into my car, I think about her again, how the dark red shirt that she wore the other day was pulled so tautly across her perky, full boobs. It makes me wonder what they look like naked. Her nipples are probably pink and tilted toward the sky. My dick gets hard again.

Fuck.

Mila

"Why are you giving me such a hard time about this?" I demand of my sister.

Madison looks up from where she is sitting at a small table in my shop, browsing my latest black and white prints of the lake.

Her blonde hair is draped over her slender shoulder, her body curled up into the chair. I had gotten our mother's dark hair, while Maddy had inherited our father's. She is taller than me, model tall. Lanky, thin, gorgeous. I'm the small and dark one. The baby of the family. Only now, she and I are our only family. The Hill family, party of two.

Right now, Maddy looks surprised by my question.

"Why? Because you haven't mentioned a guy to me for, like, two years. Maybe even longer. That's why. It piques my interest."

I roll my eyes and wipe my hands on my smock, smearing the gray and black paint across my hips. I'm painting the full moon and landscape from the other night, and it seems like it should be portrayed by varying shades of black. A dark landscape, a dangerous night. I only hope that I can do it justice on the canvas.

"Of course I'm going to mention saving a guy's life," I tell her matter-of-factly. "Anyone would. It doesn't mean anything."

"Doesn't it?" Maddy arches one perfectly waxed eyebrow, her gaze glued to mine.

I shake my head.

"No. It doesn't. A guy overdosed. I gave him CPR and called an ambulance. The End."

Maddy smiles the kind of smile that means she's just getting started.

"Yes, but you've elaborated several times about how good-looking he is. How dangerous. How fascinating. Seems to me that that doesn't mean *The End*. And that both interests me and concerns me. This guy overdosed. *On drugs*. You found him convulsing in his car. That's not exactly what I would consider relationship material."

Maddy pauses here, her face strict and stern. I roll my eyes.

"Mila, I'm being serious," she insists, perturbed that I'm not paying enough attention. "I haven't personally met him, although I've seen him at the restaurant a few times. From what I've heard, he doesn't even work. He's a trust fund baby; a spoiled brat who doesn't have to be responsible. Apparently, he's a mess. A true bad boy. He would eat you for breakfast."

And this has gone far enough.

"Maddy, let it go," I sigh. "Seriously. It was just an interesting situation and I wanted to tell you about it. I won't make that same mistake again, trust me, not if it's going to earn me an unfounded lecture. You said yourself that you haven't even met him. Besides, I'm not considering him for relationship material. I'll probably never even see him again so you can turn off your mama bear instincts. Now, can you get back to telling me about the restaurant? What's wrong?"

Madison turns serious now and sets the portfolio to the side, unfolding her legs from beneath her. Her deep blue eyes are troubled and that gets my attention. She's been taking care of our parents' restaurant ever since they died and if she's concerned, then I should be too.

"What's wrong?" I ask her again. I'm nervous because Maddy never shows her concern. As the big sister of our relationship, she always hides it. Always.

She sighs, her voice thin and wispy, before she turns to me.

"I may have miscalculated the risks involved with doing those renovations."

I stare at her, confused. "You said the budget was fine, that it would be paid for by spring, and that it would practically pay for itself because it would increase business."

She nods, troubled. "I know that's what I said. And that's what I thought. But I didn't anticipate that business would drop so much this Fall. I don't see it picking up again through the winter, because it never does. It will be tourist season before we see enough business to really bring in enough revenue to start paying on that loan."

And now I'm startled. "What does this mean? Is The Hill in trouble?"

That thought sends me into a panic. Our parents started their little Italian restaurant when they got married and it has become a staple of Angel Bay. Situated directly on the beach, it is a popular place for tourists and locals alike in the summer.

After our parents died, my sister came back home to run it. Since she had just earned a business degree, it seemed logical. This arrangement allows me to run my little art shop, where I sell art supplies and my own paintings and prints. It's a win-win situation. As part-owner of The Hill, I get a share of the profits every month, while still getting to do my own thing.

But apparently, things aren't looking so good.

"Don't freak out," Madison instructs me calmly. "It's not doomsday or anything. We're just going to have to tighten our belts around the restaurant this winter. If you can pull a few shifts, that would really help. That way, we can cut wait-staff until summer."

I nod.

"Of course. Whatever I can do to help." Madison and I had

both waited tables for our parents in high school and when we came home for summers in college. It wasn't a big deal. I could do it with my eyes closed.

"We might also have to decrease our own pay for a while," Madison adds slowly, her face serious as she watches for my reaction. I don't hesitate, I just nod again.

"That's fine," I tell her. "I can survive on what I make here."

I glance around at my shop, at the paintings exhibited on the walls under the spotlights and the prints hanging by thin steel cables from the ceiling. There are chic sitting areas and modern lighting, there are easels and shelves of art supplies, all perfectly arranged. It's a trendy little shop, exactly what I had wanted, and it does alright in the winter. It does exceedingly well in the summer when tourists are here. I nod again.

"I'll be fine," I confirm. "Will you?"

She nods. "Yep, I'll be fine. Since I live rent-free, I'll be okay."

When she had agreed to run our parents' business, I had told her that she could live in their house. I have an apartment above my shop anyway, so it seemed like the right thing to do. Although, in the first months after mom and dad died, I spent a lot of time with her at their house anyway. It made it seem less real, like they might come walking in the door at any time.

Surprise! We were just away for a while. But we're back now.

Of course that never happened and eventually, I went back to my little apartment. I love my sister, but we don't live very well together. I'm a clean freak and she's a tornado waiting to happen.

"Thank you for being so calm about this," Maddy tells me, her mouth widening in an appreciative smile. "Like I said, it's not the end of the world. The Hill will be just fine and by summer, we'll see the return on our investment. But until then, consider your belt cinched."

I roll my eyes. "I don't wear belts. But okay. It's cinched up tight. No shopping sprees for me."

Madison nods, satisfied, and picks up my portfolio again.

"I like this one," she tells me. "I want to buy it."

I lean over her shoulder, staring at the gray cloudy sky and full moon. I can perfectly see the rippling sheen of the dark water shining in the black and white contrast. It's perfect. I smile.

"This one is gorgeous. And it's from the other night. I'll frame it up for you and you can pick it up next time you're here."

She grins at me. "Or you can drop it off during your shift tomorrow night at The Hill."

I stare at her. "What?"

"You said you wouldn't mind pitching in. You can do a shift tomorrow. That would help out a bunch. Then maybe we can go out and get a drink afterward. It's been far too long since we've blown the cobwebs off. We need to de-stress."

I don't have time to argue about the short notice or to remind my sister that I seldom drink, because the little bell above my door jingles, signaling a customer. I glare at Maddy quickly before pasting a smile on my face and turning around.

And then I freeze.

Pax Tate is strolling through my door in jeans that look like they were tailored just for him and with a shopping bag in his hand. His eyes glimmer mischievously as he smiles in greeting, a slow grin that curves his lips and crinkles the corners of his eyes. In the course of one day, I had forgotten exactly how devastatingly sexy he truly is.

My knees buckle.

Madison turns to stare at me in shock because what are the odds of Pax showing up here? Particularly after I just said that I would probably never see him again.

"Hey there, little red riding hood," Pax drawls, setting his bag on the counter in front of me. "I owe you a sweater."

Chapter 6

Pax

"Little Red Riding Hood?" Mila cocks an eyebrow at me, a whisper of a smile flitting across her full lips. I nod.

"For some reason, that's how I think of you," I admit to her. "You were strolling out on the beach, all alone, and came along just when I needed you."

My eyes are glued on her face. I know that there is someone else in the room, but to me, it's just me and Mila. She stares at me uncertainly.

"That would make you the Big Bad Wolf," she points out.

I laugh. "Now you're catching on," I tell her.

Her gaze remains locked with mine, her eyes clear and dark. My gut wrenches at the sight of her clean and clear expression. There is no drug induced haze in her eyes, a marked difference from my usual companions. It's both refreshing and terrifying. I'm not sure how to interact with her. But since I woke up this morning craving her company, I knew I had to seek it out.

So here I am.

"Is this for me?" Mila motions toward the shopping bag and

I nod. She delves into it with interest and then her face lights up when she sees all of the sweaters.

"They're all red," she laughs. "Every one of them."

I feel my lip twitch. "Of course they are. I have to keep you in character somehow, don't I? I didn't know what style you liked, so I bought you a bunch of them. I wanted you to be fully stocked the next time you come along and save me."

She visibly startles and stares at me, her movements frozen, her fingers dangling limply at her sides. I can't help but notice her slender hourglass figure. She's proportioned absolutely right to drive a man crazy. Full tits, tiny waist, lush hips. My groin tightens.

Fuck. I quickly think of dead puppies, nuns and cold pork. It seems to do the trick and my dick calms down. For now.

Mila is still staring at me, an intense, charged gaze.

"Do you need saving?" she asks quietly.

The air between us practically crackles with energy as we stare each other down. Her eyes are fathomless and deep, the kind of eyes that a man could fall into and lose himself. Permanently. I am flustered for a moment, trying to find the words to answer her when the other person in the room clears her throat.

An escape.

Thank you, God.

I turn gratefully to find another woman there, a pretty blonde woman that I've seen before, but I can't place where. She seems to be waiting for an introduction, but Mila isn't giving her one.

I hold my hand out.

"Hi," I tell her. "I'm Pax Tate."

She shakes my hand firmly. Perhaps a little too firmly.

"Madison Hill," she answers. "Mila's sister."

Oh. Then her stern handshake makes sense. Big sister is looking out for little sister, trying to protect Mila from the Big Bad Wolf. I can't really blame her.

Madison is staring at me now with blue eyes that are nothing like her sister's. In fact, nothing about her resembles Mila, except for maybe the shape of her nose. She's tall and blonde, while Mila is petite and dark. Mila is sexier, although for some reason, I'm guessing that she doesn't think so. She's quiet now, allowing her sister to do the talking. It is clear that she is used to her sister taking charge.

"So are you feeling better?"

Madison cocks an eyebrow, her question a not-so-subtle way of telling me that she knows that I OD'd the other night. That she thinks I'm a fuck-up who isn't good enough for her sister. I can see that in her icy blue eyes. The thing that she doesn't understand, though, is that I don't give a shit what she thinks. She doesn't know me and that is my biggest pet peeve- when people judge me without knowing what the fuck they're talking about.

"I am, thank you," I tell her. I smile pleasantly. I won't bow to her. She's crazy if she thinks that. "Your sister was a lifesaver."

Literally.

Madison doesn't know how to respond. I can see that she wants to say more, but there's really no way she can without seeming completely rude. She's disgruntled as she turns and kisses Mila on the cheek.

"I've got to get back to The Hill. I'll see you tomorrow, okay?" she looks pointedly at her sister, as if to silently warn her away from me. Then she glances at me.

"It was... nice to meet you."

And then she walks out, her stylish boots clicking on the tiled floor. The bells above the door jingle and then she's gone.

I look at Mila.

"I don't think your sister likes me much."

It's a statement, not a question. And even I can hear the ambivalence in my voice. It's obvious that I don't care.

Mila actually smiles.

"Well, I'm glad you're not all broken up about it."

I shrug. "I'm used to it."

Mila studies me quietly.

"Why are you really here?" she asks. "I didn't need for you to bring me a sweater. Or six." She chuckles. "Obviously I'll be all set in red sweaters for Christmas though. So thank you."

She pauses and looks at me and her face is very delicate. I hadn't noticed before how delicate she is. I can't imagine her trying to pull me out of a car. I must outweigh her by a hundred pounds.

"So?" She raises an eyebrow and I realize that I haven't answered her question. I don't exactly know what to say, so I decide to simply tell the truth. It's a novel concept for me.

"I couldn't remember if I thanked you for what you did," I tell her. "And I can't get you out of my head."

Her breath freezes on her lips. I can hear the startled little intake of breath and I'm not sure if that's a good thing or not. Did the truth scare her? Or has she been thinking about me too?

I look at her.

And for a moment, we are suspended in the moment. She drags her bottom lip into her teeth and her green eyes are liquid. She turns her face slightly, the curve of her cheek catching the sunlight from the window.

We are frozen.

And then she breaks the spell.

"You've been thinking about me?" she whispers. "Why?"

"I don't know," I tell her honestly. "Maybe I feel like I owe you."

"You don't," she answers quickly, her voice clear and sure. "You don't owe me anything. I'm glad I was there to help, but it was purely coincidence and anyone would have done the same. "

Her hands flutter around her nervously as she shuffles paper on the counter. I shake my head and smile.

"Not everyone would have done that," I tell her. "Not at all."

She's hesitant now, probably remembering that night and how I had apparently puked all over her. Finally, she smiles too.

"Okay, fine. Not everyone would have given you mouth to mouth. Maybe you do owe me. What are you going to do about it?"

Her sassy words seem to startle her as much as they startle me. She looks surprised as soon as they are out of her mouth. But she's nowhere near as surprised as I am. Is she flirting? With *me*?

My, what big teeth I have.

I once again feel like the wolf as I smile at her, as I turn on my charm. I have it, I just seldom care enough to use it. I'm baffled as to why I'm using it now. But I am. Because her sassiness was an invitation.

"Hmm," I answer, grinning my best flirtatious grin. "What would you like? A pint of blood?"

She laughs, nervous and musical, before she shakes her head. "No, I gave up drinking blood a long time ago. I developed an allergy."

Warmth floods through me before I can stop it. She has a sense of humor. I love that in a woman. I grin back.

"Okay, noted. No blood for you. Okay, I've got it. Clearly, you're an artist who likes to feature the lake in your work. I happen to have one of the best views in Angel Bay from my beach.

It's private and quiet and no one will bother you. You can use it whenever you'd like. How about that?"

I don't know why I just offered that. There is utter silence and I can feel my heart pound as I wait for her to respond. Why do I care what she says? But I wait, holding my breath, until she speaks.

"That's quite an offer," she finally says, her gaze still holding mine. We seem to be doing a lot of staring today. "Do you live alone? I'd hate to disturb anyone."

I'm more relieved by her answer than I care to admit. And then I'm amused.

She's fishing.

"You're very direct," I answer, my lip twitching again. "Most girls try to be more subtle when they ask if I have a girlfriend. But the answer is no. I'm not married. And I don't have a girlfriend. You won't be disturbing anyone."

She blushes now, a faint pink that spreads from her cheeks down to her chest. I like it. It's seems very soft, very feminine. Once again, I fight the urge to reach out and trace the delicate color with my thumb. What the fuck is wrong with me? I jam my hand into my pocket instead.

"Hmm," she answers. "It seems a shame to waste a view like that on one person. I bet sunrises are amazing there. Something like that should be shared."

I laugh now, loudly. She completely just walked into this and I'm pretty sure she didn't mean to.

"You don't have to beat around the bush about it, Mila. If you want to be there at sunrise, just pack an overnight bag when you come out."

No one could miss my suggestive tone.

And she doesn't.

She blushes again, her cheeks bright red.

"That's not what I meant," she mumbles. She's embarrassed and I like it.

"No?" I ask, my eyebrow still cocked. "Because I can certainly arrange a sleepover."

"I'm sure," she says wryly. "But no. Thank you for the invite, though." She's laughing now, her blush fading. "Truly, thank you for the offer of your beach. I can paint the lake from memory, but it's always nice to actually be there looking at it. A new view will be great. Artists are visual people."

The air seems to whoosh out of me for some reason and I don't even know why. Perhaps it is the thought of her sleeping over. Or maybe it is the sound of her voice. It seems to have a profound effect on me.

I step toward her and she looks uncertain, but she doesn't move away.

"Men are visual too," I tell her softly, my eyes frozen on hers. "So I understand. But there is something that bothers me, something that puts me at a disadvantage. And I really don't like feeling disadvantaged."

"What is it?" she asks, her eyes not leaving mine.

"You've seen me at my worst. Maybe you should see me at my best."

My words hang between us, heavy and charged, and I don't know what the fuck I am doing.

"When are you at your best?" she asks hesitantly. And I can see from the determined look on her face that she is trying hard not to feel intimidated. I'm impressed. She's like a kitten standing up to a lion.

"In bed."

My answer is simple. And her eyes shoot sparks in response.

"You're kind of arrogant, aren't you?" she demands, her hands on her slender, paint-spattered hips. "A simple *Thank you for saving my life* would suffice. I don't need for you to carry me off to your bed to show your gratitude."

I pause for a minute before I try to smooth her ruffled feathers.

"Calm down," I tell her quietly. "I'm sorry. It's a habit. I was just joking. Sometimes I have an inappropriate sense of humor. Thank you for the other night. I'm sorry I didn't say it before."

She purses her lips and then sighs.

"It's okay," she answers. "And you did say it in the hospital. You didn't need to come here and say it again. I have been wondering though…" and her voice trails off.

It's her turn to stare at me now and her gaze is contemplative. I stare back unflinching.

"What?" I prompt. "What have you been wondering?"

"Why did you do it?" she asks softly. "Why would you do that? It seems like you have a wonderful life."

I'm surprised again. This girl is very direct and doesn't hesitate to say what she's thinking. And she thinks that I purposely tried to kill myself. What the fuck?

On the one hand, her direct attitude is refreshing. I have a feeling that she doesn't play games. But on the other hand, it's annoying as hell. Because sometimes I like to get lost in games so that I don't have to provide any real answers.

But I have a feeling that Mila doesn't tolerate bullshit.

"It was an accident," I shrug. "I was being careless. It won't happen again."

She's still staring at me and I fight the urge to flinch. It's like she's looking inside of me, trying to pick me apart and examine me. I don't like it.

"Really?" she asks. She sounds doubtful, unsure. "I hope not.

If you're lying, I hope you get help. I might not be there next time to save you."

She turns on her heel and heads for the back room. And just like that, Mila the artist with the wholesome smile walks out of my life.

I'm surprised by how much I don't like the feeling.

Chapter 7

Mila

I'm dreaming again.

As I walk down the aisle of a local church with the morning sun slanting through the windows, I know that I'm dreaming. I know it because I've visited this place a thousand times since my parents died.

The dream is always the same.

Nothing changes.

Because of this, I know that I won't be able to wake up until it is finished.

I sigh and glance down.

I'm wearing the same black dress that I wore to their funeral. It is fitted, yet flowing; somber, yet feminine. It is what I wear each time I have this dream, an endless reminder of that horrible day.

With one black-slippered foot in front of the other, I pad down the aisle. I have no control of my feet. They are moving on their own accord. I couldn't stop if I wanted to. My right foot settles into the carpet, then the left. Then the right.

Propelling me forward.

Before I know it, I'm standing in front of two caskets, basking in sunlight, at the front of the church. One is white and lustrous, one is black and gleaming.

Good and evil.

When I first began having this dream, I thought this meant that one of my parents had been bad, deep down, and I'd never known about it. I put a lot of stock into dreams. I know that they mean significant things. So this thought, that one of my parents might be a troubled dark soul, weighed heavily upon me for quite a while. But then I realized that I had the meaning wrong.

Because even though this dream is set on the day of their funeral, my parents aren't here. They were cremated. They were never in caskets at the front of a church.

This dream isn't about them.

It's about the doubts that were formed in me the day they died, the doubts about the value of life itself. Life seems pointless if it is all for nothing; if everything ends in a fiery car crash, leaving only sadness behind.

It is one reason I grew so adamant about being an artist. I wanted to create beauty to cancel out the ugly. Yin and Yang. Dark and light. Good and evil.

My conscious self doesn't dwell on this stuff anymore. But my subconscious has issues. And it clearly hasn't settled them yet, thus the recurrence of this confusing dream. And to be honest, I haven't completely figured it out yet.

What I can see so far is that life consists of good and evil, black and white. And everything in between is a struggle for dominating the other. Life is a struggle.

And I hate that it all ends with nothingness. That one day, you simply aren't here anymore. No more smiles, no more tears, no more anything.

Poof.

Lights out.

I sigh and run my finger along the black casket. The one housing the evil. It's beautiful, even as it is bad. But as my arm moves, I catch sight of something different. Something that has never been here before.

I have a jagged scar on my hand, right where my index finger meets my thumb.

An X just like Pax's.

I startle and stare at it, noting how it is old and thick, just like his. In the sunlight, it seems sinister somehow, although I can't imagine why. It's just a scar. A hundred different things could have caused it.

But why is it on me?

I turn my hand in the light, rotating it in the sun, illuminating how it is as familiar on me as it is on him, as if I had worn it for years. As though it is comfortable on me, as though it is marking me for something.

X marks the spot.

I have no idea what it means. But something in my subconscious wants me to think on it, that much is true. There is something for me to ponder, something for me to solve. But I don't know what.

I shake my head and walk to the white casket. What I do know is that I have to finish this out so that I can wake up. So, I carefully open the lid of the good casket, exposing a million glistening sunbeams.

They shoot from the casket and merge with the light pouring in from the window. The rays are beaming, sparkling, radiant. I stand in them, bathing in the warmth and the goodness, absorbing the light.

And when I wake up, I know I will feel that energizing radiance for some time to come. It's my subconscious way of boosting myself up. It's how I coped with the grief after my parents died.

It is how I cope with any kind of uncertainty now.

And judging from the scar on my hand, I'm guessing that it is Pax's appearance in my life that has given my subconscious pause. He is what has triggered this dream once again.

While I can't figure much of this dream out, at least that fact can only mean one thing.

I'm more interested in Pax than I would like to admit.

With a sigh, I roll out of bed and pad down the hall in my pajamas. There's no way I'm going back to sleep now. Annoyed with myself for allowing a strange man inside my head, I bang everything around as I move around the kitchen. It doesn't help my annoyance, but it does serve to wake me up.

Thankfully, my day passes quickly. After four cups of strong coffee, I venture into the shop and visit with friendly customers. When business slows down, I work on a new painting…something bright and cheerful. Like always, a good piece of art lifts me out of my funk.

I am humming as I duck out of the shop to grab a sandwich for lunch. As I pause to lock the door, I notice Pax's black car parked on the street twenty yards from my shop. My head snaps up and I stare at it, my fingers frozen. He's not in it. I don't know if I am relieved or not.

"Looking for someone?"

Pax's voice is right behind me.

You've got to be kidding me. This is too coincidental. I slowly turn to find myself face to face with the very man who has invaded my thoughts. Pax smiles, a slow panty-dropping grin.

"Are you stalking me again, Miss Hill?" He cocks an eyebrow.

My heart hammers.

"What?" I choke out. "This is my shop."

Pax shrugs. "And that's my car. You were staring at it like you were hoping I would get out of it."

I'm guilty of that. I can't say a word in my defense. Instead, I stare at him like an idiot.

"What are you doing downtown?" I finally manage, changing the subject.

"I don't cook," he explains. "I'm making a food run. The bar down the street makes good burgers."

"Oh," I answer dumbly. "That's what I'm doing too."

He lifts his eyebrow again.

"Not the bar," I add quickly. "I'm going to the deli, next door to the bar."

Pax smiles again. "All by yourself? Haven't you heard that there are some bad things going on in Angel Bay? Just a while back, some dumbass overdosed on the beach. Apparently, they're letting all kinds of assholes in nowadays. It's probably not safe for you to walk alone."

I have to grin now, at his audacity.

"Oh, really? Wow. That does sound bad. Assholes are just running loose on our streets? I guess I'll never know now when I'm going to bump into one."

"How very true," he answers softly, his golden eyes frozen on mine. Sweet Jesus. The man has beautiful eyes. So bottomless and warm. Like hot caramel. I gulp.

"Is this when you take your lunch every day?" he finally asks, breaking the silent stare.

"If I go out," I answer. "Are you planning on stalking me again?"

We're still standing in the middle of the sidewalk, but Pax doesn't seem to care. Instead, he grins.

"Maybe," he answers, before holding his arm out like a gentleman.

"Since I'm here and you're here and we're both going in the same direction...I'll walk you today. I'll keep the wolves at bay."

I stare up at him as I slip my fingers into the crook of his leather covered elbow.

"I thought you were the baddest wolf of them all?"

He grins again, wickedly. It lights up his eyes with a gleam.

"That's probably true," he admits. "Are you afraid?"

"I should be," I tell him.

But I'm not.

He walks me to the deli's door and steps away from me. I feel the absence of his warmth immediately.

"Have a good day, Mila Hill," he tells me, his eyes flickering up and down the length of me. "Watch out for those wolves."

And he's gone. He disappears into the bar and I realize that I'm standing alone outside. I shake my head and sigh, going inside to order my sandwich. I have no idea what just happened, but Pax Tate is firmly in my head now. And I have the feeling he's not going anywhere. My stomach flutters and I realize that I like that thought.

Pax

I walk Mila to the deli all week.

I have no idea why.

All I know is...I'm drawn to her. She's everything that I'm not and it fascinates the hell out of me. And it fascinates me that she hasn't told me to leave her alone. She seems as entranced by the situation as I am.

So every day, at 11:00 a.m., I roll out of bed and shower, then make my way into town. I park in the same place and wait until she comes out.

Every day, she teases me about stalking her.

Every day, I tell her that she's the stalker, because she's choosing to walk past my car. Never mind the fact that I'm parking directly in front of her shop now. She giggles and flushes and looks into my eyes and I swear to god, I have no idea what I'm doing.

But I keep doing it.

And she seems to like it.

Yesterday, she mentioned that she was taking today off, just in case I needed to know for my 'stalking calendar.' I love a girl with a sense of humor. And I have to admit, today feels a bit empty because I know that I won't be seeing her. She gave me something to get up for, something to look forward to.

But not today.

I woke up early this morning from a restless sleep, roused by my own tossing and turning. I've always been a bit of an insomniac and actually, it's why I started taking pills in the first place, years ago. I realized way back then how easy it was, how very easy, to swallow a pill and slip into oblivion.

I had a therapist after my mom died, and even though I can't remember what he looked like, I can remember that he prescribed me sleeping pills. It helped keep the nightmares away.

All I remember now about the nightmares is that they were horrible. Bad enough that I used to sneak down and sleep in the doorway to my father's room. He would wake in the morning and find me sprawled on the floor. And I would wake not remembering my dreams.

My therapist told my father it was my mind's way of protecting itself from the emotional trauma. Well, my mind has done a good job. To this day, I don't remember the events surrounding my mother's death.

My phone buzzes on the nightstand. I pick it up to find a text from my father.

You need to come sign your papers.

Fuck. It's that time already?

I toss the phone back on the stand, where it skids across the mahogany, coming to rest against the wall. Every quarter, I have to sign papers for my trust fund, since it is fed by my mother's family business. I am technically the sole heir to her shares. It's a pain in the ass, but it's a necessary evil.

I am on the way to the shower when my doorbell rings and I pause. I'm not expecting anyone. It had better not be someone trying to sell me religion or they might find their teeth knocked into their throat.

Because fuck that.

Glancing through the window of my door, I see Jill the bar whore on my porch, nervously shifting her weight from left foot to right. I sigh. I'm really not in the mood for her, but I open the door anyway. I guess I feel sorry for the desperate look on her face. She pretty much always comes to me when she doesn't have money to buy from her dealer.

A blow job for a line of blow. It's our running deal. And the deal was her idea. Who am I to pass that up?

Jill smiles as the door opens, revealing grayish teeth. It's a sign that she has been using harder shit, like meth. I cringe. Even I won't touch that shit. It's the devil, or so I'm told. One time and even the strongest user is addicted. I don't need that.

"In the mood to get your dick sucked?" she asks with a smile, her fingers jittery as they thrum her leg. She's agitated and restless, a sure sign that it's been awhile since she's used and she's craving it bad.

"Not really," I tell her honestly. "I just woke up. And to be honest, my dick is a little pissed off that you left me to die on the beach. A stranger had to call for help. You ran off like a chicken shit."

Jill looks stricken.

"Pax," she whines. "I didn't mean to. I just can't go to jail, you know? I've got two kids. I'm a single mom. I can't be in jail."

She's desperate now, whining even louder and I stare at her in surprise. Shocked horror, actually.

"You've got two kids?"

After all this time, a couple years, I didn't know that. She's never said anything, never mentioned them even once.

She nods. "Yep. A girl and a boy. Five years old and seven."

All I feel is disgust now and I shake my head.

"Then what the fuck are you doing on this shit, Jill? And hanging out in the bar all day and night? It's one thing to fuck up your own life, but it's entirely different when you're fucking up someone else's. You need to get your shit straight."

I start to close the door in her face but she lunges inside, clutching at me. Crying. Wailing. Panicked. I grab her wrists and hold them to prevent her from scratching me.

"Please, Pax. I need it. I'll stop. I promise. But I need it one more time. Just one more. And then I'll go get help. I promise."

Tears are streaking down her face in black streaks from her makeup. The sunlight exposes the hardened lines on her face, the lines that nighttime hides for her. In the light of day, she looks hard and used.

Because that's exactly what she is. I sigh again.

"Fine. I've only got a little. I'm not going to use for a while. You can have what I have left, which is probably only one line. And then you need to go get help. Get your shit straight."

She's shaking now, her breath catching in her throat as she waits for me to lead her to the coke. It's all she can focus on right now, so I shut up and save my breath with the lecture.

I lead her to my kitchen table, and cut up the one little rock I have left. I drag it into a line and watch as she inhales it in two snorts. She slumps into the seat and lets it take affect and when she turns to me, she is visibly calmer.

"Ready for that blowjob?"

She's looking up at me, expectant, familiar. And for a second, the thought of a blowjob does make my groin automatically react, shifting against the constrained crotch of my jeans. But I shake my head.

"I'm not really in the mood, Jill."

I turn around and pad across the stone in my bare feet, toward the living room. She grabs my arm.

"You can't give it to me for nothing, Pax. I don't feel right about that. Besides, I feel bad for leaving you the other night. Just let me pay for it. Please."

A woman is begging to suck my dick. Oh, the irony. And it's particularly ironic that I just don't want it. My mind has been consumed with Mila Hill lately. The thought of this bar whore frankly turns my stomach a bit now.

I shake my head.

But Jill shakes hers too, and now she leaning against me, running her hands over the bare skin of my chest, trailing her fingers down to my waist band and unzipping my jeans. She bends and runs her tongue around my nipple and then she's got me in her grasp. I'm instantly horny.

I inhale a little as she runs her fingers up and down my shaft, outside of my underwear. Fuck. I curse my testosterone.

"Fine," I sigh. As if getting a blowjob is a hardship. I drop my pants and she sinks to her knees in front of me, taking all of me into her mouth. And as I lose myself in the moment, in the pleasure of her lips forming a vacuum around my dick, sliding, moving, sucking, I stare at the lake.

As Jill's head bobs, I watch the current and the waves, the occasional sailboat. I watch the seagulls fly, I watch the sun. And then Mila's face forms unbidden yet again in my mind. Hers is as different from Jill's hardened face as it can possibly be; fresh and innocent. I focus on it, then picture her lush tits with the pink nipples that point to the sun.

It makes me come a lot faster than normal. I groan and spurt into Jill's mouth and I don't even look. In my head, it is Mila's mouth. It is Mila's hands cupping my balls, lightly squeezing them as I come.

And as I open my eyes, I am horrified to see Mila's face.

For real.

Staring up at me from the stretch of beach below my house. She can see perfectly into my home, and can see perfectly that Jill is bent in front of me sucking my dick.

And she looks as horrified as I feel.

Chapter 8

Mila

Oh, my God.

I feel like a freight train just plowed into my chest, knocking all the air from my body. I don't know why. I don't own Pax, not in the slightest. But he's been coming to see me every day so I felt like there was a mutual attraction there. I mean, he drove into town just to walk me the length of one block every day. Frankly, it's all I've been able to think about. He's even invaded my dreams.

But clearly, I was wrong. My fascination with him isn't reciprocated.

He's getting a blowjob from the girl who left him on the beach.

I can't even think. My head is swirling in a blur of anger and hurt. I just grab my supplies, fold up my easel and bolt for my car. I think I might hear his voice behind me, calling my name, but I don't turn around. I start to run, and when I reach my car, I dump my things into it and peel out.

I chance a glance into the rearview mirror and he's not there. I exhale.

I'm not sure if I'm disappointed or not. A sick part of me kind of wishes that he'd cared enough to chase after me. But he didn't. So he doesn't care. I feel like crying. And that's ridiculous. But then I cry anyway.

I cry for the end of something that didn't even have a chance to begin.

And then I cry because I feel even stupider for having such stupid thoughts.

I'm an idiot.

I drive to my shop and sit there for a bit inside of my car. I pull myself together and finally walk inside. I flip the sign to Open and put my apron on. And then I do what I always do when I'm happy or sad or bored or well, anything.

I paint.

With swooping strokes, I paint the sun hanging over the edge of the lake by Pax's house. I paint the gray choppy water and then I turn the sun black, allowing the paint to drip toward the water. It's a dark scene and it perfectly fits how I feel. Stormy, black, angry. All are words that can be used to fit both the scene and my mood.

The shop door jangles and I sigh. I usually don't hope that customers don't come, but today I'd sort of like to be alone. I turn, my paintbrush still in hand, ready to smile at the customer.

But it's Pax.

The smile dies on my lips and I am frozen.

He is freshly showered, I can tell. His hair is wet and I can smell the scent of soap as he approaches. His face is oh-so-serious and I clench my jaw. This guy just got a blowjob. He has no right to come and talk to me.

Then why am I so happy that he came?

It defies logic.

"I'm sorry you had to see that," Pax says quietly, forgoing a greeting. "Please, Mila. I'm really sorry."

I grit my teeth and turn back to my painting, smearing the sun into the gray sky.

"What you do is your business," I tell him curtly. "It's not mine."

Pax sighs and I can hear it from here, even though he stopped moving several steps away from me.

"I could tell you that it wasn't what it looked like, but that would be a lie. It was exactly what it looked like. I could explain it, but you wouldn't understand."

"Then why are you here?" I whisper, confused. If he doesn't want to explain, then what's the point? I don't look at him, instead I just stare at the movement of my paintbrush. I notice that my hand is shaking.

And then I feel him behind me.

His hand closes around mine, steadying it. His is warm and large. And I should pull away, but I don't. His warmth is all around me and I want to be absorbed by it.

"I don't know why I'm here," he admits softly, and his voice is so close to my neck. "Because I can't stop thinking about you, I guess. And because I'll never get that horrified expression on your face out of my head. I'm sorry to have put it there. Just know that she doesn't mean anything to me. She was persistent and I didn't say no. It was a habit. I'm sorry."

My heart hammers hard in my chest. I don't know what to say. I know that I should tell him to get far away from me, but my heart is a traitor and wants him here. My heart must have issues. But I can't say that.

"You don't even know me," I tell him instead, finally turning around to look at him, pulling my hand away as I do. I stare up into his hazel eyes and find an expression there that I haven't yet seen. Trepidation. "Why would you apologize to someone that you barely even know? You don't owe me anything."

He shrugs and his movement stirs his masculine scent. I inhale it and fight the urge to close my eyes so that I can better enjoy the smell.

"I don't know. All I know is that ever since I met you, I've *wanted* to know you. That's why I've been coming into town this week to see you. Something about you makes me think that I can be better, maybe even get my shit straight. I haven't felt that way in a very long time. And I feel like I *do* owe you something."

Hell. His words strike a chord in me and I swallow hard. His tone is hesitant, soft. And it melts my heart. I can't help it. Sometimes, there is such a broken look in his eyes. And deep down, I just want to fix it.

"Why?" I ask, my gaze firmly locked with his. He shakes his head.

"I don't know. You just seem so *good*, so wholesome. It draws me to you. I can't explain it."

I laugh now, thoroughly amused.

I gesture toward my painting. "Does that seem good and wholesome to you?"

We both study the angry black and gray canvas. It looks like something that someone in a Psych ward might have painted. Pax finally smiles.

"Well, then, Red, it looks like you've got a dark side. But the difference between you and me is that you channel yours in a healthy way. I don't."

I stare at him, trying to decide what to say, how honest to be. But this moment seems like a good time for honesty, so I don't hesitate.

"I don't know if it's all that healthy that I'm attracted to you," I admit finally. "I've never been attracted to a bad boy before."

He is so close to me that his proximity is a bit intoxicating.

I feel almost dizzy from it as I stare up at him, waiting for his response. It also seems as though I can feel the danger emanating from him...it's charged, electrical, fascinating.

Pax thinks on it for a moment, his jaw covered in day-old stubble.

"Well, I've never wanted to be good before, so I guess it's a first for both of us."

We stare into each other's eyes for what seems like forever.

I don't know if I should believe him, but he seems so sincere. I do know that I *want* to believe him, even if it's a stupid feeling.

I don't know what to say and apparently, he doesn't either.

Without a word, he ducks his head and his lips meet mine.

It is as unexpected as it is amazing.

His lips are soft and he tastes like mint. Gone is the taste of ashtray and vomit. Gone is the limp man from the other night, the one who convulsed on the pavement. In his place is someone vibrant and alive, someone who smells delicious and is devastatingly sexy.

Someone who is bad for me.

His tongue delves softly into my mouth and I fight the urge to sigh into his. His hands grip my back and I don't know when they got there, but I lean into his embrace, clutching his waist. I revel in the way his fingers knead at my skin, at the firm pressure he places against me, at the hard rigidity pressed against my hips. It's dizzying.

When I finally need to breathe, he pulls away.

I am shaky from the kiss, from his absence from me. From the idea that I enjoyed that way too much.

I look up at him.

He looks down at me.

He's waiting for a reaction and I'm not sure what to do. The kiss was perfect. Pax is sexy as hell. But he's so different from me. *And he just got a blow job from someone else.* The vision of that horrible girl on her knees in front of Pax springs into my head and I cringe. He could very definitely hurt me if I give him the chance. I've already had enough pain in life. I don't need more.

"I don't think this is a good idea," I finally say reluctantly. And the words are so very hard to say.

The warm light dims in Pax's eyes as he stares at me and I see the disappointment in them, the rejection, before he hardens it into a cool expression that makes me want to weep.

"I'm sorry you feel that way," he says calmly. "Because I think it's a very good idea. The best I've had in a long, long time."

He turns around and walks away, out of my shop.

Away from me.

Without another word.

I watch his wide shoulders as he walks away, out of my sight.

Then I sink to my knees right in the middle of my shop. My hands are shaking and my head is spinning.

What did I just do?

Am I insane? I met someone who made me feel something for the first time in the two years since my parents died, and I'm too chicken-shit to pursue anything?

I'm pathetic.

I reach for my phone and call my sister. I speak before she even has a chance to.

"I'm ready for that drink tonight."

Chapter 9

Pax

Fuck her.

My head is spinning as I walk woodenly from her shop and to my car. I can't believe that just happened, actually. I bared myself to someone for the first time in forever and she stomped on it. I don't know who I'm madder at—her for rejecting me or me for putting myself out there for her to reject.

But either way, fuck her.

I jam my keys in the ignition and turn the volume up. Hard rock vibrates my chest as the bass rumbles and I tear out of the parking lot and toward the highway to Chicago. Since I'm in a bad mood anyway, I might as well get this over with.

The highway stretches in front of me and the loud music calms me as I drive. I lose myself in it, actually. I allow it to numb me, to absorb the negative thoughts. I almost reach for my vial, which is safely ensconced in my jacket, but I don't. I told myself that I wouldn't, not for a while, and I won't. I'm not weak. And I'm not a pussy.

As the miles are absorbed by my rearview mirror, the sky swallows the road in the horizon bit by bit until I'm finally crossing the bridge into Chicago and onto the Skyway.

By the time I arrive at my dad's downtown office, I have managed to put my agitation away, to tuck the image of Mila's face far away in my mind.

Because fuck her.

I have the urge to punch a wall, but I don't. Instead, I make my way to the eighteenth floor and my father's receptionist lets him know that I am here. I make myself comfortable in his sitting area, taking a mint out of a bowl and popping it into my mouth.

My eyes are closed when my father finally appears twenty minutes later.

"Pax, get your feet off of the furniture."

His voice is tired and I open my eyes. He looks older since I saw him last quarter. His dark hair is just beginning to gray at the temples, and he has lines around his eyes. And his mouth. His navy blue suit seems to hang a bit on him, like he lost weight and hasn't taken the time to have his clothing altered. I stare at him, amazed at the idea that my father is growing old.

And then I yank my feet off of the table in front of me.

"Sorry," I mumble. My father nods and leads me to his big office.

I sit in a chair in front of him and wait until he slides a few papers across his desk toward me.

I don't even read them, I simply sign my name. I trust him.

"You should always read anything that you sign your name on," he admonishes me for what seems like the hundredth time regarding this subject. And for the hundredth time, I reply in the same way.

"I do, when it's a stranger. But you're my father. I know you aren't going to fuck me over."

Dad sighs again. "Can you at least try to watch your language? It's the respectful thing to do."

"Sorry," I mutter again.

For Christ's sake. He acts like I'm a child. But that's part of our problem. Our relationship will always be frozen in his head- back to a time when I was a child and he was the adult. He doesn't seem to understand that we're both adults now.

"Alexander Holdings had an exceedingly good quarter," my dad remarks, taking back the papers and shuffling them. "So your income has increased this time. You really might want to consider investing. You're twenty-four years old. It's time to grow your portfolio. And maybe take an interest in your family's company. Your grandfather has contacted me, wanting to know how to reach you. He's an old man, Pax. He won't be around much longer. He wants to know that his company is in good hands."

I stare at him, fighting the urge to curl my lip.

"I don't want anything to do with the business," I tell my father. "I don't agree with anything they stand for. As far as I'm concerned, I'll hire a CEO to run the place after he finally kicks it. And as far as my grandfather goes, it's his fault that he's all alone. He basically disowned me when we moved away. He's got himself to blame."

My father's eyes glaze over and he turns to stare out his window.

"Pax, your grandfather wasn't the same after your mother died. None of us were. You can't hold that against him. When we moved, he felt like he was losing you too, and you were the last connection that he had with your mother. Since your grandma died so long ago, you and Susanna were all he had. When he lost her and then you, he felt like he lost everything."

"Yet he didn't have to lose me," I spit angrily. "His fucking temper is what caused him to lose me. He chose to be angry and cut off contact. I was just a kid. I didn't even choose to move.

You did. But he took it out on me. So, as far as I'm concerned, he can rot."

My father stares at me, his gaze thoughtful as he temples his fingers in front of him. Finally he sighs and nods.

"I guess I can understand your feelings. Your grandfather is a formidable man. And stubborn. He used to make your mom want to pull her hair out sometimes."

And now his eyes really do glaze over as he thinks about my mom, lost in his memories. If there was ever anyone who didn't get over her death, it was most certainly my father.

"Dad, you look like you aren't eating right," I tell him, pulling him from his thoughts and back into the present with me. He doesn't look happy about it, either. He prefers to live in a world made from memories.

He shakes his head, shaking away my concern.

"I'm fine, Pax. Just stressed about some big cases that I'm handling. How are you doing? Are you pulling things together?"

"You mean, am I still using?" I stare at him harshly. I mean, fuck. If you have a question, just ask it. Don't beat around the bush. Dad nods, tired again.

"Fine. Yes. Are you still using?" He asks the question haltingly, as if the words taste bitter in his mouth. And he doesn't really want to know the answer, I can tell. He thinks I'm a fucking addict who can't quit.

It's fucking annoying.

"No, I haven't used," I tell him, rolling my eyes. "I said I wasn't going to and I'm not. Not the hard shit, anyway. I'm not an addict, dad. Seriously. I use it because I like it. Not because I have to."

My father stares at me with his best hardened attorney gaze.

"That might be so," he tells me. "But eventually, when a person keeps using, they become addicted. You're pushing it."

"Whatever, dad," I sigh, pushing away from his desk and standing up. "It's been good to see you. I'll see you next quarter."

I stalk out, away from his disapproving stare and his doubts. What he doesn't understand is that if you constantly expect the worst from someone, that's probably what you're going to get. He should have learned that by now. I've certainly shown him time and time again.

I am headed back toward the Skyway when I decide to take a quick detour, into a seedy little bar that I know of. I've had to stop there numerous times after heated visits with the old man. The bartender knows me and calls out a greeting when I enter. I never can remember his name. Dave? Dan?

I make my way across the dingy room, glancing around at the split vinyl seats and dark walls. This place hasn't changed. It still has a hole in the paneling back by the pool table where somebody punched it and it still smells like piss and old grease. It's not what you would call upscale, but it's perfect for drinking away a bad mood.

I nod at the bartender.

"I'll have a Jack."

The bartender nods back and fills a tumbler with the dark golden liquid, sliding it towards me. It sloshes a bit onto the bar, but he's not concerned. Cleanliness isn't exactly his highest priority. You can tell that by his stained shirt and greasy hair. But that doesn't bother me. The whiskey will taste the same regardless of the bartender's personal hygiene habits.

Before he can attempt to talk with me, he's distracted by another customer, a dirty old man who is clearly far too drunk. I watch with interest as the bartender tries to cut him off, then just gives up and pours him another drink.

"Hey, big fella. I'm Amber."

I stare down at the big-busted woman who has just slid up to me. She's got bar whore written all over her, from her extremely tight jeans that exhibit camel toe to her garish overly done makeup. Her tits are practically busting out of her top because it's three sizes too small.

I cock an eyebrow and take a gulp of whiskey.

"Big fella? The 1940's called. They want their phrase back."

Amber throws her bleached blonde head back and laughs as though it is the funniest thing she's ever heard.

"I'm from Iowa. I guess we still talk that way back home."

"Charming." I knock back the rest of my drink and motion for another. I look at Amber. "Would you like one?"

I figure it's the polite thing to do, even though I'm not much in the mood for company. She nods.

"I'd love one." She looks up at the bartender. "Dan, can you make it two?"

Dan the bartender. I've got to remember that.

But I'm sure I won't.

Amber slides her hand up my thigh. "Thanks for the drink. But if you don't want me to call you big fella, you've got to tell me your name."

I eye her, at the way her eyes are already dilated because she's already had a few too many. "Do I?"

She examines me for a moment, before she laughs. It's a slutty laugh. A fake one. I almost shudder, but don't. I don't know what's wrong with me. This is an easy woman who is mine for the taking. If I wanted to take her, that is, but I find that I really don't. And I think I do know what's wrong with me.

Mila Hill is in my head, wholesome and sweet. But I'll be fucking damned if I let her invade my life when she doesn't even want me in the first place.

I knock back my glass of Jack and signal for one more. I knock that one back too.

A comforting sense of calm descends upon me, the familiar numbness that I love so much. When all else fails, the obscurity prevails. I almost laugh at my deep thinking, but instead, I reach over and grasp Amber's thick thigh, enjoying the fleshy feel of her leg in my fingers. If this chick wants me, she can have me.

And then I do what I always do. I block out logical thought with drugs or women. In this case, a bar slut and Jack Daniels.

"Come with me," I whisper into her ear. Amber smiles knowingly and nods. She clings to my hand as we pick our way through the dirty bar, down the dingy back hall and into the women's bathroom.

The bathroom is exactly how I figured it would be—disgusting. A single light bulb hangs from the yellowed ceiling, casting a dubious light around the small room. There is evidence of puke on the sides of the toilet, the tiles are grimy and the walls look as though they haven't been washed since 1969. But it doesn't matter. I lock the door behind us and turn to Amber.

She reaches for me and I let her, sliding my hand up her thigh and under her tight shirt, gripping her fat tit. I squeeze it hard and she moans.

I squeeze it harder and she moans again.

I want to roll my eyes at this stupid game. I know what's going to happen because I've played it a thousand times before. She's going to pretend to enjoy anything that I do, and I'll pretend not to know it's fake.

But who gives a fuck? Pussy is pussy.

I pull a condom from my wallet and rip it open with my teeth, but discover a problem. I'm not hard.

"Suck me," I tell Amber. And then I smile charmingly.

She smiles back and immediately drops to her knees on the dirty floor, her head bobbing. It's not long before I'm hard enough for the condom, in spite of myself. I slide it on, help Amber to her feet and turn her away from me. And then I enter her from behind, with no preamble, no foreplay.

She doesn't seem to mind.

She moans as if my dick is the best she's ever had. I close my eyes and picture all of the porn scenes I've ever watched, all of the tits and ass and masturbation and shower scenes. But something is off. The smell in here is putrid, I'm tired, I'm pissed. Things aren't coming easily tonight and I know that having an orgasm isn't going to be easy, particularly with whiskey-dick.

So I picture Mila.

And immediately, I feel a gush of warmth. I picture her small waist, her lush hips. Her full lips. Her soft tits. Her feminine smell, clean and floral. It immediately floods life into my dick and I'm back in the game.

As I envision Mila, I bang Amber hard and I hear her forehead thumping against the dirty tiled walls. She allows it because, like me, she doesn't feel like she deserves anything more than this... this dirty fuck in a dirty bar bathroom.

It's pathetic on both our parts.

I picture Mila again, and then for some reason, it stops working. It's doesn't feel right. Amber isn't Mila. And even thinking of Mila while I'm in this pathetic place with this pathetic chick feels wrong on a hundred different levels.

I pull out abruptly and Amber turns to look at me in confusion. Her eye makeup is smeared from sweat. In fact, I can smell the sweat from here and I fight the urge to shudder.

"It's not you, it's me," I tell her. "Whiskey dick."

It's a lie, but it doesn't matter. She nods knowingly, as if she encounters this problem all of the time. She pats my shoulder sympathetically, as if I give a flying fuck what she thinks about me.

But I smile as if I'm grateful for her understanding.

I toss the condom into the trash and walk out.

As I do, I hand Dan the bartender a twenty.

"To cover her drinks the rest of the night," I tell him.

Dan smiles. "Sure thing. See you next time!"

I nod and make my way into the parking lot, collapsing into Danger. My car is familiar and comfortable and I feel calmer now that I'm in it. I rest my head against the seat and inhale the leather smell and the fresh air. It's so much better than the stale, smoky air in the bar. And then I drive home with the windows open and my music blaring.

The road is black and long as it flies beneath my car, but I am home before I know it. Before I am even ready, actually. I stand in my driveway and face the dark house, and for the first time, I have the feeling that I don't want to go in, simply because it is so empty.

Living alone is great, but sometimes it is just so fucking lonely.

I stand still for a moment, my hands dangling at my sides, before I head back to my car. I've still got agitation to burn, I guess.

I don't know why I head to the Bear's Den, the little bar in town. I know that Jill is probably there or her other bar whore friends, and if I want to spend time with them, I'll call them. I don't want them hanging on me when I'm not in the mood.

And I'm definitely not in the mood for that tonight. I just want to walk in, draw up a seat at the bar and be around people, without actually having to interact with them. Is that so much to ask? I'm not in the mood for bar whores.

I nose my car into a parking slot and slam the door, taking

a deep breath of the night air as I walk inside. It's the last clean breath I'll get once I cross the smoky threshold of the bar.

I walk in and glance through the smoky haze that floats through the dim room. Locals sit and chat, while others play pool or darts in the back. I know their faces, but not their names. I'm not much of a socializer.

True to form, Jill is here. I see her situated in the back, perched on the edge of a table, her half-naked ass shoved into some poor sap's face. So much for her promise to get help. Quite honestly, now that I know she has kids at home, all I feel is disgust for her. What a waste of oxygen.

She notices me looking at her and her heavily made-up face lights up and she practically leaps from her table to come to me.

But I shake my head, mouthing the word *No*.

She looks startled, then hurt, as she stops in her tracks. I turn my back and head for the bar. As I sit down on a stool, I can see from my periphery that she sat back down at her table. I can feel her wounded gaze, but I don't look at her. I think my time with her is over. Someone else can be her supplier and contribute toward her wasted life.

I know the bartender's name here, because he wears it on his nametag. I guess that makes it easier for the drunks to remember. Or people who don't really give a shit. Like me.

"Hey, Mickey," I greet him. "I'll have a Jack. Double, neat."

Mickey nods, a wiry guy who looks like he's seen better days and more than his share of bar fights. He's got a scar running from his ear to his chin. I've never asked him how he got it, and he's never offered to say.

"How you doin', Tate?" he asks as he sets the whiskey in front of me. I pick up the glass, drain it in one gulp and thump it back down.

"Better now," I tell him. "I'll take another. In fact, just keep 'em coming tonight."

He nods, pouring one and then heads down to help someone else. I take a small gulp from my glass and set it down, closing my eyes. It feels good to be surrounded by people, but still lost in them. No one will approach me other than Jill and I shut her down already. I'm alone here, but it's less lonely than it is at home.

Feminine giggling invades my hearing and my eyes pop open. Because I know that laugh.

I turn in my seat to find Mila and her sister stumbling from the hallway leading to the bathroom. It looks like they are holding each other up and I roll my eyes. You've got to be kidding me. I run into her even here? This was the last place I would have expected to find her. She and her sister both look as out of place in this little hole as they can possibly get.

Mila glances up and stops, her giggle dying on her lips as she recognizes me. Her eyes widen and she looks like she wants to come over to me, to possibly say something. But her sister is pulling on her arm, and even though Mila looks over her shoulder at me, she allows Madison to steer her away. I'm pretty sure Madison is moving her away from me on purpose and I clench my jaw. Mila's an adult. She can make her own decisions.

Not that her decisions are always wise.

I come to this realization very quickly as she and Madison rejoin a couple of local guys who are playing darts.

The darts aren't the problem, the guys are.

I roll my eyes again. What the hell does Mila think she's doing? Either one of those guys would eat her for breakfast. She probably thinks she's safe because she's most likely known them her whole life. But they are both snakes. I've seen them with a million women in this very bar, none of them twice.

I sigh and drain my glass, signaling for another. It's not my problem. She made that clear when she said I wasn't a good idea. So fuck her.

I turn away as I watch one of them wrap his meaty paw around her slender waist and pull her close, supposedly showing her how to properly throw the dart. It makes me want to hurl so I turn my back to them.

I do everything I can to ignore them. I make small-talk with Mickey. I watch ESPN on the overhead TV. I close my eyes and listen to the conversation around me. And even though I know that it would be much easier to just get up and leave, something in me wants to stay. Something in me thinks I *need* to stay.

I can't explain it.

And then I realize the reason in a sudden rush of clarity. I'm staying because I think she'll need me.

Holy shit, what kind of idiot am I? I slam my glass down on the table and toss some bills on the bar. I head to the bathroom to take a leak before I go, but then I'm out of here. She's made it clear what she wants. And it isn't me.

When I come back out, Madison is already at the door of the bar with one of the guys. She's leaning into him, laughing into his ear. She's clearly very drunk. I shake my head and fight the urge to say something.

It's one thing when a bar whore goes home with random men. Bar whores know exactly what they're doing. They're giving something for getting something, be it drugs or drinks or even just attention. It's a conscious decision. But Madison isn't a bar whore and that jackass is taking advantage of her. But it's not my place to interfere.

Until I see Mila grab her purse and stumble toward the door. The guy she's with tags along at her heels and she turns to grab onto him, unsteady on her feet. He laughs, his hand brushing her perfect ass as he steadies her.

My blood boils. And since I'm already on my way out the door, I can't do anything other than trail behind them, something that causes my blood to burn even hotter. Fuck this.

They stumble out and I even hold the door open as Mila's jacket gets caught on the handle. Her eyes meet mine, and hers are blurry and unfocused. She's in no condition to be choosing a bedmate. My gut clenches, but I keep my mouth shut.

She made her choice.

She made her choice.

She made her choice.

I repeat it in my head, as if it will make it an easier pill to swallow. It doesn't. It still pisses me off. I step outside and turn to walk to my car.

I hear their voices behind me, fading into the distance. Mila is laughing, the guy is talking to her, low and deep. As I turn to open my car door, I glance in their direction. They are standing next to what must be the guy's car because he's opened the passenger side door, but Mila is trying to shake his hand instead.

What the hell?

I pause and watch. Mila is slurring her words by now, but she is definitely trying to shake this guy's hand. And say goodnight.

A feeling of satisfaction wells up in me before I can stop it.

Until the guy smiles like a piranha and pushes Mila against the car, where he shoves against her and sticks his tongue down her throat. His hands are all over and she is pushing at him, struggling.

"No," she cries out.

I see an explosion of red and I close the gap between us in three strides.

I yank the guy off of her and slam him onto the ground. Before I can think or breathe, I stomp on his hand as he grasps for my leg. His bones crunch and he howls in pain, clutching his broken hand to his chest.

Mila gasps, her eyes wide, as she huddles against the car. As my attention is on her, the guy kicks at my leg, connecting with my knee.

Fuck. But I don't feel it with all the adrenaline pumping through me.

He kicks again, but this time, I see it coming and move. He only connects with air.

"Fuck you, man," he slurs. "Fucking prick. This isn't your business. You broke my fucking hand, man."

He is scrambling to get up now and I put my boot on his chest.

"Don't," I tell him, as he tries to grab at me. "You're lucky that's all I broke. The next time a woman tells you no, stop whatever the fuck it is that you're doing. Now go home and sleep it off. And don't come near Mila again. If you do, I will break your dick off and feed it to you."

The drunk guy glares up at me. "What the fuck is your problem? You don't know what she wants."

I turn to Mila, my foot still firmly planted in the guy's chest.

"Mila, do you want to see this guy again?"

She shakes her head. "No."

"There you have it," I tell him calmly, removing my foot. "Get the fuck out of here."

"Fuck you, man," he mutters as he struggles to his feet. "I don't need this. Fuck that slut, too."

That's when I punch him.

Hard. In the side of head. He goes down like a bag of rocks.

Mila gasps and I shake my head, bending to make sure he's still breathing.

He is, so I turn to Mila.

"Come on. Let's get you home."

"Why did you do that?" she whispers, her eyes frozen on the unconscious asshole on the pavement. "Jared didn't mean to hurt me. He was just drunk. I've known him for a long time."

I stare at her as I walk to her side.

"You have no idea what he meant to do. Trust me. It wasn't good."

I take her arm and lead her to my car, opening the door and tucking her into the passenger seat before I strap her in.

As I'm getting into the driver's seat, Mila is rummaging through her purse. She looks up at me.

"Uh-oh," she says quietly. "I can't find my keys. My apartment is locked. Can you take me to Maddy's?"

Her words are seriously slurred by this point. It sounded more like she said *I cent fine my keel. Miz part is lock. Cent you take me to Man's?* I shake my head.

"You're seriously fucked up," I tell her. "You're probably going to get sick soon. And I don't think your sister is going home. I'll take you to my house."

Her eyes widen and she shakes her head. "Pax, no. It's not a good idea. I don't trust myself around you." Her words are completely garbled of course, but I can make them out.

I startle and stare at her.

"You can't trust yourself around me?"

She shakes her head pathetically, then leans her head on the cool window glass.

"No. I can't let you break my heart. I don't have much of it left."

My gut clenches yet again, something that it seems to do a lot of when I'm around her. I ram the key in the ignition.

"Don't worry," I tell her. "I won't be breaking your heart tonight. You can sleep it off in my bed. I'll take the couch."

She nods, her face planted firmly against the window and I know that she's not long for the conscious world. And I'm right. By the time we reach my house a scant five minutes later, she has passed out in the seat.

I stare at her for a minute, at her shiny dark hair, her tight jeans, her full breasts, which I can just barely see through the opening of her jacket. Her lips puff out with each little breath that she exhales in her passed out state. She's going to feel this tomorrow. If she hadn't been so stupid, I'd feel sorry for her.

I scoop her out of the car and carry her to the house, trying to ignore the soft way she melts into my body, and the way her head leans against my shoulder. She can't weigh more than a hundred pounds soaking wet.

I set her on my bed, pull off her boots and cover her up. I drag my bathroom trashcan next to her, just in case, and then sit in a chair and watch her for a bit. I have no idea if she's going to wake up and be sick or if she's definitely passed out for the night.

She remains still and quiet, with a little snore erupting from her every once in a while. I can't help but smile just a bit over that. I'm guessing she would be embarrassed to know that she's snoring, even though it's actually cute as hell.

I sigh.

I'm fucking tired and I could easily sleep right here in this chair, but I know that if she wakes up and finds me here, it might be startling, particularly in the dark. So I head downstairs and find that once again, I'm just not ready to sleep. I'm worked up now, from all of the shit at the bar and by the fact that Mila is in my bed at this very moment. Alone.

And I'm downstairs. Alone.

And my hand hurts.

Fucking A.

I grab a baggie of ice for my hand and a bottle of whiskey from my garage and make my way out to the beach behind my house. I drop onto a chair and stare up at the stars as I listen to the rhythmic crash of the waves. I take a gulp of the liquid fire. I feel the warmth all the way into my belly and I take another swig.

I fall asleep humming a song that I don't know the words to or even where it came from. The last conscious thought I have is that the night is so very, very black.

Minutes, or days, or years pass before something wakes me. Time has run together.

"Pax," the soft voice murmurs, intruding upon my sleep.

And for a minute, just a scant minute, it seems like it might be my mother. In the blur of sleep, the voice has the same soft timbre as hers. But it can't be. Even in sleep, I know that. It's only the wishful thinking that comes from that grayish, half-awake place. It isn't my mother. I know that before I even open my eyes.

But I'm surprised, when I do, to find Mila standing in front of me.

She seems uncertain, but she's so fucking beautiful in the morning sun. Radiant, actually. She doesn't seem hung-over at all. Her dark hair is loose and flowing and the morning breeze carries her scent to me. I inhale it and stare at her.

"What are you doing out here?" I ask groggily. I squint into the light, then rub my forehead. As I do, I wince because my fucking hand hurts. And then I realize that I must have fallen asleep here. The night air made my throat scratchy, so I clear it, then clear it again. "Are you feeling alright?"

I glance down and find that my bottle of whiskey is beside me on the beach, its contents spilled onto the sand. I think. I certainly hope I hadn't drunk the whole thing. If I did, I'm going to feel it later today, just like Mila.

Mila looks even more uncertain now.

"I…uh." She shifts her weight from one foot to the other nervously. I look at her and cock an eyebrow. "I feel fine. Mostly. My mouth is dry and I have a headache. I don't, um. I don't remember exactly what all happened last night. But I sort of remember that you punched Jared and brought me here. And I think you might have broken his hand."

I eye her. "Yeah, that happened. Do you make a habit of getting trashed at the Bear's Den and going home with assholes?"

It came out a little harsher than I meant for it to and Mila flinches.

"No," she answers quickly. "In fact, I don't usually drink much at all, unless it is wine at dinner. Maddy has been bugging me to go out with her and blow the cogs off and after yesterday, I just felt like I needed it."

I stare at her with interest now, my lip twitching.

"I think you mean cobwebs. And what about yesterday? When you rejected me, you mean?"

Color floods her cheeks and she stares at the sand.

"Yes."

"If that was stressful for you, then did you ever think that maybe you made a mistake? That maybe you shouldn't have rejected me? And that maybe you should give this thing a chance?"

I stare at her, trying to force her to meet my gaze.

"Well," I prompt. "Have you?"

She lifts her chin, her green eyes bright.

"That's all I've thought about since you left my shop yesterday," she admits. "All I can think of is you. Even when I was with Madison and Jared last night. And then when you were there at the bar, it was all I could do to keep from running over and jumping in your lap."

I cock my head. "Why didn't you? I think I would have enjoyed that."

She blushes again, her cheeks and neck flushing prettily.

"I think it might be considered socially inappropriate," she replies wryly. "Thank you for coming to my rescue last night. I guess we're even now. I saved you, then you saved me back." She pauses and looks at the ground before she looks back up at me.

"And I *have* been thinking about you. It's probably not smart or good for me, but it's all I seem to do lately. I think about you. Is your apology still on the table from yesterday? Because if it is, then I think maybe you were right. Maybe this is worth taking a risk for."

She fidgets with her hands nervously.

I raise an eyebrow, deliberately obtuse.

"*This*? Can you be more specific?"

She doesn't answer. She just bends down without hesitation and kisses me square on the mouth.

The lips that I fantasized about last night are on mine, her tongue in my mouth. I know that I taste like whiskey and smokes, but I don't care and she doesn't seem to either. She tastes like heaven.

Finally, she pulls away and I can see that she is a bit breathless.

"So, was that a yes?" she asks hesitantly.

I shake my head in bewilderment and smile at her. Having

her here like this is fucking amazing. And surprising. My chest is swelling with the amazing feeling so much that I can't believe my next words.

"That's a yes," I tell her. "My apology is still on the table. But I think I probably owe you another one."

Chapter 10

Mila

I stare at Pax.

Even though he's gorgeous, he looks rough, like he had one hell of a night. He's got two-day stubble now and he's wearing the same clothing that he was wearing yesterday. His eyes are rimmed in red, like he didn't sleep much. Or he had way too much to drink. Or maybe he even did too much of something else.

I narrow my eyes.

"What do you need to apologize for now?" I ask hesitantly. I'm not sure if I want to know. And he looks like he's not sure that he wants to tell me. I back away a few steps. It can't be worse than getting a blow job from Jill, can it?

He holds his hand up. "Wait, Mila. Just listen."

He stares at me.

I stare back.

He sighs.

I wait.

"Yes?" I ask and even I can hear the trepidation in my tone. I swallow. He dips his head, then returns my stare.

"I think we might be onto something good here and I don't want to fuck it up by starting it out with lies."

I'm confused now. Lies? He's lied to me already? As if he can hear my thoughts, Pax shakes his head.

"I haven't lied to you yet," he explains. "But if I don't tell you what I did last night, then you won't understand what kind of person that I am. And that would be the biggest lie of all."

"What kind of person are you?" I whisper. "Did you try something with me last night?" The morning breeze blows my hair into my face and impatiently, I shove it behind my ears. I need to hear this, even if it isn't pretty.

Pax is hesitant now, unsure. The look on his face drops a big iron weight upon my heart because I know that whatever he wants to tell me isn't good. Maybe coming out here was a bad idea. I should have known. I want to back away, but I resist the urge and plant my feet firmly in the sand.

Pax catches my gaze and lifts his chin, sighing heavily.

"I'm the kind of person who gets pissed and then goes off and does stupid shit to try and block out my anger. Or my hurt. I don't deal with things in a healthy way. I deal with them in shitty ways, like drugs or women. Or whiskey. Last night, I chose whiskey and a woman. Although the woman wasn't you. I didn't try and take advantage of *you*."

He stares at me and the breath is caught in my throat. And I sort of feel like he kicked me in the stomach. I tortured myself all day yesterday and he had slept with someone else? When he didn't even want me enough to try something with me when I had been in his bed last night?

I am stunned and so I do the only thing any self-respecting woman in this situation can do.

I walk away.

"I'm out of here," I mutter.

One foot in front of the other, I retreat down the beach, my feet sinking into the sand. My heart feels like it is sinking too, more and more with each step, and I focus on the ground in front of me, trying to ignore the piercing pain coming from my heart. I know it's illogical to be upset that he hadn't tried to take advantage of me. But under the circumstances, it is a bit hurtful. And it wouldn't have been a violation because I want him.

And that's why the whole thing is so hurtful.

"Mila, wait!" Pax calls from behind me. I hear his steps right behind me and I stop when he grabs my arm. "Please, just wait. I need to explain something. And then, if you still want to, you can go."

I turn slowly, staring at him in the face. His is so anxious, his mouth tightly drawn. I nod.

"I can leave right now, if I wanted. I don't need your permission. But I'll hear what you have to say."

His lip twitches, almost as if he finds my little show of independence funny. I don't see the humor. I press my lips together, my hands on my hips as I wait.

It looks like Pax is trying not to laugh again.

"Well, obviously you can leave right now. But you'd have to walk, unless you want to wait until I drive you. Your car is still at the bar."

I feel my face fall. So much for being feisty. I'm at his mercy right now.

He stares at me, all traces of amusement gone from his face.

"I need you to know something," he says patiently. "Can you come back and sit?"

I glance at the beach chairs where he had apparently spent the night and nod again, curtly, following him back. I settle into one and instead of sitting in the one next to me, he sits on mine, beside my legs. I wait.

It is a moment before he begins.

"I've never talked about this with anyone, so it's difficult to know where to begin," he tells me with a wry smile. "Bear with me, okay?"

I nod yet again, silent as I wait for him to just spit it out.

"I'm fucked up," he says bluntly and I can't help but smile a little.

"Well, that's one way to start," I tell him. He smiles a little too, but it's a sad smile, and my heart twinges a bit.

"I know. But I want to be completely honest with you. I'm seriously fucked up. I have never had a real relationship. All I've ever dealt with are bar whores, pardon the term, and I don't really know how to be in a real relationship with a normal woman. Yesterday, when you said that we weren't a good idea, it hurt. I don't take rejection well. And then I had to drive to Chicago for some business with my father and overall, it was just a shitty day. I stopped by a little bar in the city and I ended up having sex with a woman there. Because that's what I do. I block out any kind of hurt or anger that I feel with drugs or women."

He pauses and I'm numb as I stare at him.

"You didn't even know her?" I whisper.

Pax shakes his head.

"No. I didn't even know her. But the strange part is that I couldn't bring myself to finish. All I could see in my head was you. And all of a sudden, the dingy little bar closed in on me and I couldn't get out of there fast enough. I thought about you the entire drive home. Then, when I saw you in the Bear's Den, I almost couldn't breathe. But you were there with someone else, and you had already said that you didn't want me.

"Mila, when that guy had you against his car, I saw red. For the first time in a long time, I cared about something other than myself. It didn't matter to me if you wanted me or not, but I couldn't let that guy hurt you. That tells me a lot about myself. And you. It tells me that you are good for me, that trying to be with you is something that is worth my time and worth any kind of wait that it might entail, until you're ready to be with me, too."

He pauses now, his eyes frozen upon my face. He's waiting… for a response, for an answer, for another possible rejection.

My heart is beating frozenly, as though the numbness of my emotions has spread to my chest. I can see the broken little boy in his eyes again, the one that screams that he has been hurt, and once again, I long to fix it. To fix him.

Even though he just had sex with someone else last night in some dirty bar.

Shit. He just had sex with someone else last night in a dirty bar.

I gulp hard at that ugly fact and stare at him. What he did might have been ugly, but he's absolutely beautiful right now with his fragility shining in his eyes. My gut twists.

Against my deepest misgivings, I somehow believe him. I believe that it didn't mean anything to him. I don't know if that makes me as twisted as he is or what. The whole thing is crazy and I don't know what to say. All I know is what I feel.

I want to take a chance.

My heart feels like it might stop beating if I don't.

"Did you at least use protection?" I ask hesitantly. "With the girl, I mean."

Pax nods. "Of course."

"I'm probably crazy. We aren't even dating and you've cheated on me already. But I have this insane attraction to you," I tell him. "When I'm not with you, I'm thinking about you. I've never been attracted to someone like this before. It has to mean something, right? So, maybe we should see where this goes. But I need your word that you won't be with anyone else while you're with me. I can't tolerate that. You're going to have to find some other way to deal with your issues. I'm really afraid, Pax. You've got issues that I don't know what to do with."

Pax stares at me, his hazel eyes more gold than green in the morning light. He nods slowly.

"I will try very hard not to hurt you," he says. "I'm fucked up. So I can't promise that I won't. But I promise that I will try."

"Okay," I whisper. "But try very hard."

Pax chuckles, low and husky and my belly twinges with warmth from the sound of it. "And I did not cheat on you. We weren't together. You rejected me, remember?"

He dips his head and kisses me again. This time, it is a kiss with promise. Of things to come, of things that might be. It fills me up with hope and I realize with a start that this is the first time I've felt truly hopeful in quite some time. It's quite a feeling and for just a second, I think that I might not be crazy after all, because it feels right.

As Pax pulls away, he holds onto me, looking down at me and I see warmth in his eyes. So there really was warmth there the other day. I hadn't been imagining it.

"I remember," I tell him. "But it was because I was trying to listen to my head, not my heart. My head is usually the smarter of the two. For once, though, I'm going to do the crazy thing."

Pax grins. "I've done the crazy thing more times than I can count, usually to my detriment. Trust me, I know crazy, and this isn't it. This is…just nature. A man and a woman who are attracted to each other when they logically shouldn't be because they're opposites. But opposites always attract, you know, so it makes total sense."

He says this knowingly, as if he's an expert and I laugh.

"Okay, Dr. Phil. We'll just pretend that it makes total sense and then just go from there."

"Where exactly do we go from there, though? How do we go about a real relationship?" he asks wryly. "Because I truly don't know."

I can see that he doesn't. He looks at a loss and he's not even trying to hide it. I find that refreshing, so I don't make fun of him.

Instead, I simply say, "Well, we start with a first date. Then a second and a third. We'll take it slow. I'm not going to jump into your bed tonight, Pax. I meant it when I said that I'm afraid to trust you to not break my heart. I'm going to need some time for you to prove that you won't."

"I'm okay with that," he tells me, amusement in his voice. "I think you'll be worth the wait."

I smile, then lean into his arm and we watch the lake, at how the foamy lip slides onto the beach and then sucks back away. The sun glistens on the surface like a million prisms of light and I look up at him.

"I bet this is the earliest you've been up in a while."

He laughs. "Maybe. I'm not admitting to anything, though. I will tell you that I need a shower. Desperately. So I'm going to drive you to your car, then take one. When can I see you again?"

When can he see me again?

The way he words that question causes my heart to twinge a bit once again. It seems so vulnerable and tender, like him. Like somewhere, deep down, behind his tough-looking exterior, he's fragile. But I don't say it because I'm sure that he wouldn't appreciate being described with that particular word.

Instead, I reply, "I have to work a shift at The Hill, my family's restaurant. My sister runs it. I'm helping out during the slow winter months. But if you want to come over around the end of my shift, we can have our first date. Do you like Italian food?"

Pax smiles. "I love it. And it's a date."

He walks me to his car and then kisses me again, leaning me against the cool metal door as he wraps his tongue with mine until I feel weak-kneed from his nearness. But I finally pull away like a rational human being and watch him walk around to his side. I can't help but notice the way the muscles in his back flex as he moves. I sigh.

He's gorgeous, and flawed and sexy. And I have no idea what I'm getting into.

* * *

I had forgotten how tiring waiting tables truly is. I've only been here for five hours and it feels like a million. I pause tiredly by the kitchen door to rub my ankle after banging it on a table leg.

"Tired already?" Maddy asks with a grin as she passes by. She pauses next to me, a tray of food in her hands. "Don't worry. The night is almost over."

I roll my eyes. "Yet the blisters will last all week. Oh, the things I do for you, big sister."

She giggles and delivers her food while it is still steaming, balancing the loaded tray expertly. Even though she has been here every bit as long as me today, she still looks flawless. Her blonde ponytail is still perky, her makeup is still perfect. She doesn't look for even a minute like she is hung-over. I don't know how she does it. It's annoying.

I sink into a nearby chair to rest my weary legs.

"Is this seat taken?"

Before I even look, my heart knows that the husky voice belongs to Pax.

I turn and find Pax behind me, freshly showered and dressed in slacks and a button-up. Holy Hell. He looks amazing. I hadn't been expecting him to dress up and I instantly feel at a distinct disadvantage. I'm grimy and smell like garlic. Why can't I look perfect at all times like Madison?

"Hi," I tell him softly. "You clean up really well."

He smiles, bright and brilliant. "Thanks. Am I early?"

"Only a bit. Why don't you come sit at the bar and get a drink while I finish up?"

He nods and I lead him to the bar, introducing him to our lion-haired bartender. Tony's thick black hair stands up in an uproarious mess all over his head.

"Pax, this is Tony. He's been with us for years, back when my parents were still alive. Tony, this is Pax. Can you keep him company while I finish up my shift?"

Tony, a forty-year old true Italian, looks interested in this venture. As I walk away, I hear him begin interrogating Pax.

I turn around. "I'm sorry," I call to Pax. "I won't be long."

Pax rolls his eyes good-naturedly and returns his attention to Tony's inquisition. I turn back around, only to bump directly into Maddy.

"What are you doing, little sis?" she asks sternly. "What's *he* doing here?"

I eye her. She's got her sternest big-sister expression on and I sigh.

"He's here for a date. He saved my ass last night. And if you'd like to come with me while I change clothes, we can talk about it."

"Oh, you bet I will."

Madison calls out to another waitress to watch things in the dining room, and then she accompanies me down the long back hall to her office, where I'd stashed my bag.

As I take off my garlicky restaurant shirt and apply fresh deodorant, Maddy starts firing questions at me. With each word that leaves her mouth, I sympathize even more with Pax, who I know is answering just as many questions in the other room.

As I pull on a soft white long-sleeved shirt and jeans and spray perfume on my neck, I look at my sister.

"Look. I know you're concerned about me. And I don't honestly know if I should be taking this chance with Pax. But what I do know is that he makes me feel things I've never felt before. He makes me feel alive and hopeful that life truly can turn out amazing, if I only try hard enough. And last night, he saved me from Jared's drunk ass. So please. Just give me some space to try and figure this out and see where it goes. It's just a freaking date. We're not eloping or anything."

Madison sighs, loud and long. "I think you're insane. The guy has a drug problem. Among many other problems, probably. I don't think you should be giving him the time of day, much less a few hours for a date."

I glare at her.

"Maddy, you shouldn't judge someone that you don't even know. I don't think he actually has a drug problem. I think he uses, and of course I hope he stops. He made a mistake the other night by using too much. And again, I hope he stops and that never happens again. But there's something in him that seems so real and genuine, I can't help but want to get to know him better. There must be something good in him. He saved me last night. He didn't have to."

I stare at her and Maddy sighs heavily once again as she strums her red nails on her desk nervously.

"There's something I should remind you of—something our mother always said. You can't change a person, Mila. Not ever. A person will always be what they are. So don't go into this thinking that you can change Pax, and that his good qualities will overtake his bad. Things don't work that way. You don't even know him."

I'm quiet as I brush my hair and pull it into a low ponytail.

"No, I don't," I finally say as I turn to face her. "But you don't either. I'm going to get to know him because I'm an adult and it's my decision. Can we please drop this now?"

We have a stare down, me into her blue eyes and her into my green. Finally, she sighs and looks away. I smile at her concession.

"Thank you," I tell her as I bend to kiss her cheek. "Just be polite to him, okay? I'm not asking you to be best friends."

Maddy scowls at me, but I pay her no mind as I hurry out to the bar to save Pax from Tony. As I approach, I see that he doesn't appear to need saving. Tony is chuckling at something that Pax said, and Pax seems to be perfectly at ease.

I relax.

That is, until Pax turns in his seat and smiles at me. He's got a cleft in his chin that I somehow didn't notice before and his golden eyes are sparkling.

The world tilts on its axis and my heart slams a crazy cadence against my ribcage. I'm probably in way over my head, but for the moment, I don't care.

Chapter 11

Pax

I've never seen anything as beautiful as Mila looks walking toward me across the dining room. It's not just because she's gorgeous. *It's because she's walking toward me.* To be with me. Even if it's only for tonight or for now.

I gulp and grin at her.

She smiles back and everything seems right with the world, a strange and unusual feeling for me.

When Mila is halfway to me, Tony says quietly, "Don't hurt that girl or you will answer to me."

I glance at him and he's got a gruff, rigid look on his face, very different from the congenial bartender he was a second ago. But I understand it. He's protecting Mila and I've got to respect that. I nod.

"I'll try not to."

Tony nods back as he towels off a glass. "Do that."

Mila slides up next to me, breaking the sudden tension.

"Hi," she murmurs and she places her slender hand on my shoulder. I fight the urge to lift it into mine and kiss it. It's a strange inclination for me. But she seems to bring out strange things in me.

"Hi," I answer. "You ready for our date?"

She grins again. "Absolutely. Why don't we put our food orders in before the kitchen closes and then we'll open a bottle of wine. I'll show you the best table in the house."

She grabs my hand and leads me through the quiet dining room to an even quieter table for two by the windows. The entire back of the restaurant faces the lake which is easily visible through the windows. To the left, I see an Italian-style patio, which I must assume is used for dining in the summer months. It's too chilly to eat out there now.

"Will this be all right, monsieur?" Mila asks with a smile and an exaggerated accent. I grin back.

"French? I thought this was some fancy Italian joint."

She giggles, handing me a menu as I sit. I catch a hint of her perfume as she moves and I inhale it. She smells like heaven, just the way her mouth tastes.

"We're not aiming to be fancy. We're aiming to be an authentic Italian place. We just did a bunch of renovations this past summer to improve the ambiance and make it feel like you're in Italy."

I look around at the rough stucco walls, the Italian art, the rustic charm. It does seem like we're sitting in an old-world kitchen. So I tell her that and she beams. Apparently, that's exactly the look they were going for.

"I'll have the lasagna," I tell her. "Is it good here?"

She gives me a look. "Everything's good here. Make sure to tell all your friends."

I laugh. "I don't have that many. But I'll try and pimp your restaurant for you anyway. How do you feel about the rougher type of crowd?"

She gives me a dry look and darts away, presumably to turn

our food order in. She's back within a minute with a bottle of wine and she settles into the chair across from me. The candlelight flickering on our table casts a soft light onto her face.

"Wine?" she asks as she pours me a glass of red. I nod, which is good, because she's already pouring.

"Thank you," I tell her. "It's a beautiful night, isn't it?"

I glance out the windows, at the lake that is calm and dark in the night. Mila follows my gaze.

"I love the lake," she tells me quietly. "I know that most of us do that live here, but I really love it. It's so comforting. It's always the same no matter what else changes in my life."

I have to stare at her, because I feel exactly the same way. It's one of the reasons that I choose to live here, perched on the very edge of it. The lake symbolizes continuity to me. And it is comforting.

Mila stares at me, her gaze pensive. I notice now that her eyes are the softest shade of green, almost like jade.

"Tell me about yourself," she instructs softly as she sips from her wine. Her fingers almost stroke the wine glass and I find that I am jealous of it. I also notice that she's wearing a deep red ring on her middle finger that is the exact shade of the wine. I take a breath.

"Well, my name is Pax Alexander Tate. You know where I live now, but you probably don't know that I grew up in Connecticut and we moved to Chicago when I was seven. My father is still there. He's an attorney downtown. But I moved here a few years back. I love the lake, just like you. I love the peace and quiet and the solitude. I'm not the most social person, and I knew that people in lake towns are used to leaving other people alone. Locals know that sometimes people come here for exactly that reason— to be alone, away from the noise of the city. That's why I chose to move to Angel Bay."

Mila smiles encouragingly, as if she knows how hard it is for me to talk about myself. And honestly, I don't know why it is. What I'm doing right now is just rattling off facts. It's not like I'm getting into anything deeply personal.

"What about your mom?" she asks curiously. "Are your parents divorced? Is that why you moved to Chicago?"

And now we're in deeply personal territory. I inhale again and realize that my hand is clenched tightly against my thigh. I relax my fingers. This is just a conversation. No big deal.

"My mom died years ago. When I was seven. My dad and I moved to Chicago to get away from the memories."

Mila freezes, her gorgeous green eyes glued to mine.

"I'm…I…I didn't know that," she finally stammers. "I'm really sorry. You didn't say anything earlier at the hospital when I told you about my parents."

I stare at her. "I know. I don't usually talk about it."

"Was she sick?" Mila asks. "Did you have a chance to say good-bye? I think that was the worst thing about my parents' deaths. I didn't get a chance to say goodbye. It was so sudden. So shocking. The shock of it was the worst."

I try to think back to when my mom died, and like always, I draw a big blank. The only thing I ever see when I try to think on it is a bunch of vague whiteness. No memories.

"Do you ever remember things by colors?" I ask her off-handedly. "See, because I was so young, I apparently blocked all the memories of my mother's death. She died suddenly, also in a car crash, like your parents. But I can't remember anything about it. When I think about it, all I see is a big whiteness, like a blank screen, almost."

Mila seems shocked. "I do that too," she whispers. "I associate colors with pretty much everything. I think it's because I'm an artist. I paint for a living, so I naturally see things in paint. I don't know how to explain you, though."

I smile. "No one knows how to explain me," I tell her wryly.

"So, you were a little boy when your mom died," Mila says slowly. "That must have been horrible for you. No wonder you suppressed the memories. How did your dad handle it? Do you have any other family?"

Normally, I would be put off by someone probing into my personal life. But I know that Mila doesn't mean any harm. I think she's just trying to figure me out, to see what makes me tick. I almost laugh, because that's pretty impossible to do, I think.

"I was a little boy," I confirm. "And I think it probably was horrible. But like I said, I pretty much don't have any memories of it at all. I don't remember much until I turned nine or so. My old therapist, the one I had when I was a kid, said that it was my brain's way of protecting itself from the trauma. My dad didn't handle it well, either. It's one of the reasons that we moved away. He's never been the same. My mom took a little piece of him when she died. And no. I don't have any family other than him. My grandfather, my mother's father, is still alive. But he was pretty pissed when we moved and stopped talking to me. He runs an oil company, which is how I make my living. I inherited my mother's shares."

And just like that, I've shared more with Mila than I've shared with anyone in a long time. I guess I really hadn't realized how secluded I've become until this moment. It's pretty sad. I've never really had a use for anyone else. Until now.

I stare at Mila.

"So, now you have my life's story. What about you? I know your parents died. What else is there to know about you?"

I reach for the bottle of wine and fill our glasses up again. I have a feeling that we'll both need it by the time the evening is out. I glance around and find that the restaurant has pretty much cleared out, except for some clattering in the kitchen.

"Well, I'm still fascinated by the fact that we have more in common that I had thought," Mila admits, her cheeks flushed from the wine.

"Yeah, we belong to an elite club," I roll my eyes. "We know what it's like to lose a parent at a young age. Lucky us."

"You were much younger than me," she tells me seriously. "I was grown and in college. I can't imagine what that would do to a little boy- to grow up without his mama. Was your grandma alive for a while at least? Did you have any kind of female influence at all?"

I shake my head. "No. My grandma died before I was born. And no, I didn't have any kind of female influence, other than teachers as I was growing up."

And right there, with one breath, Mila touched on something that I'd never thought about. Had the fact that I didn't have a mother (or any other female) affect me more than I had known? Is that why I'm not good at relating to women?

From the look on Mila's face, I think she's wondering the same thing. But she doesn't say anything. There's a bit of sympathy in her eyes though and I hate that.

"Don't feel sorry for me," I tell her. "There are millions of people who have had their mother die. You did, as well. I'm not so unique. We all get through it as best we can."

She stares at me again, her face pensive. "So you don't cut yourself any slack at all that you grew up without a mother?"

I roll my eyes. "Are you trying to find some sort of reason that I've become such an asshole? The reason is…I'm an asshole. There are some things in life that can't be explained. Period. Assholes are assholes. Rainbows are pretty. Kittens are cute. Chick flicks are sad. It's the way of things, no explanations."

And now she rolls her eyes.

"Things are the way they are, but everything has a reason. Kittens are cute because they're tiny fur-balls with smushed faces. Rainbows are pretty because they have every color in the world in them and they're made from refracted light. Chick flicks are sad because chicks sometimes just need a good cry. And assholes are always assholes for a reason."

She stares at me again, her eyes full of determination, and I can see that she truly wants to pick me apart and see what makes me tick. I suddenly feel naked beneath her gaze. But as luck would have it, our food arrives at this most perfect of times, and I almost sigh with relief.

Her sister Madison sets our plates down in front of us. Lasagna for me, penne for Mila. A basket of bread between us.

"You should be all set," she tells us, but she's looking at Mila, not me. "If you just want to put your dishes in the kitchen and lock up when you're done, that would be great. Everyone else will be leaving soon. Are you good here?"

She raises an eyebrow at her sister and I know she's really asking Mila, *Are you okay here with him?*

I fight the need to glare at her. She's the one who left her little sister alone and drunk with an asshole last night. I didn't.

Mila nods and smiles. "We're good, Maddy. I'll see you tomorrow."

Madison nods and leaves without looking at me again. I look at Mila.

"Your sister's an ice bitch," I point out politely.

Mila throws her head back and laughs. "Why don't you tell me how you really feel, Pax?" She giggles again, then adds, "Maddy's just protective. She's all I have now and she takes that role pretty seriously."

I raise an eyebrow. "She didn't last night when she left you alone with Jared the asshole."

Mila shakes her head. "She feels badly about that. She can't handle her liquor very well either and she made a mistake."

I shake my head, but let it go as we dive into our food.

"This is very good," I tell her. "It's no wonder this place is swamped in tourist season."

She smiles. "Thank you. It was my parents' dream. And Madison is keeping it alive for them."

We continue eating by the candlelight, the silence surprisingly comfortable. I've never been with someone before when I didn't feel the need to fill the awkward silence. With Mila, nothing seems awkward. She's got an easy way about her that puts me at ease.

When we're finished, we carry our plates to the kitchen and Mila turns to me, her slender hand on my chest. I glance down at her in surprise.

"I'm not ready to say goodnight yet," she tells me softly. "Would you like to go for a walk on the beach?"

I nod. "Of course. Let's get our jackets though."

I help her shrug into hers and then I follow her outdoors, over the worn trail leading down to the water.

Mila grabs my hand as we walk and holds it, and it feels really intimate.

"I used to play here on this beach when I was a kid," she tells me as she gazes around at the frozen wild-grass and gray water. "Maddy and I used to run up and down this stretch of sand while our parents worked in the restaurant. It was a great childhood. Where did you play?"

I think on that as I guide her around a piece of driftwood.

"I don't really remember," I tell her. "I have bits of memories from my grandfather's estate. I think my mother maybe took me there from time to time. And I remember a few Christmases. But nothing more than that."

She looks at me sympathetically again, but doesn't say anything. I have a feeling she knows that I wouldn't like it.

"Do you think there's a God?" she asks, changing the subject. And it seems so out of the blue. I stare at her.

"What kind of question is that? It's so random."

I smile and we continue to walk and I feel the moisture of the wet sand permeating my dress shoes. I wish that I would have worn my boots, but they would have looked out of place with slacks.

Mila sighs.

"I don't know. It's not really random. I just wonder from time to time. Don't you? I never really thought about it until my parents died, but now it crosses my mind sometimes. I can't help it. And we were talking about other deep things tonight, so I just thought I'd ask. I'm trying to get to know you."

She smiles and squeezes my hand and my heart softens a bit. There's something about this girl. I know that she could ask anything, and I'd probably answer.

"I don't know," I tell her. "I don't know about God. I'm sure he's there somewhere. Out there. Probably looking down on all of us and wondering why we're so fucked up. And if he's there, I'm sure he forgot about me a long time ago."

Mila's breath catches in her throat, I can hear it. And she stops, turning to me, her hand on my arm. She looks up at me, her eyes filled with something that I can't identify.

"Why would you say that?" she asks quietly.

I shake my head. "I don't know. There's something missing in me, Mila. It's just not there and I'm not sure if it ever was. And I'm pretty sure that God doesn't mess around with someone like that."

For some reason, there's a lump in my throat and I have no idea why. I swallow it and stare down at the delicate, beautiful girl on the beach beside me. Anyone else might have tucked tail and run. But not her. Her feet are planted and her eyes are wide.

She reaches up and touches my chest, then my face.

"You're wrong," she tells me softly. "About everything. You don't see yourself the way I see you. But if you did, you would know that there's nothing missing in you at all. I think that you've always used drugs to block out questions that you've had about yourself, or doubt or fear. I'm not sure what all your reasons were. But I know that you've got things you've never dealt with or thought about, and that's probably why you feel a void now. But once you discover what it is that you need to deal with, you'll feel whole again. No more holes, no more voids. That's what I think."

My eyes burn as I stare down at this incredibly perceptive woman. I do have a lot of shit that I've never bothered to think about. In fact, I went way out of my way to avoid thinking about it. And maybe *that* was what was most to my detriment—not doing crazy shit, like I thought.

"I think you know me better than you should," I tell her gruffly. She smiles her delicate smile.

"I don't know you nearly as well as I'd like to," she answers, wrapping her arms around my neck. "But I'm going to remedy that."

And then she kisses me. As she does, everything seems right in the world, like it always does when she's in my arms. It's like holding a ray of sunshine. I kiss her until we can't breathe and when we finally pull away, we take a breath and kiss again.

The stars twinkle overhead, the lake is soundless and calm to our left and for the first time in as long as I can remember, I feel like I'm home.

Chapter 12

I wake up craving coke for the first time in a week.

I don't know why, because last night was fucking amazing. Mila and I had walked along the beach until we were exhausted. We held hands and kissed, then held hands some more. I had walked her to her car, where we kissed yet again. But I didn't invite her to my place and she didn't invite me to hers.

This is too good to fuck up. Even an asshole like me knows that. If she wants to take it slow, that's exactly what I'm going to do. I'm not going to rush her. I have a hand for a reason and I'm not afraid to use it.

Just thinking the word *use* makes me remember my craving, the one where I want my nose to burn and the numbness to spread through me.

But it's just habit. Because for the first time since I can remember, I don't want to be numb. Mila makes me want to feel things...with her and for her. She makes me want to be a better person simply so that I can be around her.

So, I throw my covers back and do an impetuous thing.

I take the lid off of my vial and dump every pill inside it into my toilet, flushing them down. As I watch them swirl around, I'm overcome by a moment of panic.

What the fuck am I doing?

I almost thrust my hand into the toilet water to yank them out.

But then Mila's face appears in my head and I am calm again.

I'm doing the right thing. That's what I'm doing. And I can do this. I'm not a pussy.

I pad down to the kitchen and find my backup pills in the freezer, and I toss them into the garbage disposal, turning it on. I listen to it grinding up the pills, grinding away my escape from reality.

I even dispose of my sleeping pills. Anything that can be a crutch to me, I pitch. Except for the three bottles of whiskey that I have in the kitchen. I'm trying to turn over a new leaf- I haven't gone fucking insane.

My cell phone rings and I see Mila's name light up. I smile and answer it.

"Hey, babe."

There is silence for a second, as though the endearment caught her off-guard, but I hear the smile in her voice when she finally answers.

"Hey. Just calling to say good morning. And to thank you for last night. It was really nice. I had a fantastic time. What are you doing now? Did I wake you?"

I laugh. "No. You didn't wake me. You won't believe what I'm doing, actually."

Pause.

Then she laughs. "Well, are you going to tell me or are you honestly wanting me to guess?"

"I was wanting you to guess," I tell her. "But if you want to lack creativity, then I can just tell you. I'm turning over a new leaf. I won't bore you with the details, but I think you'll notice a change around here."

Another pause.

Finally she answers.

"Pax, what do you mean, a new leaf? What kind of change are you talking about? Because if it's something significant, I don't want you to do it because you think I want you to. That will never work. Change only happens if *you* want it to happen."

I chuckle. "You're fairly wise for such a young little thing," I tell her. "But I do want to make this change. You were right last night. I've used drugs to cover up emotions before- to block them out. Only a pussy does that. I can handle whatever life wants to throw at me. I don't need a crutch."

"Okay, one, I'm not much younger than you. I'm twenty-three. And two, I'm really happy for you, Pax. This is amazing. And I'll help you in whatever way you need. If you want, I can recommend a therapist. I used one after my parents died. He was really good with helping me deal with the grief. But I'm sure he can help you with kicking this, too."

"Fuck that," I tell her automatically. "I'm sorry. I didn't mean for that to sound rude. I just meant that I'm not an addict. I don't need help kicking the habit. I really don't. But thank you for the offer."

Pause.

Longer pause.

"Okay," Mila finally answers. "I can respect that. But let me know if I can do anything to help. I can listen if you want to talk, or try to keep you occupied, or whatever you need. In the meantime, would you like to have another date tonight? I have something in mind."

"Oh, really?" I ask, raising my eyebrow even though she can't see it. "And what are you thinking?"

"Well, it involves my shop and paint. Since we're getting to know each other, I thought maybe you'd like to see what I like to do."

I'm intrigued now, so I tell her that and then agree to meet her at her shop at 7:00. I'm supposed to bring take-out.

I smile as I head to the shower. If this is what being in a relationship is like, I think I can handle it.

Mila

They say not to wish your life away, but that's exactly what I do all afternoon long as I wait for 7:00 p.m. to roll around.

After I close the shop at 6:00, I rush up to my apartment and shower, dressing in a pair of jeans that fit me just right and a soft red sweater, a gift from him. This particular sweater has a plunging neckline and I don't wear a camisole underneath. I can see the swell of my breasts as I examine myself in the mirror and a flush spreads along my cheeks.

"God, you're ridiculous," I tell myself as I dab on perfume. "You're an adult, he's an adult. You can dress sexy if you want to. It doesn't make you a slut."

And now I'm talking to myself.

Great.

At 7:00, I make my way back down the stairs, pretending to be calm while I wait for Pax in my shop. He's right on time, thank God. I watch him walk up the sidewalk and quite honestly, he takes my breath away.

Tonight, he's freshly showered again and wearing jeans and a black shirt that clings to his chest beneath his coat. His slender waist makes me ache to wrap my arms around it, so I drag my gaze up to his face. He winks at me.

My heart flutters as I unlock the door and let him in.

"Hi," I say softly. He brings with him the cool winter air and his clean scent. I take a deep breath, then stretch up to kiss him on the cheek.

"Hi," he answers. "Is that all you've got for me?" He grins.

I shake my head, rolling my eyes. "For now. Be patient."

"Oh, I'm very patient," he tells me. "Trust me."

He stops in the middle of my shop and looks around. He's so big, but he manages to not look out of place in the midst of all the delicate furniture, easels and paint.

"So, what's the plan? What are we doing?"

"Well, first, I'm going to take your coat. And then you have two choices. I can either teach you to paint and you can paint with me, or I'll paint you. You can be my model. Either way, it should be fun."

Pax stares at me thoughtfully, appearing to truly think about this.

"Well, I'm not much of an artist," he finally says. "I don't even know if you could teach me, to be honest. I'm just not artistically inclined."

"I think I could teach you," I tell him smugly. "But if you would feel more comfortable, I'd be happy to paint you and we can chat while I do."

"I've never been painted before," he announces. "Can I choose the setting and pose and whatnot?"

I'm surprised that he would care. But I nod.

"Of course. This is just for fun. I'll do it any way that you want it."

He beams. "Great! I'd like to be nude."

I'm shocked as I stare at him, but as I see the sparkle in his eyes, I know that I walked right into that.

"That was a trap!" I roll my eyes. "You set me up."

He shrugs and looks very proud of himself.

"I'm sorry that you're not more street-wise," he says, and I can tell that he's not sorry at all. "But you already agreed to it. So, I guess you'll be painting me nude." He narrows his eyes. "Why? Does that bother you? Are you worried that you won't be able to control yourself as you gaze upon my sexiness?"

He waggles his eyebrows now and I giggle.

"Oh, I'll try hard to manage," I tell him. But quite honestly, it might be a feat. I can't believe I've gotten myself into this.

I gulp a big breath of air and glance around, trying to calm my quaking nerves.

"We'd better take this into my studio in the back. I don't think you want to be naked in front of the windows. Or maybe you do, you exhibitionist freak."

I laugh, remembering that he has entire walls of windows at his house which doesn't deter him from walking around naked. Then I remember watching him get a blowjob through one of those windows and it sobers me up. My cheeks flush and Pax looks at me.

"What's wrong? Does the fact that I'm a freak bother you?"

He's still kidding and has no idea that I have a picture of he and Jill firmly implanted into my head. I shake my head, trying to shake the image away.

"Of course not," I joke back. "I like it."

I turn my heel on his shocked expression and lead the way to my private studio. As I walk in, I inhale the familiar smell...of oil paint, acrylic and wood floors. I turn to Pax.

"I give private lessons in here and this is where I do my own work."

He looks around appreciatively. "It's perfect. I can see you in here, working away."

He points at a painting hanging on the wall, one of a woman with her head bowed. It's fairly abstract and you can't see the details of the woman's face. No one would know that it's my sister, and her head is bowed because she's crying at my parents' funeral. That particular moment imprinted on my heart and I knew I had to paint it. The painting hangs in here, in my private studio, because it's too personal to be sold.

"Is that Madison?" Pax asks curiously. I stare at him in surprise.

"How could you possibly know that?" I ask. "It's so vague."

He walks over to examine it. "Well, I can see that the features are delicate, like hers. Her hair is blonde and there's just something haunting and personal about it. I figured it had to be Madison. It's beautiful."

"Thank you," I murmur.

He runs his finger along the bottom edge of the frame, still examining it.

"She's crying, isn't she?" he muses. I nod.

"Yes."

He turns to me. "You've been hurt in life, Mila. I know that. And I swear to you, on everything that is sacred to me, that I will try not to hurt you, too."

I stare at him as I pull out a smock.

"On everything that you consider sacred?" I'm trying to joke now, to pull us out of this serious conversation. I'm just not in the mood for deep right now. "What exactly do you consider sacred? Jack Daniels?" I laugh, and he finally laughs too, allowing me to lead this conversation elsewhere. I'm silently grateful.

"I'll have you know, Miss Smarty Pants, that Jack has gotten me through some hard times. And thankfully, I'm not giving him up yet. So, yes. Maybe Jack Daniels is sacred to me."

He grins at me cockily, daring me to say something. So I raise an eyebrow.

"You can drop trow now."

His jaw practically drops instead.

"Drop trow?"

His shock makes me giggle. "Hey, you're the one who wanted a nude picture, you freak. In order for me to do that, you're going to have to drop your trousers."

Pax regains his composure and smiles charmingly.

"Well, if you think you can control yourself."

He unfastens his jeans and lets them drop to his ankles. He steps out of them, then his underwear follow. I fight the urge to look. He grins.

"Oh, you know you want to," he teases, as he pulls off his shirt. "Go ahead. Take a peek. You're going to have to eventually anyway."

I swallow hard as I stare at his chest. He's got a tattoo on each pec, and one on each bicep. I notice that he's also got words on his right side. All of it is perfectly show-cased by his amazingly sculpted body. Holy hell.

I fight not to look below his waist. I don't want to give him the satisfaction right now and he's certainly waiting. I smile.

"All in good time, Mr. Tate. Why don't you go up there and stand under the light?"

I motion toward the front of my studio, a safe and respectable distance from my easel. He confidently strides naked into place. I inhale. His backside is as sculpted and perfect as his front. How is that even possible?

"How do you want me?" he asks as he stands facing me, his hands dangling at his sides. What a loaded question.

I can't help but look below his waist now and am sufficiently impressed, yanking my eyes back up to find that he is staring at me in amusement. My cheeks immediately flush, hot and quick.

"Um. Why don't you turn a bit and look into the distance?"

"Your wish is my command," he drawls, turning. The muscles of his back ripple and I stare at the words on his side. They are bold and black, scrawling across his ribcage. I read it aloud.

"Go placidly against the noise and haste."

I stare at him in disbelief.

"Isn't that from the poem *Desiderata*?"

He nods and I'm stunned. I must look it because he laughs.

"What? You think I'm illiterate?"

He cocks an eyebrow and I laugh.

"No. It's just not how I think of you. Placid. Or calm. Isn't the next line something about peace?"

He nods. "It's *And remember what peace there is in silence.* I almost had that inked on me, too, but decided against it. It's enough that I know. Pax means peace in Latin, you know. So it's fitting."

I pull the canvas toward me and begin to paint his silhouette, deciding to do it in an abstract, like the painting of Madison.

"I guess I didn't know that. That's interesting. And your tattoo is beautiful. I just don't picture it as something that you would choose. It says a lot about you."

Pax stares at me thoughtfully. "Why? Because it's deep? I'm deep. Sometimes. Although most of the time, I'm just trying to block out reality. I'll give you that. But there's peace in that, you know."

I eye him, then paint the line of his butt and thigh.

"Maybe. But that's not true peace. It's a false sense of peace, brought on by oblivion and denial. That's not real."

I look up again and he seems to be considering that.

"You might be right," he says quietly. "But it's still a peace, nonetheless. It's better than nothing."

"I think you set the bar too low," I tell him. "You need to aim higher."

I paint the edge of his pec, then flow downward to his rib.

"I have," he says seriously. "With you."

I look up and into his eyes and the intense look that I find there gives me goose bumps. His hazel eyes glitter and I can't think straight.

"Anyway," he drawls with a grin, lightening the mood again. "I think you're handling this much better than I expected. Being exposed to all of this sexiness is usually disarming, but you're one cool customer, Mila. I propose that we up the ante."

I stare at him hesitantly, my hand frozen above the canvas.

"I'm almost afraid to ask," I tell him. "What do you want to do now?"

He examines me as he stands tall and proud in his nudity.

"I want you to be naked while you paint me. It's the least you can do to put me more at ease. I'm a basket case over here."

I do a double-take and my jaw drops open. He's the furthest I've ever seen from a basket-case right now. He's proud of his nudity. Cocky, even. He laughs at my expression.

"Are you chicken, little Red?"

My heart pounds so loud that I can practically hear it.

He stares at me, a dare in his eyes and against my better judgment, I lay my paintbrush down and unbutton my jeans.

"Fine," I tell him. "If you think you can handle it, I'll paint naked. Even though this isn't exactly normal second date behavior. But you need to focus on remaining still. Not a single part of you can move. Can you do that?"

He watches in utter fascination as my jeans fall to the floor and I step out of them, kicking them to the side. My black lace panties follow, and then my sweater and bra. He acts unfazed, as if it doesn't matter to him in the slightest, but the movement below his waist reveals the truth.

I smirk.

"Can you handle it?" I ask saucily. "Because you're moving."

His lip twitches.

"Oh, Red. If you want to turn up the heat, you've got to be careful not to get burned by the fire."

And as I stare into his hazel eyes, at the golden flames there, I have the distinct feeling that I could get very, very burned.

Chapter 13

Pax

My dick is harder than it has been in a long time and I know Mila can see it. I can't help but stare at her. She's so fucking beautiful.

She stares at me from around her easel and I can see the curve of her breast. It's creamy white and soft and I ache to stride across the room and stroke it, to pull the nipple into my mouth and feel it harden into a pebble. With each movement of her arm, I can see the curve of her hip, the length of her thigh. Her legs are the perfect length to wrap around my hips.

My groin tightens even more.

Dead puppies, nuns, cold fish. I envision these things, but it doesn't work. Damn. My dick twitches.

Mila smiles.

"You won't burn me," she tells me confidently as her hand moves across her canvas. "You already promised."

I swallow.

"I promised to try," I remind her. "But I'm not as perfect as you are."

She smiles again, her eyes focused intently on what she is

painting. I can only see the silhouette of her side and her slender arm moving. I strain to see more.

"I'm not perfect," she tells me. "Far from it, actually."

I roll my eyes and shift my weight. It's surprisingly hard to remain in one place.

"I somehow doubt that."

She looks at me sternly. "You've got to stay still," she reprimands me. "I need you in one position."

"What position might that be?" I ask, trying not to smile. "Missionary? Doggy-style? Shall we check out a copy of the Kama Sutra from the library?"

"No need," she says as she steps around her easel and walks toward me, absolutely gorgeous in her nudity. "I have one in my bed stand."

I suck in my breath and stare at her and she laughs, enjoying my shock.

"Kidding," she tells me as she draws to a stop in front of me and moves my arm. Her touch, although it's merely on my arm, sets my skin on fire. As she leans forward, ever so slightly, her breast presses against my chest, soft and warm. My dick is rock hard now and curved toward the ceiling. I fight the urge to grab her and bury my tongue in her throat.

"Funny," I say drily. And then an idea occurs to me.

A wicked one.

"I've changed my mind," I tell her and she is standing so close that I can feel the heat of her naked body. Her nipples are exactly as I thought they'd be. Pink and tilted toward the sky. I groan silently. This girl is hotter than any one girl has the right to be.

"Oh?" she asks innocently as she adjusts my other arm. I nod.

"Yep. I want to paint now."

She's surprised. "You do? I thought you said that you aren't an artist."

I smile, the grin stretching from ear to ear. She's walking straight into something again and I'm enjoying it.

"Oh, I think I can be," I tell her. "If I have the right canvas."

She is still puzzled and I break form, grabbing her hand and leading her back to her easel, to the little stand that holds her tray of paint. She's staring at me in confusion, one eyebrow cocked as she waits for me to explain.

I stare into her eyes, which is incredibly difficult to do since the rest of her body is naked. I deserve a medal for this show of restraint.

"I know that you want to go slow and I respect that. I promise to stop at any time that you tell me to, okay?"

She looks uncertain and I fight the urge to look at her tits again.

"I promise," I assure her. "I have an idea for something fun. But it involves me touching you. Do you have a problem with that?"

She looks even more hesitant, but she shakes her head. She trusts me. I don't know how or why, but she does. That knowledge clenches my gut into a vise-grip.

"No," she says quietly. "I don't have a problem with that."

I smile and will my stomach muscles to relax.

"Good. I'm going to need you to stand still. An artist needs to concentrate."

Mila rolls her eyes and stands still, her hands dangling beside her perfect hips. I swallow hard. My dick is so fucking hard it could cut glass.

Reaching around her, I scoop a glob of red paint onto my fingers. And then without hesitation, I touch her chest, gliding the crimson color in a swoop across her skin. It looks like a red bird is flying in a V across her chest.

At the contact, she gasps and her eyes fly to mine.

"Finger painting," she manages to eke out. "Interesting. I did this in kindergarten."

"Oh, not like this," I answer confidently, as I slide my fingers down her soft side, toward her hip. "I guarantee you that."

She looks like she swallows her tongue as I trace the outline of her butt, and then slide my fingers down her slender thigh toward her knee. I bend on my own knee and kiss the back of hers. She inhales shakily.

I can hear it, and I smile.

Reaching over, I choose black paint this time, tracing the color across her back and up to her shoulders, in swirls and swoops. I don't have a particular picture or word in mind, I simply slide the color across her flawless skin. I enjoy the friction of my skin against hers, and I can't help but wish that she was pressed against me.

I reach around and pull her toward me, my palms flattened against her flat belly as I press my lips against her smooth back. I bury my face in the top of her butt, the soft rounded flesh against my face. Her feminine scent fills my nose and I breathe deeply, soaking her in.

"Pax," she whispers.

"Do you want me to stop?" I ask quietly and everything in me is praying that she says no.

"No," she answers, and I breathe again. "I like your hands on me."

Her voice is quiet and soft and I close my eyes.

As I slide my hands around to her hips, I can feel her pulse in my fingertips. I glance around and find my handprints on her abdomen.

"I've imprinted on you," I tell her, laughing softly. "You're mine now."

And it's true. She's mine now. She might not know it yet, but it is true.

She swallows hard. I can hear her moist tongue in her mouth and I wish it was in mine. She twists around and her eyes meet mine. I drag my fingers up to her neck, holding her chin as I bring my lips to hers.

Slowly.

Painfully slow.

Her lips are warm and soft and she crushes them harder against me, turning until she's pressed against me, naked and pliable. And I get my wish. Her tongue plunges into my mouth, quiet and needy.

She melts into me and I press my palms against her back, dragging her to my chest, holding her there tightly.

She moans and my dick is wedged against her, hot and hard.

Fuck.

I hadn't counted on this. I'm going to need a very cold shower. But it isn't over. Not yet. I've got her here, naked and in front of me. I can't let this opportunity pass by. I want her to realize that she wants me too.

I slide my hands down, down…until they reach the softness of her thigh. I stroke there, softly, barely touching her until her eyes flutter closed. Her breath is rapid and soft and I smile.

"Do you like this?" I ask quietly. "My form of art?"

She nods. "You're…very creative." Her words are a whisper.

I chuckle, then move my hand toward her very center, between her legs. She gasps as I push her legs apart and touch her, as I move circles around her most sensitive part. She leans against me, allowing me to prop her up as I stroke her.

I bend my head and pull her pink nipple into my mouth, sucking the softness in, then letting it slide back out. She tastes as sweet as I thought she would. I knead at her soft skin, inhaling her scent and warmth, all while the fingers of my other hand never stop moving.

She moans and it is almost my undoing. I've never wanted anything more than I want to bury myself in her right now. I swallow hard. I can't. But I can make her want it so much that when it does finally happen, it will be fucking explosive.

I bend her back and follow the contour of her neck with my lips and then I kiss her again, hard and deep as I quicken the movement of my fingers. She's so fucking wet now and my fingers move fluidly in her, rubbing, stroking, bringing her to the edge.

She whimpers.

"I want you," she breathes against my lips. "Please. I want you."

I gulp as hard as I can, willing myself not to cave in.

"Let yourself go," I tell her. "Right now. I want to feel you come on my fingers, Mila."

Her eyes pop open and she stares into mine, her eyes filled with unselfconscious wonder, as though no one has ever said that to her. And then I realize it is probably true. I groan and drop my head, kissing her yet again, her tongue sweet against mine. I slide my fingers in and out, quicker, faster, harder and then she gasps, arching against me, crushed against me.

I suck in my breath as I feel her shudder. She comes hard and it is so fucking sexy.

She is damp and shaky and I hold her suspended in front of me, wrapped in my arms, until she finally opens her eyes.

She and I are both covered in paint now and when she pulls away slightly to look up at me, her cheeks are flushed and she looks sheepish. I smile.

"Did you enjoy my art project? I think it was a masterpiece."

She rolls her eyes and smiles slightly, as she bends to pick up scattered art supplies from the floor. I watch her ass, since she frames it up so perfectly in front of me.

"Why didn't you fuck me when I asked you to?"

The sound of that word coming from her sweet little mouth surges life back into my dick and she notices. She raises her eyebrows.

I smile.

"Because you're not ready yet. But you will be. And when you are, it's going to blow your mind."

"I have no doubt," she answers softly as she bends again to pick up the smock that she abandoned. "But that wasn't fair. You didn't get anything out of that. I feel bad."

I stare at her incredulously. Seriously? This little episode is going to fuel my morning shower every morning from now until eternity.

"Trust me," I tell her. "I got something out of it. Don't you worry about that."

She looks at me doubtfully. "I find that hard to believe. But we have a bigger problem. Where does one go in a date after something like that?"

I shrug. "I don't know. You're the expert on normal date behavior."

She grins and blushes. "That wasn't normal date behavior," she tells me. "That was extraordinary. Just so you know."

I grin as she picks up her clothes and turns to me. "I think we need a shower now."

I grin wider and she blushes again.

"Separately," she adds quickly. "Or I won't be able to trust myself."

I laugh and follow her as she walks from the studio. My eyes are once again focused on her perfect ass.

"Obviously," I tell her. "You've shown that you can't be trusted to think clearly in these situations."

She turns and rolls her eyes. "Oh, yes. That was entirely my fault."

I chuckle. "You were the one who suggested that I paint," I remind her and she laughs. I decide that her laughter is my new favorite sound in the world.

"True," she acknowledges. "But that wasn't exactly what I had in mind." She glances at me impishly. "It was better."

* * *

After we both shower, I have to admit to Mila that I had forgotten to bring the Chinese food.

"I'm sorry, "I tell her with a grin. "I can't be trusted to think about more than one thing at once. And I was focusing on being on time."

She smiles and reaches for the phone.

"It's okay," she tells me. "I've got them on speed-dial."

After the food arrives, I show her how to use chop-sticks and laugh at her attempts. She ends up eating with a fork, her lip puffed out in a pout.

"I'll master that," she vows. "Someday."

I smile and we eat and then she talks me into watching a chick flick. I honestly have no idea how that happened, except that I am coming to realize that it exceptionally hard to say no to her.

The movie doesn't end until far past midnight and we are cuddled together on the couch, warm and comfortable.

"I don't want to get up," she tells me as the credits roll. "I want to stay right here, with you. Can we sleep like this tonight?"

Her eyes are wide, as though she's asking me for the biggest favor in the world. My arms are around her and she is settled against my chest, her slender back draped against me. I smile down at her.

"Go to sleep, Red. I'll be right here in the morning."

She smiles and closes her eyes, nestling against me. I fall asleep, more contented that I've been in my entire life.

And then I dream.

Once again, I dream about my mother and even in my dream, I am wondering what the fuck is up with this. I deliberately don't think about my mom—because it's just too painful. But here I am dreaming about her again- and I can't force myself to wake.

I am somewhere dark. And I'm afraid. I don't know why and I can't see anything, but I can hear my mom's voice. She's begging. And I hear my name.

I try to open my eyes, to wake myself, to end the sound of her voice, but I can't. And deep down, I feel a sense of intense horror, although I don't know why.

"Not him!" she cries out and I know it is her voice because I'll never forget the sound of it. "Not him!"

And then I see her arms, stretching out, reaching for me and I am clutched to her even though I can't see anything. Everything is black and I am more frightened than I have ever been in my life. I am crying and she is crying and suddenly her arms are Mila's.

I look up and I can see again. Mila is covered in light, in a thousand glistening sunbeams. And she's smiling at me.

"Pax," she whispers. "I'm here. It's alright. Everything is going to be alright."

And then my eyes are open and I'm awake and I find that Mila is really here and she is really whispering those words to me.

"It's okay," she croons to me, stroking the hair away from my forehead. I realize that I am drenched in sweat. "Everything is okay."

I look at her, at the tenderness on her face and my gut clenches. I just dreamed that my mother turned into Mila. I'm seriously fucked up.

"Babe," I tell her when I can finally speak, when my gut unclenches enough to allow me to form the words. "I think I'll take the name of your therapist now."

Chapter 14

Pax

I lie awake, staring at Mila's painting of me. She finished it a couple days after she started it and I had brought it to my house and hung it next to my bed. It's amazing, but it's a bit too personal to hang in the living room. Even though it's an abstract, you can still tell that I'm naked.

The bronzes and golds of my body are contoured into curved muscles, tightly coiled. My tats are blurs of color, more conceptual than real. My eyes are closed and my head is bowed as though I'm thinking. It's incredible and I'm touched as hell that she actually finished it for me. Nobody has ever done something like that for me before.

I study it, wondering what the Painted Me is thinking.

The Real Me is thinking that I'm fucking hungry.

I swing my legs out of bed and make my way to the kitchen to grab a slice of cold pizza for breakfast. Mila and I had ordered it last night after our third "official" date. This time, we had watched a movie here at my place, and this time, the movie was my choice. It was no chick flick. It was completely made up of gunfire and gore. A man's movie. Mila watched it like a trooper, thumping her chest and pretending to scratch her imaginary balls.

I am chuckling at the memory when my phone rings. My mouth is full of pizza, but I answer it anyway because I see Mila's name.

"Hey," she says and she sounds a bit breathless. I immediately imagine her breathing like that into my ear with her legs wrapped around my hips. And just like that, I'm hard as hell.

"Hey," I answer, adjusting my erection. "Good morning."

I smile into the phone because I can't help it. This girl makes me smile like an idiot.

"I was just calling to remind you of the therapist appointment this morning," she tells me. "I figured you'd forget. Or change your mind."

Pause.

Fuck.

She's right. I don't want to go. But I'm willing to go for two reasons. One) I want to stop dreaming about my mother because it's freaking me the fuck out. And two) I think it will help put Mila at ease. I know she's struggling with the idea of dating me. She thinks I'm going to stomp on her heart. To be completely honest, I'm afraid I accidentally will. So off to therapy I go. I can do this. I'm no pussy.

"Whatever," I tell her, rolling my eyes. "Oh, ye of little faith. I haven't forgotten. I'm all showered and everything."

She laughs.

"Oh, really? You mean you aren't standing at the windows with bedhead and in your underwear? And eating a slice of pizza?"

Startled, I look down and find Mila standing in my driveway. She holds up a white paper bag and grins.

"I brought you doughnuts," she says into the phone. "Come answer your door."

I shake my head, but honestly, I'm happy she's here. Fucking ecstatic, actually. I had been disappointed when she didn't want to sleep over last night, curled up on my couch with me. She was afraid that she couldn't trust herself not to move too fast.

This might make me a pussy, but she's been the first thing I've thought of every morning this week when I woke up. And she's the last thing I think about when I go to sleep. Not that I'd ever admit that to anyone.

I try not to break my neck as I hurry to the door and open it. Before Mila can even say a word, I grab her and kiss her hard, smashing her against my chest. I hear the crinkle of a paper bag as we smash it between us. Her arms come up and wrap around me, pulling me closer. She smells like flowers and vanilla. And winter.

"I missed you," she murmurs against my neck. She's cold from the outdoors and I pull her inside.

"You just saw me last night," I remind her as I nibble at her lip. She smiles against me and I add, "But I missed you too."

I really did.

And that scares the shit out of me.

But of course I don't say that. Instead, I just pull her into my kitchen where we eat smashed doughnuts, perched atop breakfast bar stools.

Mila eyes hers. "I guess it still tastes the same," she shrugs. "Even though you flattened it."

She raises an eyebrow and takes a huge bite of her chocolate drizzled roll. She licks her finger, which causes my gut to clench.

"What time was my appointment?" I ask, looking away from her tongue and glancing at the clock.

"It's in thirty minutes," she tells me. "Dr. Nate Tyler. He's in town. I texted you the address."

I nod. "I've still got it. Don't worry. I'm going to jump in the shower and then I'm out of here."

She stares at me. "I really just wanted to tell you good luck. And that I'm proud of you for doing this. I know you don't like to talk about personal stuff."

"You got that right, sister," I mutter as I swing around on my stool. I drop a kiss on her cheek. "I've got to get moving if I don't want to be late. Want to join me?"

She grins wickedly. "I would. If we were two months further into our relationship." She shrugs. "But as it is…no."

I raise an eyebrow. "So you can paint naked in front of me, but you can't shower with me?"

She slugs me lightly on the arm, rolling her eyes. "Now you're getting it."

I smile. "Good. I'm just trying to get all of these dating rules down. It's sort of complicated. Confusing, really."

Mila grins, wide and beatific. "It's not that hard. I still like to look, even if I'm not ready to touch yet. But good things come to those who wait, mister."

I shake my head and start off for my bedroom. "I hope so," I call over my shoulder. "My hand's getting tired."

I can still hear her laughing as I step into the shower and let the water beat down on me. I was only partially joking. My hand *is* getting tired. But that doesn't stop me from using it.

* * *

"Tell me about your drug use," Dr. Tyler instructs me. He is using the calm monotone that I always think of psychiatrists using. The one that says, *If I talk slowly and quietly enough, I'll keep the psychos at bay.*

I shift my weight from one hip to the other in an ugly-as-fuck blue plaid chair. The doctor is older, graying at his temples and he's wearing reading glasses even though he isn't reading. I sigh. I really don't want to be here. I feel like a bug under a microscope and the dark paneling of this doctor's study seems to be closing in on me.

"My drug use isn't the problem," I tell him. "The dreams that I've been having are my problem. They're fucked up. I'm sorry," I quickly correct. "They're *messed* up."

Dr. Tyler smiles a bit as he makes some sort of note on his notepad.

"Why do you think your dreams are messed up?" he probes, his dark eyes assessing me. "Have you ever dreamt them before?"

I shake my head. "They're about my mother. And I haven't dreamed about her since I was small. As an adult, I make a conscious effort to not think of her. I'll admit it, I try to avoid painful things."

The doctor nods as he takes notes. "That's not unusual," he tells me. "Avoidance is human nature. But tell me more about these dreams."

So I do. I tell him how my mother is pleading. And how I am scared but I can't see and how my mother has turned into Mila in them.

The doctor studies me yet again. "It sounds like you are somehow associating Mila with your mother. Was your mother like Mila in some way?"

I think on that. And even though it's been a very long time since I've seen it, I can still remember my mother's smile.

"My mother had a pretty smile," I tell him. "It was very warm, like Mila's. Maybe that's it."

The doctor scribbles. "Anything else?"

"I don't know," I muse. "Mila seems soft and graceful. I think my mother was the same way. My mother was actually a ballet dancer, before she retired when I was born. Mila is an artist…so they are both artistic types."

More scribbling.

"Was your mother very accepting of you? She loved you unconditionally?"

I stare at him. "I was only seven when she died. But I'm guessing that, yes, that was the case."

"Is Mila very accepting of you?" Dr. Tyler asks quietly, his pen paused above his pad. I stare back at him. He might have hit upon something.

"Yes," I tell him. "For whatever reason, she's been very patient with me."

"Just like your mother," the doctor says pointedly.

"Yes." I agree, my heart pounding for a reason that I don't understand. My hands are sweaty, too. I wipe them on my jeans.

"Tell me about the drug use," Dr. Tyler says now, without looking up. I sigh again.

"You're not going to give up on that drug use thing, are you?"

He smiles and shakes his head.

"People use drugs for many different reasons," Dr. Tyler says. "I'd like to uncover yours."

I try to hide my annoyance. I want to get to the root of my current issue, not dig into something useless. But I do my best to humor him.

"I started taking sleeping pills when I was little, after my mother died. My therapist prescribed them because I couldn't sleep without nightmares. As the years went on, I realized that I liked the way I could take them and slip away from reality. I starting using different kinds of drugs. I've never stopped, until recently."

Dr. Tyler stops scribbling and looks up.

"You've stopped using? Why?"

I nod. "I dumped everything out this past week. I don't want to feel numb right now. Like I keep telling everyone, I'm not an addict. This isn't a big deal."

He lays his pen down and studies me. "You don't consider drug use a big deal?"

I exhale and fiddle with my hands. "Of course it isn't legal and it isn't healthy. But what I meant is that I've never been addicted. I've barely craved anything since I dumped everything down the drain."

The doctor nods. "Some people do have more addictive personalities than others. It must be harder for you to become physically addicted to narcotics than others. That's in your favor. But I'd like to talk about why you've done drugs for so long if you haven't been addicted. You've just told me that you know it isn't healthy. So why would you inflict that kind of thing on your body if you could've stopped at any time?"

I stare at the floor, at my feet, at the patterned rug.

"I don't know. Because I craved oblivion, I guess. Because it's easier to fade out of reality than face it. My reality as a kid wasn't that great. My mother was dead and my father might as well have been, because he sure as hell checked out when my mother died."

The doctor nods. "It sounds like you're a little angry about the way he handled things."

I think about that. "Yes. I'm angry about it. He had a little kid to raise and not only did he pretty much neglect me and spend every waking hour at work, but he uprooted me and moved me across the country to live in a place where I didn't know anyone.

He couldn't have made a worse choice. I needed normalcy, I needed to be around people that knew and loved me. But instead, I got nothing."

"So, you took drugs to cope?"

"I guess," I answer. "Although that makes it sound like a cop-out."

Dr. Tyler looks up. "It's not a cop out. Everyone has their reasons. Is that yours?"

"I suppose," I admit, and the feeling of admitting it is huge. I don't know why. But there is something freeing about saying it out loud. "I took drugs to cope with the void that I feel."

Does that make me a pussy, after all?

Dr. Tyler looks interested. "Did it help? Did it fill the void?"

I stare at my hands. "Yes."

"When the drugs wore off, did the void come back?"

"Yes," I answer quietly.

"Is the void still there?" The doctor is definitely interested now, his dark eyes staring into mine. I look away, at the wall, at the clock.

"Yes," I answer honestly.

It's quiet now, the only noise coming from Dr. Tyler's pen scratching across the page. I have the urge to reach over and grab it, to snap it into two. But I obviously don't. That would be crazy and I have no reason. I don't know where my sudden anger is coming from. I flex my fingers against my knee.

"You don't like talking to me, do you?" Dr. Tyler observes without lifting up his head.

"No, I don't."

"Then why are you here?"

I think about that, trying to come up with a somewhat polite answer.

"Because Mila asked me. And because I'm tired of the messed up dreams."

The doctor looks at me, his eyes kind. "What exactly bothers you the most about the dreams? It must be something substantial to get you to come see me."

My foot bounces up and down with nervous energy.

"I don't know. I think it's because my mom seems to want something and I'm not able to give it to her and it seems important. And because she turns into Mila and that freaks me out."

The doctor smiles. "I wouldn't worry about that aspect. Many people associate others in their dreams and it doesn't mean anything significant, at least regarding that person. Most of the time, it's symbolic of something else entirely. If I had to guess and at this point, it's an early guess, but if I had to guess, I would say that your mother turns into Mila because you have a deep-seeded fear that Mila is going to leave you like your mother did."

Shock slams into me and I suck in my breath. It's quite a concept and one that I hadn't thought of.

"My mother didn't leave me," I manage to answer. "She died. There's a difference."

"Yes, there is. But to a seven-year old boy who has been uprooted from everything he knows, there's not much difference. And it was at that point, when you were seven, that that idea was formed. In your head, she left you. And it was perfectly normal to feel angry about that. It's one of the normal phases of grief, actually. But since you blocked it out and didn't deal with it, you've never successfully gone through those stages. You might be stuck in the anger phase."

"Fuck," I breathe.

"Indeed," the doctor answers. "You've got some work ahead of you."

He scribbles some more and I pull at my collar as the room seems to get hotter and hotter. Then thankfully, my hour is over.

On the way out, the doctor scribbles something on a little paper and hands it to me.

"It's for Xanax," he says. "If you get the urge to use something again, to block out the stress or anger, get this filled instead."

I give him a hard look.

"I told you. I don't need this." I start to hand it back, but he holds up his hand.

"Take it," he urges me. "Just in case."

I roll my eyes.

"Whatever." I crumple it as I shove it into my pocket. "See you next week."

Chapter 15

Mila

Why in the world did I agree to help with the lunch rush at The Hill? For one thing, there isn't a lunch rush, not during this time of year. And for another, I should've known that Maddy only wanted to get me here to lecture me.

"I don't like it," she tells me now, referring to Pax. And me seeing Pax again last night. "He's not good for you. He's going to break your heart and leave me with the pieces to put back together."

I stare at her. "We've been through this. Your opinion has been noted. Is there anything else?"

I stand in front of her desk with my hands on my hips and what I hope is a defiant expression on my face.

Madison purses her lips, then shakes her head.

"No."

"Good. I'm going to go finish my side-work, then I'm out of here for the day."

"Can you come back and help tonight?"

I shake my head. "No. You didn't schedule me and I have plans."

She glares. "With our resident drug dealer?"

I glare back. "He's not a drug dealer and it's not your business."

"You're my sister, so it is my business," she tells me snappily.

I don't bother to answer, I just head out to the dining room. Tony is whistling at the bar and I edge up to him, perching on a bar stool.

I smile at his tuneless song. "Tony, you're always happy. Why is that?"

He glances at me as he slices limes. "Why shouldn't I be? I've got everything I need and a pretty little wife at home. My life is good."

I nod. "Good point. It's the simple things in life that are best, right?"

He nods and examines me, his knife paused mid-slice.

"Why the long face, mia bella? Do I need to break someone's legs?"

My gaze flies to his and he is laughing.

"Are you talking about Pax?" I ask. "Has Maddy been trying to get you on her side?"

Tony sobers up. "I'm on your side. And her side. I'll break the legs of anyone who gives you a hard time, period. Either of you. It doesn't matter if it is this kid or someone else."

I eye him and he seems to be serious. I picture big, gruff Tony swinging a bat and shudder.

"What do you think about 'this kid'? You talked with him the other night. How did he seem to you?"

Tony seems to consider that as he leans on his burly arms against the bar.

"It's hard to say. He seemed nice, polite. Respectful. That says something right there. At least his jeans aren't hanging around his ass, like some of the other punks his age. But he's got baggage. You know that already, though. You always were attracted to things that needed fixing. Remember that old stray dog you dragged in when you were little?" He looks up at me and then without a beat adds, "Oh, and by the way, the kid is here."

"What?" My head snaps up and I turn to find Pax walking through the restaurant door. I have no idea how he knew I was here.

Tony smiles and hums and continues wiping the gleaming wooden bar down as I head toward Pax.

"Hi," I say as I stop in front of him. I stare at his face, trying to assess his mood. Did the therapist appointment go well? I'm not sure if I should ask.

"Hi," he answers, then he smiles. He seems tired, but definitely okay.

"Did you come for lunch?" I ask. He shakes his head.

"Nope. I came for you."

"For me?" My questions comes out more like a squeak and Pax smiles.

"Yes, for you. I want to get out of town for a little bit, to clear my mind. You game?"

I stare at him, into his hazel eyes. He seems troubled and tired. "You want company?"

"If it's you."

If it's me. My heart lurches.

I nod, knowing that I would agree to anything now.

"What do you have in mind?" I ask, knowing that it doesn't really matter.

He stares down at me. "The lake hasn't begun to freeze yet. I was thinking we could take my boat out one last time before I have it winterized."

I'm nodding before I really even think about it and head for the door.

Pax tugs on my elbow. "You might want to get your coat."

He's laughing now and I have to laugh too. I'm an idiot. It's cold outside, and even colder on the water. I head to the back and grab my coat, ignoring Maddy sniping about my side-work.

When I return to Pax's side, I grasp his arm. I can't help but notice that my fingers fit perfectly inside the crook of his elbow.

I leave my car at The Hill, and ride with Pax out to the Pier.

"The vomit smell cleaned up nicely," I observe, as I sniff the interior. It smells like leather and pine car freshener. Pax shakes his head.

"Yeah, a good detailing will do that. I'm never going to live that down, am I?"

"Probably not," I answer absently, as I stare out the window. The wintery trees blur past as we leave The Hill behind us.

It only takes a few minutes to drive to the pier and the boardwalk looks so lonely this time of year. Most of the boats have already been taken out of their slips for the winter. It almost seems abandoned here.

Pax heads around to the trunk of his car and after burrowing around for a minute, pulls out a heavy blue parka.

"It's going to be cold on the water," he tells me needlessly. "So why don't you bundle up in this?"

He helps me pull it on and when I look sufficiently like the abominable snowman, we head toward his large speedboat.

I decide it must have costs thousands and thousands of dollars, but I don't say that as he helps me climb aboard. I choose to sit on the floorboard, out of the wind, and he starts up the engine. The roar slices through the silence and we are quickly puttering out of the bay.

Before long, Pax's face is red from the wind. It's been a mild winter so far, but it's still frigid out here. The water makes the wind absolutely bitingly cold.

"We'd better not go too far out," I yell to him. "You're going to freeze to death."

He rolls his eyes and continues to steer us past the huge lonely buoys that mark the channel-way into the bay. When we're out in open water, he finally cuts the engine and the silence seems enormous.

He drops down onto the floorboard next to me.

"You're right," he says, leaning into me. "It's fucking cold."

I giggle as he rams his hands into my pockets, trying to absorb some of my warmth.

"We're crazy for being out here today," I tell him. "We're going to get frostbite."

He grins. "I'm crazy for many things, but not this."

The rest of me might be cold, but my heart warms at his words. And then I feel like a sap. A freezing cold sap.

I huddle together with him, enjoying the way we seem like the only two people in the world out here as we bob with the current. The cold air stings my lungs, but I take a deep breath anyway, enjoying the briskness.

"Do you come out here a lot?" I ask.

Pax nods. "I come out here when I want to get away from the world. No one can find me here, although not that many people come looking."

I laugh and lean against him, and he wraps his arm around my shoulders.

"I should've brought some hot chocolate from The Hill," I moan, trying to warm up my red fingers. "I think I might lose a hand or my toes."

Pax rolls his eyes. "A little melodramatic, aren't we?"

"Speak for yourself. I need my toes." I squeeze into his arm tighter, then look up at him.

"How was your appointment today? Are you glad you went?"

He goes still and his jaw is clenched. I stare at him and try to decide how to handle this delicate situation.

He still hasn't said anything, so I ask, "Are you going back?"

Pax sighs. "I don't know. I don't see the point, really. He seems focused on my drug use and I just want to figure out my dreams. It's pretty startling to dream about your dead mother all of the time."

"Maybe he thinks the two things are connected," I suggest, trying to keep my voice light, but in reality, I'm dying to know what the doctor might have said.

"Doubtful," Pax answers. "The only correlation that he seemed to draw was one between you and my mom."

This startles me and I stare at him.

"What? He compared me to your mom?"

For some reason, this horrifies me. Being compared to his mom isn't exactly how I want him to see me. He shakes his head.

"I don't know what he's thinking. He's got some crazy ideas."

"But your dreams didn't start until you met me, right?" I ask slowly and I know the answer before he nods.

"Yes. But that doesn't mean anything."

"Okay." My voice is quiet here in the boat buried under the lip of the fiberglass. He squeezes me tight.

"Don't worry about it. I'm the fucked up one, not you. Trust me, I don't think of you as my mother, if that's what you're worried about."

I smile a bit, in relief and he laughs, looking at my face. "That's what you were worried about? I'm fucked up. But I'm not *that* fucked up."

I relax and sag against him and he rubs my hands to warm them. We can see our breath, the white wisps floating away as we talk.

For at least an hour, we chat about nothingness; high school, family and old pets. He laughs because I was a cheerleader for a while. And then I laugh because he owns every Star Wars movie ever made.

"What?" he demands imperiously. "They're good movies."

I laugh and try to pretend that my feet aren't blocks of ice and that I can't hear his phone. It's been buzzing every few minutes for at least an hour. He looked at it once, then shoved it back in his pocket and hasn't looked at it since.

"Do you need to get that?" I ask him as it buzzes again. "Whoever it is really wants to talk to you."

He shakes his head, clearly annoyed. "No. It's no one that I need to worry about."

I'm dying of curiosity, but I don't push it. He clearly doesn't want to talk about it. But I realize for the first time, that when he gets like this, so secret and closed-away, that it makes me nervous. What other parts of his life don't I know about?

I guess I fall silent because after a while, Pax nudges my foot.

"Why are you so quiet? Are you upset?"

I really want to say no, to pretend that I'm not unnerved, but I don't want to lie. Nothing good can come from lies and the deck is stacked against us already.

"It makes me nervous when I feel like you are hiding something," I tell him hesitantly. "I don't want to think bad things of you, but when I don't know what you're thinking…"

"Then you automatically assume the worst?" he interrupts, his eyes narrowing. "You automatically assume that I'm trying to hide something if I don't want to talk about it? That's a bit judgmental, isn't it?"

He's ticked now, I can tell, because he's clenching his jaw. It's a habit that I've noticed he has when he is angry. I see the muscle in his cheek tick and I swallow.

"I'm not trying to be judgmental," I tell him gently. "It's just that we started out on the wrong foot and I've been trying to gain ground here with the trust thing, and I'm sorry. I'm just a bit nervous. I'm out of my element."

He abruptly removes his arm from my shoulders and stands up. The boat rocks and I clutch the side.

"If you don't want to be with me," he says coldly. "Just say it. If you can't trust me enough, just tell me now. I'm trying to change for you. But I don't want to waste time on this thing if you can't get over my past."

I'm frozen, not by the bitingly cold wind, but by his words, by his angry face. He seems so ready to discard me, as though I'm not worthy enough of even a conversation. It's enough to suck the air right out of me.

"You'd throw this away, just like that?" I'm incredulous. "I didn't say that I can't trust you. But your phone has been blowing up for an hour and you clearly don't want to deal with it and you don't want me to know what it is. Your 'past' isn't very distant so you have to understand that I'm a little nervous. And you shouldn't be changing for *me*. You should be changing for *you*."

Pax stares at me and his eyes are cold now, like they were when I first met him. All traces of warmth are gone and I shudder, hating the look on his face and hating this conversation. I don't know how it went downhill so fast.

"Don't be mad," I tell him. "I'm just trying to talk about this with you. This is what people do in a relationship."

"People attack each other?" he asks, his voice raised. "Because that's what I feel like you're doing. You don't know who is texting me, so you're insecure. And all of a sudden, your insecurity is my problem."

Pax is seriously pissed. He is flexing his hands so tightly that his knuckles are white. I gulp and try to figure out how to calm the situation down. I hate conflict, but I hate even more that he has misunderstood.

"I didn't attack you," I begin. "I was just curious about who was trying to reach you."

He raises an eyebrow angrily. "Really? If you were that curious, then why didn't you just ask to see my phone?"

I am flabbergasted and stumble around for something to say as the wind whips my hair around my face. "Because in a relationship that is built on trust, people don't ask to see each other's phones."

"Yet you really want to see mine, don't you?" he challenges, his eyes spitting. "Because you don't trust me."

He digs in his pocket and pulls out his phone, turning the screen to me. There are 57 unread text messages.

"Here you go. Look to your heart's content."

"Holy shit," I breathe. "Did you see how many there are?"

And they're all from one number.

"Who is it?" I ask hesitantly, afraid he's going to yell again. He shakes his head.

"It's Jill. I told her that I'm not going to see her again and that I'm not going to supply her habit. But from these texts, it looks like she's desperate and she's begging for it."

"But you don't have anything to give her, right?" I ask slowly. He'd told me that he dumped it all out.

He stares at me harshly.

"I didn't lie to you," he says abruptly. "I said I dumped it, and I dumped it."

"Have you seen her since you had that conversation with her?" I ask slowly. It just doesn't seem normal that someone who had been rejected would be this persistent. Unless they were insane. "Is she crazy?"

He shakes his head again.

"No, she's not crazy. She's just a desperate addict who needs help. I should have cut her off long ago, but I was too much of a dick to care. And no. I haven't seen her."

As he speaks, his phone lights up again, with yet another text. 58. He rolls his eyes and I eye him uncertainly.

"Shouldn't you at least answer her?"

"No. It won't do any good. She's desperate. She's not thinking logically so it wouldn't matter what I say. I've seen her act like this before. She gets hysterical and there's no reasoning with her. Fuck this. I'm not going to let this stupid wench cause problems with us."

He raises his hand and I flinch.

He freezes, as hurt washes over his face.

"What the fuck? Did you think I was going to hit you?" he asks, his voice both wavering and furious. "Do you really think I would ever hurt you, Mila?"

He stares at me, waiting for an answer, but I don't know what to say. I doubt that anything I say would help so I just look at him limply. He shakes his head again.

"I was just going to get rid of this. *Fuck*, Mila."

He throws his phone into the lake. I watch it sink into the frigid depths and then turn to him.

"Pax, I—"

"Don't," he snaps coldly, turning his back on me to take the wheel. "Just don't. I can't talk to you right now."

He fires up the engine and guns it. The force of it throws me back onto the sidewall and I grip it with freezing hands. He's pissed and I know there's no reasoning with him. He needs to cool down.

We speed toward the shore and after each swell we crest, we land hard on the surface of the water. It's bone-jarring.

And as we speed along, I get more and more pissed.

"What makes you think you have the right to be mad at me?" I shout above the wind. "I was curious, that's all. I have a right to be curious, Pax."

He doesn't answer. His hand just pushes the throttle even more and we speed faster.

I grit my teeth.

"Would you slow down?" I demand. "You're going to kill us both."

No answer.

He doesn't slow down.

I grit my teeth again but before I can say anything, we hit another huge swell. And this time, before I can think or move, we come down hard.

Only instead of staying inside the boat, I am thrown right over the edge, right into the frigid, churning waters of Lake Michigan.

Chapter 16

Pax

"Fuck!"

I barely have time to react before Mila is gone, over the side and into the icy water. I kill the motor and turn about, scanning the top of the choppy water.

"Mila!" I shout as I rush to the side. "Mila!"

She's gone. I can't see her. The gray water churns and spins, creating frothy whitecaps that lap onto the side of the boat. There is no sign of Mila among the depths.

Holy shit. Without another thought, I dive in after her.

The shock of the frigid water knocks the wind out of me and I thrash about, trying to fumble for Mila and trying to keep my lungs from automatically sucking for air. I've never felt such an incredible, bone-shattering cold in all of my life. Every cell in my body, every bit of self-preservation, is trying to force me to get out of the freezing water. But I've got to find her.

I plunge further down and my body actually goes numb. I don't feel it anymore. I wave my arms blindly in front of me, desperate for some sign of her. This can't be happening. Mila can't drown here, not in the lake that she loves so much, not because of me. I force my eyelids open and the frigidity assaults the tender tissue of my eyes, but I have to see. Although the water is so murky in its frigid state that I honestly can't see anything at all.

I continue to flail about until my hand bumps something hard in the water.

I grab at it, my numb fingers grasping at something fleshy.

Mila.

The down-filled coat is dragging her down and she can't kick to the surface. She seems to be struggling to take it off.

I pull her with me and we break through the water. I shove her hair away from her face. She sucks in air and claws at me out of instinct, trying to get out of the water.

"Calm down," I tell her quickly, kicking us toward the boat. "Calm down or you'll drown us both."

I shove her up and over the side of the boat, and then pull myself up after her. We both collapse into a heap. She's in a pool of icy water on the floor of the boat, her teeth chattering and her lips blue.

"What the hell were you thinking?" I snap at her. "Are you insane? Why weren't you holding on? "

I strip off the heavy full-length parka because it is soaked and then I look around the boat to see if there is anything to wrap her in, but there isn't.

"Fuck," I mutter. "I don't have anything to keep you warm." Her wet hair is standing up in clumps and dangling down her back and I rub at her arms. "We've got to get back to shore. Stay over here next to the edge."

She clings to the side, under the lip where she is partially protected from the wind.

"I'm s-s-sorry," she chatters. "I should have held on t-t-tighter. But y-y-you shouldn't have been d-d-driving so fast."

"I know," I tell her limply. "I'm sorry, Mila. It was my fault. We'll just get to shore and get you dried off."

I start the boat up and turn it toward shore, going as fast as I can. The wind cuts through my wet shirt and no lie, icicles form on the hem. By the time I pull into my slip, my fingers are purple and I'm shivering almost uncontrollably.

I'm no sooner docked than I am helping Mila out of the boat with numb fingers. She's stumbling so much that I can tell her limbs are numb, too. So I just scoop her up, figuring I can carry her faster than she can walk.

"I c-c-can w-w-walk," she chatters. I shake my head.

"I can walk faster."

Her fingers gripping my shoulders are like ice and I shake my head again.

"You're probably going to get pneumonia," I tell her as I unlock the car and settle her into the seat. For the first time, I wish my car was new instead of a classic. A new car would have seat warmers.

I jam the key into the ignition with frigid, shaking fingers and we make it to my house in just a few minutes. My guilt makes me drive faster on the ice than I normally would have.

The car is barely in the driveway before I hit the button for the garage so that I don't have to fumble with the front-door lock. I am out of the car and to her side within seconds, pulling her out and carrying her through the garage and into the house.

"Your lips are still blue," I tell her. "We've got to get you in a hot shower."

"You need one t-t-too," she tells me, her chin shaking. I can't decide if she is just freezing or if she's in some sort of shock.

I don't put her down. I just carry her straight upstairs, to my bathroom. I set her down on the toilet and turn the water on, turning back to help her peel off her icy clothes. I can still barely feel my fingers. They are so cold that they almost feel hot against her frozen skin.

"Mila, I'm so sorry. I lost my temper and I saw red and I shouldn't have been driving like that. I'm sorry."

She nods. "I know. It's okay. W-w-we were mad. It's d-d-done now. It's okay."

I pull off her shirt without another word, then help her unclasp her bra. She's not an invalid, but I know how difficult it is to move my fingers, as frozen as they are, so I know hers are the same. I pull her to her feet and tug her wet jeans off, then her underwear, then point her toward the shower.

"Get in," I instruct her, as I peel off my own clothes and step into the steam behind her. She's under the water now, holding her hair back as the hot water breathes warmth back into her bones.

"Oh my god," she breathes. "This feels so good. It hurts, too, but Oh. My. God."

Her eyes are closed, but color is returning to her lips. I breathe a sigh of relief and slip up next to her, under the nozzle to her left. She's right. The hot water is more amazing than it's ever seemed before.

"Holy shit, that lake was cold," I mutter as the water cascades over me. Feeling returns to my toes in a thousand painful needles. "Fuck, my toes hurt."

Mila moans in agreement next to me and honestly, we just stand under the water for another ten minutes, with our eyes closed and without speaking, just enjoying the warmth. When the door fogs over and I am no longer shivering, I turn to Mila.

She is naked and wet and gorgeous, but I don't care at the moment. All I care about is one thing.

"You thought I was going to hit you," I say simply. She looks guilty as she turns to me, her skin a healthy pink now.

"No," she protests quietly. "It was just a reflex. I just reacted."

"So you didn't think I was going to hit you?" I raise an eyebrow. "Because you flinched." She drops her head.

"I don't know what I thought."

I suck in a breath at her honesty and am deflated at the same time. Reaching out, I tilt her chin up with my fingers.

"I don't care how mad I am, I will never hit you. Do you understand?" I stare her in the eye. "Not ever."

She swallows and looks at me and her eyes are so wide and green. "I'm sorry," she tells me. "I don't know why I would think that."

And there is something in her eyes that gives me pause.

"Did your dad hit your mom?"

The question hangs between us and she stares at me. And then she nods slowly.

"Not often. But sometimes. I saw it a few times. He slapped her, she slapped him. They had a very passionate relationship."

"Holy shit," I mutter in shock, before I pull her to me. "Mila, even one time is too many. I will never hit you. I need you to believe that."

She nods silently, and I see that she's crying. And I don't know if she's crying about her dad and mom or if she's crying about our fight on the boat.

I drag her more tightly against my chest, dropping my lips to her forehead. She is pressed against me, wet and firm. I slide my hands around her back, cradling her tightly.

"Mila, I will never hurt you. Not like that."

She nods and reaches for me and just like that, we are inhaling each other, like we need each other to breathe.

Her tongue plunges into my mouth and my hands are every-where on her body, sliding up and down the smooth wetness of her back, and down over her hips. I suck her lip into my mouth, pulling it with my teeth. She whimpers into me and I inhale it, enjoying the sound.

Desperation hangs heavily around us, a consuming need. I whirl her about, pinning her to the stone shower wall, pressing into her as I plunge into her mouth yet again. I could taste this girl forever and still not have enough.

She brings her leg up and hooks it around my hips. My hands slide up her thighs to cup her ass, her amazingly perfect ass, and she wiggles into me, pushing ever closer. My dick is wedged against her and I know she feels it.

Hard.

Wet.

Warm.

"I want you tonight," she tells me in my ear. Her teeth nip at my earlobe. "Please, Pax."

I groan and pull away, looking at her.

"I thought you wanted to wait?"

She smiles an endearing and wicked smile.

"Fuck that," she says. "I want you now."

I crush her close again and pillage her mouth, and her lips are so fucking soft against mine. My fingers slip inside of her and she gasps into my mouth, panting softly. She tastes like sunshine.

"You are so fucking beautiful," I rasp against her throat as I kiss a trail down to her full breasts. "So beautiful."

I slip her breast into my mouth, sucking softly. She pulls at me, clutching me, thrashing, her hands scraping down the shower stones. Her breath is coming in pants now, I can hear it, jagged and raw.

I move to her other breast and suck there; teasing her, enjoying it. Her skin is wet and soft and when she opens her eyes to look at me, her gaze is unfocused and wild.

She wants me. That notion is almost incomprehensible to me. She wants me just as I want her. I groan and bury my face in her neck.

Her hand is on my dick and it throbs in her hand, hot and heavy. I want her like I've never wanted anything. I moan and she smiles as she slides her hand up and down the length of me.

"You're so big," she murmurs softly.

My, what big teeth I have.

I am once again the wolf as I hover above her, her back shoved against the tiles. She is innocent and beautiful. And I am...not.

I don't deserve her. I swallow hard.

"Do you want me?" I ask her, my lips just a breadth above her.

She nods, her eyes squeezed shut as she runs her hands over my back and down my hips.

"Then open your eyes and say it," I instruct her raggedly. "Say my name."

Her eyes flutter open and she stares into mine.

"I want you," she murmurs. "Pax."

My tongue twists around hers, wet and hot. I may not deserve her but she wants me anyway. My gut clenches.

"Say it again," I tell her quietly.

She looks at me with her wide, green eyes.

"Pax," she breathes. "I want you."

"Fuck," I mutter and pull away from her for only a moment, to reach out the door and pull my wallet from my pants on the floor. I fumble with the condom and then I am back under the water, pulling her against me.

And then I slide into her.

Light explodes behind my eyelids because she feels so fucking good. So wet, so fucking tight. I could die right here and never regret a thing.

Mila gasps as I push into her, and then she clutches my back, pulling me to her.

"You feel so good," she whimpers into my ear. And warmth tightens my chest.

I groan and try to focus on anything that will prevent me from coming already, but I know it's useless. Her tits are smashed against me, wet and soft, and every time I slide against her, the friction brings me that much closer to the edge.

She pulls me closer and in this moment, I know that she is everything that is light and good in the world.

I slide in and out, the heat between our wet bodies driving me to madness.

"I'm going to come," I rasp against her wet neck.

She opens her eyes and looks at me.

"So come," she says simply.

And then she buries her tongue in my mouth and I can't stop myself. My dick pulses inside of her and she clenches around me. I breathe raggedly as I hold her to the wall, and after what seems like an hour, we both slide to the floor. She's in my arms and the water is beating on us.

I can't even speak. I just hold her in my lap, cradled to me, and the moment seems huge. We sit this way for the longest time, until the water begins to turn cool.

Mila lifts her head.

"That was amazing," she murmurs. She pulls away a bit and strokes the side of my face. I lean into her hand and close my eyes. "You're beautiful," she adds. My stomach clenches.

"I'm not beautiful," I answer. "Far from it."

"You are," she insists. "You'll just have to take my word for it."

I shake my head, but I don't release my grip on her and she lays her head back against my chest.

"The water is getting cold," she says drowsily. Her legs are entwined with mine as her body drapes against me. She doesn't seem to care about the water, but we've both had more than our fair share of cold water for the day.

Reluctantly, I sit up and pull Mila to her feet. I lead her from the shower and towel her off before I head to my bedroom and find her a t-shirt to wear. I pull it over her head and stare down at her.

"Stay with me tonight," I urge her. "You're tired, I'm tired and it's cold outside. Just stay here."

She grins up at me.

"That was the plan all along," she answers impishly. "I have my overnight bag in my car at The Hill."

I stare at her. "You mean...you were going to...tonight?"

She laughs. "Spit it out, Pax. It's not that hard to figure out. Yes, I was ready tonight."

I have to chuckle and shake my head.

"Do you like to keep me guessing?" I ask her as I drag her to the bed and onto my lap.

She nods, her green eyes glimmering. "It keeps things interesting, doesn't it?"

I lower my lips to hers, silencing anything else that she thinks she's going to say. Covering her body with mine, I push her onto the softness of my bed and trail my lips down her neck, then down her arms to her hands. I kiss her palms and then glance up at the windows.

"There's a winter storm blowing in across the lake," I tell her, and she turns to watch it with me.

"It's a good thing we're not still out there," she points out as we watch the dark clouds build and roll in across the water. Lightning flashes across the blackness and the air seems charged with the power of the storm.

I glance down. "It's a good thing. It's definitely more comfortable being naked here."

She giggles and pulls me down to her, her tongue in my mouth again. I decide that it's where her tongue always belongs. My hands slide to her ass, bringing her leg up around my hip.

"This is where your leg belongs," I tell her firmly. She smiles against my lips.

"That might make walking difficult," she answers, as she trails her fingers down my back.

"We'll figure it out," I growl and I slide my fingers inside of her. She whimpers and arches against my hand, just as the thunder cracks outside. And then our talking dies as a storm of our own rages in my bedroom.

Chapter 17

Mila

The last thing I think about before I cross the hazy threshold into sleep is that Pax's arms are so strong and warm. And safe.

I'll never forget what it felt like when he dove into the lake after me and pulled me to safety. The stupid coat was weighing me down and I couldn't get it off. He probably saved my life. It's ironic that he is so reckless with his own life, but seems so protective of mine.

I snuggle more closely against him, against the strength of his chest. My face is pressed against his heart, and it beats loudly against my ear. It's that thrumming cadence that soothes me to sleep.

And then I dream.

I look down and find sunlight bathing me, glimmering over my skin.

I'm in the church again.

But this time is different.

Instead of the black dress that I wore to my parents' funeral, I'm wearing a white one. A simple cotton shift that is basically transparent. And my father is sitting in the front of the church, in place of the caskets. And instead of sunlight shining in, he is sitting in the shadows.

My pulse races because this is the first time either of my parents have appeared in a dream. It's so good to see my father's face. I rush down the aisle toward him, but my feet will only move one speed. It's so frustrating because I want to run and my feet just won't cooperate. But eventually I reach him.

I stand in front of him and simply stare. He's wearing his favorite faded green flannel shirt and broken in blue-jeans, the ones that he always used to work in the yard in.

He smiles.

"Hi, peanut."

"Hi, daddy," I eke out. I have a lump in my throat that I can't seem to swallow. "It's so good to see you."

He smiles the same smile that I have seen a million times over the years and holds his arms out. I fold into them and he smells just the same, like Old Spice and mints. I inhale and cry and hug him tight.

But after a few minutes, he pulls away.

I stare at him, at the large hands that have held me a thousand times, that have bathed my dog and pushed my bicycle and slapped my mother. I gulp and stare into his eyes.

"Daddy, why did you hit mom?"

He seems startled and holds his hands up, palms up to the sky.

"I don't know," he says quietly. "Because I'm not perfect. Your mother and I should've gotten some help with our marriage. We loved each other, but we were unhealthy together. I'm sorry you saw that."

"How can you love someone, but still hurt them?" I ask, and as I do, I feel the tears streaming down my face. Dad reaches over with a large hand and wipes them away.

"That's a travesty of life," he tells me softly. "Sometimes we hurt those that we love the most."

"But you should never hurt someone in that way," I tell him. "Having that kind of temper is being a coward."

Dad stares at me. "Maybe I was a coward, then. But I was still a good person who just happened to have a bad temper. I love you, peanut."

I feel rooted to the ground and then numb as realization floods over me. Somehow, for some reason, pieces click into place in my mind and I suddenly know what these stupid dreams have been trying to tell me all along…with the black and white caskets, the sunshine and shadows.

Life isn't black and white. People aren't all good or bad. I've concentrated so much on the meaning of life after my parents' passed that I forgot that fact, because deep down, even though I didn't acknowledge it to myself, my parents' volatile relationship was hard on me. And I guess I judged them.

Truly, though, life is just a mixture of good and bad, of varying shades of grays and whites and blacks. I think that I've always been afraid of getting into a relationship with someone because I was afraid I'd end up in the same kind of relationship as my parents' or that I'd make a mistake.

But life is all about mistakes.

I swallow hard and stare at my dad.

"I love you, daddy." He nods, his eyes full of kindness and love. "I miss you."

"I know," he answers. And even though he is sitting still, he begins to fade, until he is no longer here and I am alone.

But I'm not alone. I can feel Pax's presence, even though I can't see it. I turn and he isn't there.

And then I'm awake. I'm staring into his eyes.

"Are you okay?" he whispers. "You were dreaming."

His arms tighten around me.

"I just had the strangest dream," I whisper. "I dreamed about my dad for the first time since he died. I asked him why he hit my mom and he basically said that he was flawed. But he was still a good person. He and my mom should've gotten counseling, but they never did."

Pax stares at me, his golden eyes warm in the shadowy room.

"You're right," he finally says. "A person can be flawed, but still be a good person, or have a good heart, at least. Where is this coming from? Because I asked about your parents earlier?"

I shrug. "I don't know. Maybe. I've had a weird recurring dream since they died and I think this has always been one of the things that my subconscious has been trying to tell me. I struggled after they died, I missed them so much, but I also resented them because of their relationship. They loved each other- to distraction, almost- but they weren't healthy together. They didn't communicate well."

Pax stares at me. "Did your dad ever hit you?"

I shake my head immediately. "No. I was spanked a few times when I was a kid, but actually hit? No. They were good parents. Their problem was that they always pushed each other's buttons until things escalated beyond their control."

Pax is already shaking his head.

"Nothing is ever out of your control," he argues. "Not in that situation. You were right, though. Your parents' should have gotten help. I'm sorry that they didn't."

I close my eyes and snuggle against him again.

"I think my dream was a message to me, somehow. That everything will be okay, and that I should trust my gut. My gut tells me that it's okay to be with you. You and I aren't my parents and our relationship won't be the same as theirs. No one is perfect and you have issues to deal with, but we'll get through it, Pax."

He startles, I can feel it. He's stiff against me now.

"You think your dream was a message from your father that it's okay to be with me?"

I shrug again. "I don't know. Maybe."

He shakes his head. "No way. It's not that I don't believe in that kind of thing, but there's no way your dad would give his blessing for you to get involved with me. No way in hell. You dreamed what you want to believe that he would say to you. You're just trying to make sense of things. We stirred up your memories tonight, so it's normal."

I refuse to let him sway me though.

"We'll have to agree to disagree. But for now, let's just go back to sleep."

And so we do. Pax tightens his hold on me and I fall asleep in his arms.

When I wake, he is still asleep next to me. His arms are still tightly wrapped around me. I don't think we've moved at all. I blink from the sunlight that is pouring through the windows. I am so comfortable that I don't want to get up and close the blinds. But if I don't, I'll never go back to sleep.

And I'm just not ready to start the day. I want to stay in bed with Pax a while longer.

I carefully extract myself from Pax's arms and crawl out of bed, padding to the windows. I find the strings that pull the shades closed and start to pull. As I do, I glance down at the lawn behind the house and I freeze.

An icy feeling spreads from the base of my spine all the way to my neck as horror ricochets through my ribcage.

There is someone lying on the lawn, out in the cold and wind.

I peer closer, staring at the pale leg, spiky high heel and mousy brown hair.

Jill.

What the hell?

My hand drops from the blinds and I cover my mouth with it.

Jill isn't moving and her body is sprawled at an unnatural angle. Her face is turned away from me, toward the lake, but she is too still. The wind moves her hair across her face, but it is the only thing moving.

"Pax!" I shriek, running to shake him. "Wake up. Wake up! Jill is on your lawn."

He leans up groggily, trying to clear his head enough to realize what I'm saying. Realization finally crosses his face and he lunges from bed, and we both run to the back lawn.

Pax runs to Jill without hesitation, but I have to admit, I am hesitant. Dread seems to freeze me into place. I don't know exactly what's wrong with her, but I know it's nothing good.

Pax kneels and examines her, but he quickly looks up at me and the look on his face is grave.

I have to force myself to walk to him.

"Can you call the police?" he asks quietly. I look down and Jill's eyes are open. They are faded and unblinking and I know she is dead. I back away, my hands over my mouth, as complete and utter horror fills me up. I want to scream, but I don't.

There is vomit on her shirt and chin. At some point, it had run down her arm onto her hand. It is frozen there now, an orangey-rust color. I gag and turn away. Pax stands up and wraps his arms around me.

"Let's go call the police," he says gently. "Don't look again. You don't need to."

"We can't just leave her out here!" I tell him. "It's cold. How long do you think she's been here? Since last night? Do you think she was texting you from here?"

I stare at him wild-eyed and he grasps my elbow.

"Mila, she isn't feeling the cold now. We need to go call the police. And I have no idea if she was here when she was texting me."

I don't say what I know we are both thinking. If he'd only answered her, this might have been avoided. I don't look him in the eye because I don't want him to see my thoughts.

"Did she overdose?" I ask quietly as we walk woodenly into the house.

Pax shakes his head as we climb the stairs to the kitchen. "I don't know, but it sure looks like it."

He looks at me. "Can you make some coffee while I call?"

I nod and set to finding the coffee supplies. It somehow feels good to do this mundane thing, to let my hands operate automatically as I measure out the coffee and pour the water into the basket. The aroma fills my nose and I am standing there, with my hands gripping the cabinet, when Pax appears behind me.

"They're on their way. I forgot to put your clothes in the dryer last night, but I think I have a pair of sweats you can borrow."

I nod and follow him upstairs, where he finds the sweats and hands them to me.

"They're way too big, but there's a drawstring. Are you okay?"

He looks at me and I sit down on the bed, shakily.

"Pax, that could have been you. It could have been you."

I am limp and I don't know what else to say. That's the only thing I can think. It could've been him. If I hadn't come across him that night on the beach, it would've been. Seeing Jill like that just drove it home for me, like a stake through the heart.

Pax drops to the bed next to me and forces me to look at him.

"But it wasn't me. And I'm not doing that anymore, so it will never be me."

His gaze is determined and strong and I feel my lungs shake as I draw in a breath.

"I need you to promise."

"I promise." His words are firm. And I nod.

"Okay."

"Okay?" He raises his eyebrow.

I nod.

"Okay."

He leans over and kisses my forehead. I have the urge to collapse against his chest, but I don't. I pull the sweats on instead and we return to the living room to wait for the police. It doesn't take them long to arrive. Finding a body in our little town isn't something that happens every day.

Pax answers a million questions, and then they ask me a few, also. Was I with Pax last night? Had we seen Jill earlier in the night? And so on and so forth.

We answer all of their questions and then Pax tells one of them that he knows she has two kids, but he doesn't know her address or even who takes care of her kids when she is out. That part surprises me and it makes me insanely sad.

"I guess I didn't know a lot about her," Pax admits. He looks weary. Not sad really, but just very tired. He grips his coffee cup as the officers take notes and ask even more questions.

I feel frozen as I curl up on the couch and wait for it to be over. Through the window, I can see the EMT's rolling a gurney toward Jill's body and they load her up, zipping her into a black bag.

The finality of it slams into me.

Just like that, she's gone from sight. I feel so empty and sad, like in a second, everything about this woman was extinguished, without respect or fanfare. I didn't even know her, so I have no idea why it is affecting me so deeply.

Except that I know it could've been Pax.

And a part of me, deep down, is terrified now. Unsure.

I have no idea if I can handle this. What if the next body that I walk up to is Pax's? What if he underestimates his ability to stay clean? I'm just not sure if I'm strong enough to find out.

I feel Pax watching me, as if he can hear my troubling thoughts.

I look up to find his eyes uncertain and soft and he raises his eyebrows, as if to ask *Are you alright?*

I nod. *Yes, I am.*

And I smile a little to prove it.

But I don't know if I am alright at all.

So my smile was a lie.

I close my eyes.

Chapter 18

Pax

"That must have been horrible for you," Dr. Tyler says quietly as he once again takes notes in his stupid little notepad. "To find Jill like that, in your own yard. That would take a toll on anyone."

He pauses and looks at me. I've already been here for thirty minutes and to be honest, I don't know why I came. Except that I don't know what to do with everything that is happening in my life. I feel a little like I'm floundering, like I've lost control. That was one thing about using. It always made me feel as though I was in control...even when I wasn't.

"Of course it was horrible," I answer. "There was a dead person at my house. It was startling."

Dr. Tyler stares at me. "There was a dead person at your house whom you have been sexually involved with. She tried to contact you prior to dying. You have more than a passing interest in this, Pax. You need to deal with whatever you are feeling about it. Can you tell me what you feel?"

"I'm pissed, actually," I glare at him. "Why did she have to come to *my* house to overdose? Was it to prove a point? I told her that we were done, not that there was ever a *we*. We fulfilled a purpose for each other. That's all. I didn't even know her last name."

Dr. Tyler stares at me thoughtfully and I feel like he is trying to look inside of me.

"Are you really angry because she died at your house?" he finally answers. "Or are you angry that you weren't there with her? Or *for* her when she tried to ask you for help? Do you know what her texts said? Or did you throw your phone overboard before you read them?"

I'm pissed now, mainly because he's right. I've wondered about those very things.

"Are you trying to imply that this is my fault because I didn't answer her texts? The girl was psycho. She was an addict who needed help. I told her to get help, but she chose not to."

The doctor holds his hand up.

"Of course I'm not saying it was your fault," he says soothingly. "It wasn't. She is responsible for her own actions. I was just wondering if you were able to read any of her messages to you? It might provide you with some sort of explanation, so that you are able to get closure. I'm guessing that you are feeling some guilt and maybe even the urge to use. I want to help you deal with that."

I shake my head.

"I don't need closure. Someone that I know died. I didn't love her. I read a couple of her messages. She wanted drugs and she sounded desperate. I have no idea where she found the drugs that she overdosed with. The only guilt that I feel is based on the fact that I didn't cut her off a long time ago. I contributed to her state of mind by giving her drugs for the past two years. That's something that I am responsible for. I feel badly for her that she wasn't able to quit, but that's all. And I haven't felt the urge to use. Far from it, actually. I'm tired of talking about this now. Can we get back to my issues?"

"In a moment," Dr. Tyler answers. "I'm curious about Mila. How has this affected her?"

I pause and I feel my heart quicken. Every day this week since *the incident*, as I've been referring to it, I've felt panicky when I pictured the look on Mila's face that morning. It was a look like she somehow thought it was all my fault, like I might end up like Jill. And like she wasn't prepared for any of it.

I swallow and my throat is so dry I can hear it.

"Mila is a trooper," I reply. "She stayed while the police asked their questions and she was worried about Jill's kids. She's got a soft heart."

"So, she didn't draw any parallels between you and Jill?" The doctor sounds doubtful. I get the sudden urge to punch him in the face.

"Of course she did. She told me that it could've been me. And then I promised her that it never would be."

"And did she accept that answer?" Dr. Tyler's pen pauses.

I pause, too.

"I don't know. She seemed to. But she's been quiet this week, reserved. I don't know if she is processing it or what."

"Does it scare you that she might not be able to return to where you were before this happened?"

More than anything in the world.

But I don't say that.

Instead, I simply say, "Yes."

The doctor looks at his paper and scribbles. Someday, I'd like to see exactly what he is writing.

"I'd like to change the subject now," I tell him firmly. I'm done talking about Mila.

I steel my gaze and stare at the doctor. He sighs and nods.

"Okay. Let's change the subject. Have you had any more dreams?

I nod. "Yes. Several times this week. They are still the same. I'm in a dark room and I can't see very well. But I can hear my mom. It sounds like she's pleading with me. I can't seem to get past that point in the dream. It's frustrating, because I feel like there is more to see."

The doctor studies me, his fingers rolling his pen around on his lap.

"Sometimes, a person's mind protects itself as best it can. It does that by building barriers and suppressing memories. If I had to guess, I would say that this dream is a memory. And your mind doesn't want you to remember the rest of it because it will be very painful."

I stare at him. "You think that I'm dreaming something that really happened?"

He nods. "I'm guessing that is true. I could be wrong. But the only way to find out, is to let your dream play out."

I shake my head, frustrated. "It won't. It only goes up to that point, where I'm in a dark place and I can hear my mother. And then I wake up. Usually in a cold sweat."

The doctor nods. "There is another way, if you're open to it."

I wait, not sure if I want to know.

"Have you ever been hypnotized?" the doctor asks and I scoff.

"Fuck no. No. I'm not getting hypnotized. What kind of quack practice are you running?"

I start to stand up, but the doctor holds up his hand.

"Wait, Pax. Hypno-therapy is a very valid and useful tool available to us. It isn't quackery. It's simply guided relaxation techniques that allow the patient to focus intensely on something, blocking everything else out. Most psychiatrists are trained at using it and in fact, it is a specialty of mine. If you really want to know what you are dreaming about, it is the best way to find out. It strips away the barriers that your mind has put in place, allowing you to see what you are trying to hide from yourself."

Fuck.

He just had to phrase it that way, didn't he? Because he has to know that I'm dying to know what my mind is trying to hide.

I settle back into my seat.

"How long will it take?" I ask uncertainly.

"It's not that time consuming," he reassures me. "And I think it might be good for you."

He stares at me, waiting. Finally, I sigh.

"Fine," I mutter. "I'll do it. But you'd better not trick me into barking like a dog or anything. I don't want to do it today, but I'll do it soon."

Dr. Tyler smiles. "That only happens in movies," he tells me. "And we can do it anytime you'd like. I'll plan on it for next time, unless you tell me otherwise."

He scribbles a bit more in his notepad.

"Have you filled the Xanax prescription?" he asks, glancing up at me.

I shake my head. "No. I told you I didn't need it."

"Good for you," the doctor commends me. "You have strong fortitude. It's encouraging. It seems you really do want to change things around for the better."

I nod and for the first time today, I feel good about something that I've done. The quack doctor is right. I really am changing things around for the better. I might be going about it wrong, but at least I'm going about it.

Mila

It's funny how days blend into each other when you aren't paying attention.

It's been weeks since Jill died. Weeks since the misgivings and doubts crept in. Weeks that Pax has given me nothing at all to doubt him for. He's been perfect. Amazingly, unbelievably perfect. So perfect, in fact, that I keep waiting for the other shoe to drop. And so far, it hasn't.

I pull into my parents' driveway, or I guess I should say Madison's, since she lives here now. But to be honest, this will always be my parents' house. I think Madison actually feels the same way and I wouldn't blame her if she wanted to sell it at some point and get a new house of her own.

I yank the keys out of the ignition and make my way up the icy sidewalk to the door. Maddy opens the door before I even get a chance to knock.

"I'm glad you're here," she tells me, without even saying hello. "Try this."

She shoves a hot mug into my hand and I sniff it as I step into the house, knocking the snow from my boots on the doorsill.

"Hot chocolate?"

She nods. "The best hot chocolate you've ever had," she says confidently. "Thick Italian hot chocolate. I'm trying it out for the restaurant. It's literally so thick the spoon will stand up in it."

I sip at it and the thick, creamy chocolate slides down my throat like pudding.

"Holy cow, that's good," I tell her. "You've got a winner."

She tries to grab it back, but I yank it away. "Not on your life."

She rolls her eyes. "Fine. Now what was it that you wanted to look for today? I forget."

I take my coat off. "I just wanted to browse through mom's memento drawer. I'm feeling a bit sentimental and I miss them. So I thought I'd look through her trinkets."

Madison looks at me sympathetically. "I know how you feel. I was like that last week. I miss them so much."

Her eyes turn watery, but she moves away, toward the kitchen. Madison isn't much of a crier. She waves her hand. "You know where to find it. I'll be in the kitchen."

She leaves me alone and I pad down the hall to our parent's bedroom. Even though it's the master bedroom, Maddy couldn't bring herself to clean it out and sleep in there. She's kept her old bedroom, keeping mom and dad's exactly as it was.

As I walk in, it is so quiet that it seems almost reverent. If I close my eyes, I try to pretend that I can smell my mom's perfume lingering here. But of course I can't. They died several years ago. Her scent is long gone.

But her memories aren't.

I slide open the top drawer of her dresser and pull it out, carrying it to the bed. As I sit on the flowered bedspread, I can remember so many afternoons after school spent in here with her, sitting on the bed as she readied for work at The Hill. She'd sit at her vanity and curl her hair, spritz on perfume and talk with me about my day.

God, I miss her.

I sift through the pictures in her drawer first. They are in informal stacks, held together with old rubber-bands. Black and white ones from her youth, faded ones from mine. My favorite picture is here, the one of my dad and I both holding up huge fish that we'd caught in Lake Michigan on one perfect summer day. I was eight years old and had a chocolate mustache and he's wearing his floppy fishing hat.

I smile at the memory.

That was a really good day. Mom and Maddy had sat on the beach because they were squeamish about the fish and bait. Dad had slugged me on the shoulder and we had fished for hours. I had felt so important because I had a strong-stomach and could be his companion.

I put it back in the pile and replace the worn rubber band.

I finger through old love letters from my father to her, and even old letters from my grandmother. My mother kept everything and was a sentimental at heart. At times like this, I'm so thankful for that.

As I move the drawer, I hear a rolling sound. I feel around and find a ring in the corner. It's a wide band made from rose-colored gold and on the inside, *Love Never Fails* is inscribed. My chest tightens. I remember this ring. It was mom's original wedding ring. She had to stop wearing it after she had Maddy because it became too small. And then Daddy had gotten her a fancy diamond and she started wearing that instead.

But now, holding this simple ring in my hand, I feel buoyed somehow. *Love never fails.* What a strong sentiment. Just holding the cool metal in my hand makes me feel good, connected to my parents somehow. I slip it onto the ring finger of my right hand. It's a perfect fit.

I slide the drawer back into the dresser and find Maddy in the kitchen.

"Do you mind if I keep this?" I ask her, holding out my hand. "It's mom's original wedding band."

Maddy shakes her head. "Of course not. You gave me her diamond. It's only fair." She smiles at me now with her best big-sister grin and I can't help but give her a hug.

"I love you, you know," I tell her as we settle into her kitchen chairs, our elbows propped on the table. "Mom and dad would be really proud of you."

She smiles at me again and sips her chocolate. "Thank you. They'd be proud of you, too. They always were."

I lean into her and try to steal her cup and she slaps my hand away.

"How many of those have you had, anyway?" I demand jokingly. "Surely you can spare one cup for me."

"I already did," she answers. "And I've probably had enough. But can you ever really have too much chocolate?" She waggles her eyebrows and laughs and we chat for what seems like forever.

After we talk about The Hill, Tony, my shop, Madison's new car and the dog that she is thinking of getting, she turns to me and looks thoughtful.

"How are things with Pax?"

I roll my eyes. "As if you care."

"I do," she insists. "I'm still worried, but I'm less worried now than I was. He seems to make you happy. And I really do want you to be happy, little sis."

She wraps her slender arm around my shoulder and squeezes. I sniff at her.

"Did you put deodorant on today? Because you kind of smell."

We giggle and she slugs me and all feels right in the world.

We sit in her kitchen and talk until dark.

Chapter 19

My phone buzzes. As I pick it up, I notice that it is 7:05 p.m.

Crap. I was supposed to meet Pax at 7:00. Time got away from me.

Sure enough, I glance at the text and it is from him.

Hey, Miss Tardy. Didn't we have a date tonight?

I seriously hate to be late. As in, so freaking much. I've always been that way. So I punch in a reply, hit send and am pulling my coat on as I run out the door. "I'm late, Maddy. Gotta go, bye."

I can hear her laughing as I slam the door closed behind me.

I pull into Pax's drive ten minutes later, and am galloping to the door when he sticks his head out the door and laughs.

"You look like a lame horse, Red. Calm down before you fall and break something."

I step up onto the step and kiss him, my cold lips pressing to his warm ones. He looks sexy as hell, like he does on any other day, in his jeans that fit his ass perfectly and the black t-shirt that hugs his chest. I lean into him, soaking in his warmth. He smells like musk, and the woods and everything male. I inhale him and wrap my arms around his neck.

"I'm sorry I'm late," I tell him as I kiss him by the ear. "Trust me, there's no place I'd rather be than here."

"Really?" he cocks an eyebrow. "Then we agree. Because there's no place I'd rather have you be, either."

I roll my eyes at his corniness as we walk into his foyer. But then I push him against the wall and kiss him again, just because I want to. He drags me against him and I linger there, in the comfort of his arms. Holy cow. There really isn't anywhere I'd rather be than here.

Finally, I sigh. "So, it was your turn to plan our date tonight. What are we doing? Want to order take-out?"

He shakes his head. "I'm hungry for fried zucchini. So I thought we'd try to make it."

I stare at him. "You thought we'd try to make fried zucchini? Um. I should mention that my family owns a restaurant, but I don't really cook. Much. And who in the world gets hungry for zucchini?"

Pax laughs and drags me up the stairs. "My housekeeper used to make it when I was growing up. I loved it. So I looked for the recipe online today. I went to the grocery store and everything. What's the worst that can happen?"

"Now you've done it," I grumble as I take off my coat. "You should never ask that question."

Ten minutes later, we are both staring uncertainly at a recipe and a pan of oil on the stove. Everything in Pax's kitchen is gleaming and new. He's clearly never used it and doesn't know how. And I'm no better.

"I'm not sure about this," I tell him as the oil spits and sputters everywhere.

He watches it for a minute. "I think the oil is too hot," he decides and he turns the flame down just a bit. We roll the sliced zucchini in the flour mixture and drop it into the pan and it sizzles.

We look at each other. "Looks fine," he shrugs. "I think we did it right."

He turns to me. "Now, where were we in the foyer?"

He reaches for me, pinning me against the granite counter. I smile.

"You realize, of course, that you look really out of place in the kitchen?"

I raise an eyebrow. He grins.

"I thought women wanted men who could cook?"

"If so, I'm probably out of luck," I tell him as I press my lips to his. He laughs, which rumbles in his chest and he lifts me up, sitting me on the counter. I automatically wrap my legs around him.

"It's where my legs belong, right?" I remind him. He nods.

"You're learning."

"Oh, I'm a good learner," I tell him with a grin as an idea occurs to me. "Wanna see?

I trail my fingers down to the button on his jeans and flick it open with one deft movement.

"Impressive," he says, cocking an eyebrow teasingly. "But now what are you going to do? I think you already know how to use that."

"Maybe," I answer. "But I haven't mastered everything. And every good student needs a teacher."

He stares at me as I slide off the counter and pull his pants off, then his underwear. And then I drop to my knees in front of him.

His eyes widen.

"You're going to …" his voice trails off as I take him in my hand, sliding my fingers down his length. His penis lurches to life, instantly rock hard. I smile.

I look up at him. "I'm sure I have the mechanics down, but everyone has preferences, don't you agree?" He nods wordlessly, his eyes frozen to mine as I grasp him firmly in my hand. "So I want you to tell me exactly how you like oral sex."

He's frozen, his hands limp on my shoulders.

"Well, you should start by repeating that question, but instead of saying oral sex, say, 'Tell me exactly how to suck your dick'. No, wait. Say cock. Because that word coming from your lips will be fucking hot."

I smile at the eager look on his face. I love how he is so big and tattooed, but I can turn him on and make him speechless with just one little word. And saying that one naughty little word is turning me on, quite frankly.

"Okay, I'll play. Tell me, Pax. How do you want me to suck your cock?"

He stiffens, in more ways than one. He just got harder in my hand, although I didn't know that was possible.

"Cat got your tongue?" I tease, as I lower my head and run my tongue along his shaft. "It doesn't have mine."

He shudders as I run my tongue around the tip, then lick down the back, then back up, like I'm licking a lollipop.

"You're a freaking vixen," he mutters. "You know what you're doing."

"I do. But tell me what you'd *really* like," I prompt him, as I stroke him with my fingers again. "I want to know."

He swallows and closes his eyes, leaning back against the

counter, his hands gripping the edge. He pushes further into my mouth.

"Okay, Red. I like it when you take all of me in your mouth. I want you to deep-throat me. If you can handle it."

He says the last part like a dare.

I want to smile, but don't. He continues speaking, his voice husky.

"While you suck me, I want you to squeeze my balls, just a little. Tug on them. *Lightly.* Push your fingers against me right behind my ball sack and pull. Lightly, not too hard."

He shudders again when I do as he says. I pull his balls toward my mouth, just slightly.

I inch my lips along his length, working the entire thing into my mouth. I feel like he is practically scraping the back of my throat, but I don't gag. I just concentrate on keeping my teeth from scraping him as I slide him in and out.

"Fuck," he groans, gripping the stone counter. *"Fuck."*

I make sure my lips form a good vacuum and continue sucking, sliding, moving. I stroke his balls and pull at them and Pax's breathing gets more and more ragged.

And then, with his balls cupped in my hand, I suck on them.

He tenses up completely, his knuckles turning white. "Fuck."

I smile now as I lick at them, then suck. Then lick.

Then I plunge his dick back in my mouth, all the way. In, out, wet.

I increase my speed and he finally yanks me away by my shoulders.

"I'm going to come," he tells me raggedly. "And I want to come inside of you."

I yank off my clothes and he rolls me onto all fours, sliding into me from behind.

He fills me up, the friction nail-bitingly hot. He rocks me to and fro as he leans over me, pressing his lips to my ear.

"Tell me to fuck you harder," he whispers.

"Fuck me harder," I say obediently and my voice is strained. It's hard to form thought, let alone words while he is doing what he's doing.

As he slides in and out, he reaches around to my front, spinning circles around the most sensitive part of me. Then he presses his hand against my belly as he plunges deep inside. I cry out and he kisses in between my shoulder-blades.

"Tell me again," he says, with his lips still against my back.

"Fuck me harder," I feel like I am screaming now as he rides me from behind, his hand cupping me from beneath, driving me to distraction. "Pax! Oh my God."

I'm moaning now, but he's pulling me with him toward an orgasm that is going to be mind-blowing. I can feel it building and building and his muscles flexing against me as he moves.

"Come in me," I tell him. "I want to feel you come."

He moves faster and just as I am moaning from my orgasm, he shudders from his. He grabs my ass and holds there, shaking as he finishes.

And then I drop to the ground and he gently falls on top of me, while still supporting his weight. He kisses the side of my neck, breathing hard.

"That was fucking hot. *You're* fucking hot."

I smile. "Thank you. You're not too bad yourself."

He chuckles, and as he does, I look around and notice the smoke.

"What the hell?" I wiggle from under Pax and sit up. "Holy hell!"

Smoke is billowing toward the ceiling. I leap to my feet, naked, running for the stove. At this very moment, the smoke alarms go off.

Pax runs to disarm them and I slam a lid over the smoking pan of burned zucchini, turning the flame off.

He rushes back and we stare at it. And then he laughs.

"Well, we did say it was fucking hot. Apparently, we lit my kitchen on fire."

I giggle. "That might have been our poor cooking skills."

The entire house smells like it burned down now, so I walk around spraying air freshener while Pax scrapes out the burned mess into the disposal, running cold water over the pan.

"I think this is the end of my career as a chef," he announces as I wrap my arms around him from behind.

"That's okay," I tell him. "I think there's already a Naked Chef out there. They don't need another one."

He spins around and looks at me. "I always need for you to be naked," he tells me as he drags his hands down my sides before he grasps my hips and pulls me to him.

He kisses me, lightly and soft. "You deserve a reward."

I pull away a bit. "A reward?"

He nods. "Yep. For being such a good pupil."

I laugh. "What do you have in mind?"

"You're going to like it. Give me a minute."

He smiles and strides away, leaving me in the kitchen alone. And naked.

This is an interesting turn of events, I decide as I put away the few things that we'd left out. As I do, I let my mind wander. I think about how glad I am that I'm on the pill now and that Pax's STD tests came back negative. It's nice not having to use condoms. And then, as I turn to rinse off the paring knife, I notice a hospital bill laying on the counter. I glance at it, and notice that it was from the night Pax overdosed which was exactly two months ago today.

I'm astounded. I hadn't realized it has been this long. Two whole months. Who would have ever thought that we'd last this long?

But Pax is back before I can over-analyze it. He grabs my hand, leading me up to the guest bathroom.

"Why are we in here?" I ask as we walk inside.

"Because my bathroom doesn't have a tub," he explains. "And after that performance, you deserve a hot bath. I don't have bubble bath, but I used some of your body wash from upstairs. Is that okay?"

I nod as I stare at the steaming, claw-footed tub. It's filled with bubbles and there is a folded towel next to it. And two lit candles. I can't even believe that he thought of this.

"Thank you," I tell him, as I turn and hug him. "This is so sweet."

"It's just a bath," he murmurs as I continue to squeeze him. "It's not a big deal."

But it is. No one has ever run a bath for me, except for my mother, when I was little.

"It's the sweetest thing ever," I tell him as I step in. "Trust me."

I settle against the back of the tub and close my eyes.

"I'll let you soak for a bit," Pax tells me before he backs out of the room. I relax, inhaling the lavender scent as I enjoy the hot water. Every muscle kink fades away as I soak. And I revel in the thought that my big, bad boyfriend ran a bubble-bath for me.

Just when my fingers are starting to prune, he walks through the door again. He's got underwear on now, but his chest is still bare.

"Hi," he says as he kneels behind me on his knees, reaching in and running his fingers along my shoulders. "How was the bath?"

He bends and kisses the side of my neck and I lean into him.

"It was amazing," I answer. "Thank you. It was just what I needed."

"Want to know something?" he whispers into my ear. "You're the most beautiful thing I've ever seen. And I love you."

I freeze, my heart pounding. I can literally hear my pulse pounding in my ears.

I flip over in the water, my wet hands grasping his on the edge of the tub.

"Did you just say what I think you said?"

He nods. And for once, there is not one ounce of amusement on his face. He is completely serious.

"I love you. I love how you are so sweet and innocent and kind to people, but you are such a vixen in the sack. I love how you look at me. I love your smile. I love everything about you."

I am completely still as I stare at him in utter shock.

This is big. Huge. I've known for a couple of weeks that I loved him, but I didn't want to scare him by telling him so. But he said it first. Tonight. It's dumbfounding. And unexpected.

"Aren't you going to say something?" he asks and he actually looks nervous, as though I might reject him. My heart twinges.

"I love you, too," I tell him quickly. "I have for weeks."

And I leap out of the tub, the water sloshing onto the floor as I barrel into his arms. The velocity knocks him to the ground and I hover above him, dripping.

"I love you," I tell him again.

"I see that," he laughs, kissing me. "Simple words would have sufficed. You didn't need to knock me down with it."

I giggle. "Shut up and kiss me."

So he does.

Chapter 20

Pax

I know I'm being a pussy now.

But as I stare at Mila, at the beautiful girl in front of me, I can't help but know that I've never loved anything like I love her. It's true. The baffling thing is that she loves me back. That's mind-boggling…this beautiful girl wants me. I keep waiting to somehow fuck it up. But I haven't yet and she is still here.

She kisses me now, her lips wet from her bath and I inhale her, my hands running over her naked back.

"You're a wrinkled prune," I tell her, chuckling. I hold up the towel and she steps out into it. I wrap it her shoulders, then grab another one to dry her off.

"You're too good to me," she announces.

"Not possible," I answer.

God. I *am* a pussy.

She runs upstairs to slip into one of my t-shirts and I light the fireplace. We curl up on the couch in front of the fire and chat for at least an hour, watching the lake ripple under the silvery moon.

"This has been the perfect date," she murmurs, curled halfway onto my lap. "Even if we did almost burn down your house."

I chuckle. "Thank god I'm insured."

Her giggle is interrupted by a wide yawn. She slaps her hand over her mouth, embarrassed.

"Sorry! You wore me out tonight, I guess. Are you ready for bed?"

I nod and turn off the fire and follow her upstairs. I marvel in the fact that it seems so comfortable with her here. She makes it feel like home. And for some reason, that terrifies me and I don't know why. So I do what I always do when something bothers me. I shake it off and block it out.

I curl up behind Mila and wrap my arms around her. I fall asleep with my face buried in her hair.

But then I dream.

Fuck.

Even as I dream, I know that I'm dreaming. But I can't force myself to wake. It's been the same thing for months now.

I'm somewhere small and suffocating. There is barely any light, but I hear my mom.

"Please. Please. Please." She's begging.

Is she begging *me*?

I don't know and it's fucking killing me.

I try to call out for her, but my lips are frozen. I'm too afraid to call out.

Why am I afraid? What do I think will happen if I make a sound?

I don't know that, either.

She's begging again.

I hear my name.

And then I'm awake, gasping for breath.

"Pax," Mila is shaking me.

Mila was the one saying my name. She woke me from the dream.

I sit up, trying to stop my fucking heart from pounding, by taking deep breaths. What the hell?

"You're drenched," Mila says softly, pushing my hair away from my forehead with her cool hand. "The same dream?"

I nod. "I don't know what the fuck…"

She strokes my back and pulls me down to lie next to her. She enmeshes her fingers with mine, then lifts mine to her lips. She kisses the scar on my hand, then tucks it back up next to my chest.

"We need to figure out what this is," she tells me softly.

"I know," I answer. "But we're not going to figure it out tonight. Go back to sleep, babe. I'm sorry I woke you."

"Don't be sorry," she says quietly. "I just hate to see you so upset."

She snuggles against my back, stroking my arm. But it isn't long until her fingers fall limply against me and her breathing turns soft and even. She's asleep.

I enjoy her warmth pressed against me and I try to sleep. I count sheep. I recite song lyrics in my head. I watch the moon. Nothing works.

"Fuck," I mutter. I get out of bed as carefully as I can so I don't wake Mila. I glance down at her and she hasn't moved. Her lips puff out just a little as she breathes and I smile before I quietly walk away.

The house is silent as I make my way downstairs to the kitchen. I don't know what the fuck is wrong with me. Maybe it's my body's way of withdrawing itself from hard drugs. But that can't be it. I haven't used anything but whiskey in two months.

Whiskey.

Now, there's an idea. If ever I needed it, it's now.

I grab a bottle from the cupboard and a tumbler. Then I decide to forgo the tumbler. I carry the bottle with me to the couch, where I collapse heavily and watch the water moving under the moon from the window. I take a swig of Jack. Then two. Then three.

Before I know it, half the bottle is gone.

And I'm finally sleepy.

I close my eyes.

When I wake, it's morning and the living room is filled with light.

Mila is sitting at my feet, looking fresh and perfect. She's already dressed and her hair is pulled back neatly with a band. She's holding a cup of coffee and another sits on the ottoman in front of us.

"I brought you coffee," she says. She glances at the half-empty bottle of whiskey. "I thought you might need it."

I squeeze my eyes closed to block out the light. "Thanks," I mumble. "I couldn't sleep. I thought the whiskey would help."

"I'm sure your head will thank you today," she answers wryly.

I grunt in response and pull a cushion over my head.

"What does Dr. Tyler say about your dreams?" she asks seriously. "He must have an opinion."

I lay there silently, trying to force my head to stop hurting. It doesn't work. In fact, it feels like it's going to split in two.

"He wants to hypnotize me," I finally admit, tossing the cushion down to my feet. "He thinks my mind is trying to protect me from something that I don't want to recall. He said that hypnosis might help me remember it so that I can deal with it."

Mila looks at me thoughtfully. And then, instead of getting freaked out like I was afraid she would, she nods.

"I think that's a good idea. You should do it. Can I come with you?"

I stare at her, shocked. "You'd want to?"

She shakes her head. "Of course. I don't want you to go through that alone. If something hurt you enough to make you want to forget it, I want to help you get through it. Let's chase these dreams away, Pax."

My heart literally overflows with love for this girl.

And I don't care if that makes me a pussy or not.

Mila

Pax hasn't said anything since he picked me up at the shop. Today's the day he gets hypnotized and I know he isn't happy about it. He's driving now with a set jaw and guarded expression. I reach over and grab his hand, curling my fingers around it.

"Are you okay?" I ask softly. He glances over at me.

"I'm sorry. I know I'm not fun to be around lately."

"You haven't been sleeping," I point out. "That's enough to make anyone grumpy. But I meant, are you okay right now… since we're on our way to Dr. Tyler's? Are you sure you don't mind if I come?"

I don't know why I'm nervous about that. I guess I'm a bit worried that that's why he's upset, because I asked to come with him. I don't want to pry or to nose into things that aren't my business. But I feel like Pax *is* my business. And it's killing me that something is tormenting him so much. I just want to get it figured out so we can fix it.

Pax glances at me again. "Of course it's okay if you come. I just don't know what to tell you to expect. During the past two visits, Dr. Tyler has put me partially under to acclimate me to hypnosis, but it won't be the same today. Today I'll be fully under and apparently I won't be aware of my real surroundings. If it works, I'll be totally immersed in my memories. So please tell me afterward if he makes me do anything dumbass, like act like a duck or something."

I laugh and shake my head. "I'm pretty sure Dr. Tyler won't do that. I don't know if the man has even laughed since 1985."

Pax smiles now finally and I breathe a sigh of relief.

"You're probably right," he agrees as he pulls up to the curb. "I don't think he'd know a prank if it punched him in the face."

We climb out and walk up to the building through the snow. Apparently, in addition to not having a sense of humor, Dr. Tyler also doesn't like to snow-blow his walk. He's right on time today though and he meets us wearing his standard tan tweed jacket.

"It's good to see you, Mila," he tells me as he shakes my hand. "It's been a while. Are you doing alright?"

I smile and nod. "I've been doing fine. Thank you for asking."

"And Pax," Dr. Tyler says, turning toward Pax. "How are you feeling today?"

"Frustrated," Pax admits, his jaw clenching. "I haven't been sleeping."

"Well, let's see if we can get that straightened out for you," the doctor says soothingly as he opens his notes. "Do I have your permission to record this session, in case we want to review it later?"

Pax nods. "Yes. That's fine."

Dr. Tyler smiles. "Great. Okay, as we discussed last week, Mila can't be in the room with us as she could be a distraction. She can sit in the adjacent room and watch the TV monitor in there. Okay?"

Pax nods again and I lean up on my tip-toes to kiss his cheek. "It will be okay," I tell him firmly, squeezing his hand. He smiles to hide his nervousness.

"Thanks, Red. Just remember to watch for quackery." Dr.

Tyler pretends not to hear that as he leads me from the room and gets me settled in the room next door.

I sip the bottle of water in front of me and watch Pax and Dr. Tyler on the TV as they get settled into their chairs. Pax sprawls out in his normal way and the doctor sits with his legs crossed, his notepad balanced on his knee.

"Pax, are you ready?"

Pax nods as he stares at the red light on the recorder and it's as if he's staring into my eyes. I can see the anxiety on his face, even though he's trying to hide it. I really wish I could sit next to him, to hold his hand, to comfort him in *some* way, but it's impossible. So I sit in my own chair and watch, my hands twisting together.

"What I'm going to do is walk you through some mental imagery using verbal commands and repetition, just like we've done the past two times. Nothing will be different, we're just going to take it a little farther today. I need you to relax and breathe deeply. Can you do that?"

I notice that Dr. Tyler has changed his voice. It is even more soothing now, deep and slow. I decide that he has already started the process.

Pax nods. "I'm comfortable." He leans his head against the back of his seat and adjusts his legs.

"Good. Now I want you to close your eyes and breathe deeply. Deep breath in, deep breath out. Allow the air to rush over your tongue and past your lips, like you're breathing through a hollow reed. In, out. Deep breaths. Think about a time when you were up much too late and you grew very tired. You are that tired now, in fact. Your eyes are heavy, so very heavy and all you want to do is sleep."

The doctor's voice is smooth and calm and even I feel sleepy. I'm surprised.

"I want you to take a few more deep breaths and you are tired, very tired." He pauses and looks at Pax. "Are you tired?"

Pax nods. "Yes."

"Good. Now, I want you to think about that place, that place that you keep dreaming of. It is dark there. I want you to remember how you got there. As you remember, recite your memories aloud so that I can hear them. Are you there now?"

I look at Pax and find that he is so relaxed that his jaw is slack. His eyes are still closed, but I can see them moving behind his lids. I wish I could see whatever it is that he is seeing.

"I'm walking down a hall."

His voice is so stilted and abrupt that it startles me. A monotone. He doesn't sound like himself anymore. I watch him with morbid interest as he continues to speak.

"There is sunshine on the floor. I can see pieces of dust spiraling in the light."

"That's good," Dr. Tyler assures him. "You are doing very well. What else do you see?"

"I am stepping over a toy dump-truck with logs in the back. I almost tripped on a rug, but I didn't. There are pictures on the wall. This is my house."

"Good. Is it nice to be back home?" Dr. Tyler asks. I am utterly fascinated by this process. I have never experienced such a thing in my entire life. It's amazing.

"No. There's a noise. Something scary." Pax almost sounds like a child as he speaks.

He grips the arms of his chair, his fingers digging into the blue fabric. Dr. Tyler answers him calmly.

"It's okay, Pax. Nothing can hurt you. You are safe here. Listen closely. Do you know what is scaring you?"

Pax pauses, seeming to listen.

"My mother is crying. I've never heard her cry before, so it scares me. I'm running now, all the way to the end of the hall to her bedroom. But her door is closed."

Dr. Tyler makes notes and then looks up. He looks as fascinated as I am.

"Can you open the door, Pax? Remember, nothing can hurt you now."

"Okay." Pax seems nervous. "I'm opening the door."

He startles now, and his face turns white as he flinches.

"What do you see, Pax?" Dr. Tyler asks quickly.

"My mom is sitting on the bed and her shirt is ripped. Her nose is bleeding, and the blood is spattered onto her shirt. There's a man next to her, and he is holding a gun pressed into her side. He's got yellow teeth."

The doctor is still. "Do they see you?"

"Yes," Pax answers in his strange monotone. "My mom is screaming for me to run. And she's saying, 'Not him, not him.' But the man grabbed me. He's holding my arm so tight that I can't feel my hand anymore. I can't move. I can't run."

"Does the man speak to you?" Dr. Tyler asks slowly.

"Yes," Pax replies. "He just said, 'Lookie here, kid. Can you make your mom behave? Can you help her be a good girl?'"

Pax is silent for a minute. Even his foot, which he was banging against the chair, has gone still. He swallows.

"I want to tell him that she already is a good girl," Pax says. "But I know the man is a bad man, so I don't. My mom is still crying and she's got black streaks on her face."

It must be her mascara, I think. And I am stunned that Pax saw something like this. Who is the man with his mom?

He's got yellow teeth.

"What is your mom saying?" Dr. Tyler asks. Even his quiet

voice seems very loud in their room right now. You could hear a pin drop. Since I am utterly frozen, my room is even quieter. I think I can even hear my own heartbeat.

"She's saying, 'Leave him alone. Please. I'll do anything. Just don't hurt him.' But the man is ugly and his breath smells. He just said, 'Anything? So, you'll behave now?' "

My heart is pounding, so hard that it almost hurts. What does the man want Pax's mother to do? I almost don't want to know and I feel a big sense of dread building in my chest.

"My mom nods and she says, 'But please let my son go. I don't want him to see.' She's sad but the man is laughing and he yanks my arm and pushes me into my mom's closet. I kneel down, but I can still see through the tilted slats."

Oh, god no. I want to shout at little boy Pax to look away, to not watch whatever is about to happen, but obviously that is impossible. Whatever he sees next is going to scar him forever. My hands shake as I wait.

Dr. Tyler swallows loudly and I can hear it. His mouth is dry. He's probably hesitant to hear this, as well.

"What does the man do? Can you see it, Pax?"

Pax nods slowly, still gripping the chair.

"The man is unbuttoning his pants and they fall on the floor. He's got a tattoo on his hip. It's a black snake, coiled up. It says, *Don't Tread On Me.* He's holding the gun to my mom's head now. He says, 'Do it. Or I will kill your son as you watch."

Holy hell.

Oh My God.

Please God, no.

I am completely filled with dread now, and my blood has turned to ice. I want to rush to Pax, to comfort him, to stop this progression of events, but I know that I can't. Because until he remembers, we can't help him. I grab the arms of my chair as he continues, a sick feeling in my stomach and tears dripping onto my shirt.

"What happens now, Pax?" Dr. Tyler asks quietly. "Please remember that you are safe now. The man cannot hurt you."

"The man's back is to me and I can't see my mom very well, but I know she's still there. I can see her moving. Her head is moving up, then down. Up, then down. She's crying still and I can see her shoulders shake. The man just slapped her hard. He just said, 'Stop crying, you fucking bitch. A blowjob never killed anyone!'"

Tears are streaking down my face at will now. I can't believe that Pax saw this. He must have been terrified. It makes my heart break and I ache to fix it for him. But how can anyone truly be fixed after seeing something like that?

"No one has ever hurt my mom before and I want to help. But I'm afraid. I'm the only one home, though. My dad is still at work and I know he would want me to be brave. I'm his little man and I'm supposed to take care of the house when he is gone. So I stand up and run out of the closet.

"I jump at the man with the gun, and he turns just as I grab his hand. The gun is cold and metal. I feel it in my fingers and then there is a noise so loud that my ears ring. My mom falls onto the bed and there is a lot of blood."

I am completely frozen.

Oh my god.

Oh my god.

Did Pax bump the trigger?

Oh. My. God.

"The man is screaming, 'What the fuck did you do?' and he shakes me. Then he screams more. 'You killed your mother!' My mom isn't moving and her eyes are open, staring at me. But she isn't seeing me. The man is right. I killed my mother."

My eyes are wide and I ache to lunge into their room and hold Pax. His eyes are watery and a tear finally breaks rank and slips down his cheek. I ache to go to him and Dr. Tyler must know that, because he turns and looks into the camera—at me.

"We've got to know," he says quietly. Calmly. He's talking to me.

Fuck.

I perch on the edge of my chair, my fist pressed to my mouth as they continue.

"What happens next, Pax?" Dr. Tyler asks. "Remember, you are safe. He can't hurt you now."

"I am crying and the man slaps me. He's screaming again. 'You fucking kid. This wasn't supposed to happen. You fucking little snot nose kid. I'm not going to jail for this. No fucking way. And there's only one way to make sure that doesn't happen.' He grabs me by the neck and shoves me onto the bed next to my mom. I look down and her blood is on my shirt. I grab her hand and hold it. The man is telling me to close my eyes. The gun makes a clicking sound. I close my eyes tighter. But nothing happens."

I realize now that I am holding my breath. This can't be happening. This can't have happened. It's too grotesque, too unreal. No wonder Pax is damaged. *No. Fucking. Wonder.*

I am numb as the doctor asks Pax what happens next.

"The man tells me that he can't kill a kid. He says he just can't do it. He takes my hand and holds it down tight. He squeezes it too hard, but I don't cry anymore. He pulls a big knife out of his pants and cuts my hand with it. He makes an X. Then he dips the knife in blood and traces over the cut again and says, 'Swear on your mother's blood that you will never tell what I look like. This X is to remind you that I have marked you. I can always find you, anytime, anywhere. If you ever tell anyone about me, I will kill you just like your mom.

"Then he says, 'You're the one who killed her. They'll take you away too, you know. And bad men in prison do bad things to little boys who killed their mothers. They'll hurt you over and over, every day.'"

Pax has tears running down his face now, like the seven-year old boy that he currently is in his memory. I am literally aching. I look at the doctor and I can taste my own tears.

"Please," I beg. "Bring him out of this."

I know the doctor can't hear me. But I can't help but beg anyway. *For Pax.* For the little boy who shouldn't have to see this anymore.

The doctor nods, finally. He must have decided the same thing.

"Pax, you are safe. When I tell you to wake up, you will wake up. And you will remember everything that you have told me today. Do you understand?"

Pax nods.

"Wake up."

Pax opens his eyes and they meet mine through the TV screen. His are filled with a horror that I have never seen before and I hope to god I never see again. I leap from my seat and burst into their room, dropping to my knees next to him, stroking his back, gripping his shoulders, holding him tight.

The man with the yellow teeth scarred him in so many more ways than one. He didn't need to carve up his hand to do it. His heart will be scarred forever. I honestly don't see how Pax will ever be able to overcome any of it.

The thought makes me weep.

"Are you okay?" I whisper to him, forcing him to look at me. It's a stupid question, really. Of course he's not okay.

He stares at me. "I don't know," he says honestly. "I just don't know."

Chapter 21

Pax

I am numb. Utterly frozen as I watch the doctor write out another prescription for Xanax and hand it to Mila. She promises to have it filled in case I need it. He tells her that I shouldn't be alone and she agrees. She won't leave me, she says.

I can't imagine why not- not after what she heard today. I've always told her that I'm fucked up. But this... this is *fucked up*.

The doctor spent an extra hour talking with me after I woke up, but I can't remember anything that he said. It was all words and blurs and noise. Static. It doesn't matter. There's nothing that he can say that will help. He has to know that.

Mila grasps my elbow. "Ready?"

I nod and we walk silently out to the car. My feet feel wooden.

"Want me to drive?" she asks as she looks up at me.

"I'm good," I tell her as I open her door automatically. I'm on auto-pilot now. I'm moving, but not feeling. Mila slides in and looks up at me again. I don't know what she's waiting for. I close the door.

I buckle in and sit still for a second, staring at the snow in front of us. Everything seems to be a blur to me. Blurs of movement, blurs of shapes. Colors that bleed into each other. Nothing makes sense.

"Pax," Mila whispers. I can feel her eyes on me, waiting for something. What the fuck is she waiting for? But I don't ask. She leans over and embraces me, wrapping her arms around my shoulders and burying her face in my neck. I don't feel her warmth. I'm too numb.

"It will be okay," she finally whispers as she pulls away. She's wiping her tears away and I wonder why I'm not crying. I'm the one who should be, but my emotions seem to be gone. I can't feel a thing.

As I start the car up and drive, the silence yawns between Mila and I. I keep my eyes on the road, unable to focus or concentrate. I feel numb, every bit as numb as I felt after I dove in the lake after Mila. My heart is like a block of ice; frozen, suspended.

"Pax," she murmurs, staring at me. I can feel her gaze, her soft expression. I don't want to see it though, so I don't look. I don't deserve it. I don't deserve her goodness.

"We should talk about this." Her voice is soft, but insistent.

She puts her hand on my leg. Her fingers are cold. Normally, I would grasp it, hold it, tuck it into mine to warm it. Not now. I don't deserve to touch her with the same hands that killed my mother. So, I keep mine clenched on the steering wheel and I stare at my scar. It is jagged and deep, the edges of it white.

I have marked you.

In my head, I remember the man with the yellow teeth tracing my mother's blood into the cut. My mother's blood is literally on my hands. It's engrained in my skin forever. *I have marked you.*

I swallow. "I killed my mother. There's nothing else to say. In my dreams, I kept thinking that she was begging me to do something. But she wasn't. She was begging *for* me. For my life."

Everything seems like it is closing in on me and I suddenly feel incredibly hot. I breathe deeply, sucking in air. The white of the snow and the sky seem to be swirling around me and I can't see straight. I pull over and crack my window, and then I stare into the distance as I try to get things under control; my heart beat, my breathing, my thoughts.

Mila is silent.

I can tell she doesn't know what to do.

"Pax," she tries. "There's everything to say. You know it wasn't your fault. He was the one with the gun, the one who was forcing a violent act upon your mother. It wasn't you. I love you. I'll do anything you need me to do. Just name it. We can get through this."

Her words fade away and I stare into the silent winter day.

I can't believe the world is going on just the same as it was this morning, like nothing happened. Crows are perched in a nearby tree and I can hear them cawing. I briefly wonder why they haven't flown south, but I really don't give a fuck. The snow drifts across the road; and down the way, I see a snowplow coming slowly, it's yellow lights blinking in the slush. People are bundled up on the sidewalk, leaning into the cold winter. Everything is cold. The day, the wind, the lump in my throat.

I swallow hard, but it won't go down.

I shake my head and start the car again, driving to my house. The road passes behind us in a gray blur.

After my tires crunch on the snow in my driveway, I turn to Mila.

"I'm not going to be good company today. I think I should probably just be alone."

She's already shaking her head.

"Not on your life. I won't bother you, Pax. But the doctor said you shouldn't be alone. So you do whatever you'd like. You think about things, you process it however you'd like, but I'm staying. I'm just going to run into town and get your prescription filled and I'll be right back."

I nod curtly, and go into the house. I don't look back, even though I can feel Mila staring at me.

I stand in the middle of my living room, limply. I don't know what to do. I don't know how to process this. How would *anyone* process this?

And then, all of a sudden, I think about my father and a white-hot rage passes through me, overcoming the numbness.

He knew about this. He's known all of these years and he didn't tell me. He allowed me to suppress the memories. He had to know what it would do to me.

But everything makes sense now. No wonder he had stayed at work for such long hours after mom died. He didn't want to see me. How in the world could he have looked into my face knowing that I had killed his wife? Or even if he didn't realize the part I played, at the very least he knows that I didn't save her.

But even still. I was a kid. My logical thought tells me that Mila is right. It wasn't my fault. But I was the one who was there. It was my hand that bumped the man's gun. And it was my father who allowed me to hide it all of these years.

I punch his number into my house phone, but of course, he doesn't pick up. I leave him a voice mail.

"I know what happened to mom," I say icily. "Call me."

I hang up and throw my phone against the wall. It shatters into pieces. I guess if he wants to call, he'll have to call my cell.

Self-loathe floods through me, swirling with the anger that I feel toward my father. All of a sudden, I am consumed with so much emotion that I don't know what to do with it all. It's overwhelming. And it fucking hurts.

I head to the kitchen and grab a bottle of whiskey. I glance into the cabinet and see that I have two more. Thank god I re-stocked the other day. I gulp a few drinks, then a few more. Thankfully, the familiar haze soon descends upon me, the quiet numbness that I enjoy so much. But it's not enough.

The ache is still there.

Fuck. This.

I take the stairs two at a time and change into sweats, a sweat-shirt and running shoes. Without another thought, I dart out the back of the house, jogging down the path to the beach. The sand is packed and frozen into hard ripples that hurt the bottom of my feet.

I don't care. I deserve it.

I jog at a fast clip, sucking in the cold air that burns my lungs. I don't care. I deserve it.

The lake swirls and crashes against the shore on my right as my feet beat angrily on the rigid beach. The wind blowing from the water is frigid and wet and I suck it in, inhaling it into numb body. Flecks of the icy water hit my face and drip onto my shirt, freezing there.

I stare into the distance, not noticing as the beach falls away under my feet. I don't even know how far I go, until at last I can no longer breathe. My fucking lungs hurt so much and there is still a fucking lump in my throat, lodged so tightly that no amount of swallowing or running or heavy breathing will move it.

"Fuuuuccckkkkk!"

I turn and shout at the lake, screaming as loud as I can. The vibration of it rips against my vocal chords, bruising them in the cold.

But I don't care. I fucking deserve it. I shout again and again, until my voice grows hoarse. And then I drop onto the beach, leaning against a big piece of driftwood. I am limp and spent. My forehead is somehow sweaty, even though it is cold outside. The cold wind blows against it, giving me chills.

But I don't care.

I fucking deserve it.

I deserve to get pneumonia and die out here in the cold.

I stare blankly at the lake now, trying to tune out rational thought or logic or memories or emotion. I don't even know how long I've been here or how much time passes before I see someone making their way down the beach. I see a flash of red and a long coat.

Mila.

I can just barely see the neck of her red turtleneck sweater poking out of her heavy coat. She trudges along the beach, her slim form bent against the wind. I can tell when she sees me because her pace quickens and it only takes her a minute more to reach me.

"Pax," she shouts. "Oh my god. Thank god. What are you thinking? It's cold out here. You're going to get pneumonia."

I stare up at her. It's the weirdest feeling, but I simply don't care about anything. I don't care if I catch pneumonia. It wouldn't bother me at all.

She leans down and grabs my hand, pulling me to my feet.

"Come on," she tells me. "We're going back to the house. You don't even have a coat on."

And I don't care. But I don't tell Mila that. I just let her lead me to the house, up the stairs and into the kitchen.

"You're frozen," she says, turning to me. Her face is stricken as she strips off her coat and tosses it onto a chair. "I'm going to run you a hot bath. You have to warm up."

She disappears down the hall and I remain standing limply in place.

Nothing matters.

Not anymore.

I know now what the void was that was always in me. It was *this*. This horrible knowledge. Even though my mind was concealing it, deep down in a hidden place, I knew. It's why I've always felt empty, why I always welcomed oblivion.

Only now, the void isn't empty. It's filled with overwhelming pain and guilt. And I don't know what to do about it. I feel like I'm being pulled under.

Mila comes back and seems surprised that I haven't moved. She looks at me uncertainly, her green eyes liquid. She doesn't say anything though. She just grabs my hand and tugs me to the bathroom. She pulls off my clothes and kicks them into a pile on the floor.

"Get in," she instructs me firmly. "Your skin is bright red."

I obediently step into the tub, even though I haven't taken a bath since I was small. The hot water sends a thousand needles prickling through my limbs, but I don't care. I settle into the tub and close my eyes, blocking out everything.

"Pax," Mila begins. But then she changes her mind. "Never mind. I'll check on you soon. I have your prescription, but since you drank so much whiskey, I don't think you should take it."

I don't say anything.

When I open my eyes a moment later, she is gone. I close them again.

The problem is, when my eyes are closed, I see *her* face. My mother's.

Her eyes are wide open and staring at me. Dead. I did that to her. It was me. The guy wasn't going to kill her—I bumped his finger on the trigger.

It was all my fault.

Pain rips through me and I lurch to my feet, punching the tiled wall. I don't even feel that pain- the pain in my chest far overshadows it. I grab a towel and dry off, pulling my underwear on.

I've got to do something.

I can't live like this.

Mila

As Pax soaks, I put some water on for tea. As I do, his cell phone rings on the counter. I glance at it and see Paul Tate's name. I reach for it hesitantly. Should I answer it? My gut says yes.

"Hello?" I am still uncertain.

"Hello," a surprised Paul Tate answers. "Is Pax available? This is his father."

"Just a moment," I tell him. I want to say so much more, but I don't. I just climb the stairs to the bathroom and open the door, only to find the room empty. The tub is still full of water, but Pax isn't here.

Hell.

"He's not where I thought he was," I tell his dad. "I'll have to find him."

I start walking down the hall, but Paul interrupts me.

"Wait," he says. "How is he? I received a voicemail from him. He said he's remembered what happened to his mother."

Anger rips through me. This man concealed this stuff from Pax for years. He had to know that it was going to come bubbling to the surface at some point. Didn't he care about that? Didn't he care what it was doing to Pax all along?

"How do you think he's doing?" I ask coolly. "Not well. Nobody would handle it well."

There is a loud sigh on the other end.

"I've always been afraid of this day," Paul admits and he sounds distant and sad. "I've never known what to do, how to prevent it."

"You can't prevent it," I tell him incredulously. "Pax saw something tragic and devastating. He should have dealt with it years ago with the help of a therapist. To allow him to suppress it was unforgivable. I'm sorry. I don't know you and I'm sorry to judge, but I know *him*. And he didn't deserve this. Any of this."

There is a long silence. Finally Paul speaks again.

"You don't understand. After Susanna died, Pax refused to speak of it. I did hire a therapist and Pax refused to speak to him. He had nightmares, but he would never describe them or tell me what they were about. I couldn't help him because he wouldn't let me."

"He wouldn't talk about it because the man who killed your wife threatened Pax. He told him that he would hunt him down and kill him, that if he spoke of it to anyone, that Pax would go to jail for killing his own mother. As you can imagine, he's not dealing with it well. At all."

"Do you think I should come?" Paul sounds hesitant. I am appalled and shocked. If it was me and Pax was my child, I would be here immediately. I wouldn't ask, I wouldn't take no for an answer. But Paul Tate is hesitating. I can't believe it.

"You do whatever you feel you need to," I tell him angrily before I hang up on him. I know I didn't make the best first impression with Pax's father, but I don't care. How can he be so selfish?

As I gather my wits, I hear a thumping sound, loud and frequent.

Whump.

Whump.

Whump.

I crane my ears and follow the noise. It's coming from downstairs in the basement. Curious, I pad lightly down the wooden stairs and find Pax in his underwear, punching a punching bag that is hanging from a ceiling beam. I didn't even know it was down here. But then, I've never had a reason to be down here before.

He's sweaty and his muscles bulge and flex as he repeatedly punches at the bag. Over and over, with all of his strength. He doesn't even notice that I'm standing here watching him. He's focused solely in front of him.

Whump.

Whump.

Whump.

My heart feels shredded and I suck in a breath. I don't know what to do. I don't know how to help him. I tiptoe back up the stairs and slide to the floor, sitting against the wall. I can hear him still, punching. Over and over and over. I'm afraid he's going to hurt himself, or tear a muscle. But I know he won't stop, not even if I ask him.

I sit for at least another hour, my elbows on my knees, my face in my hands. And then the pounding finally stops. There is silence and then there are footsteps on the stairs.

I look up just as Pax emerges.

He looks down at me, then bends down and scoops me up.

He's sweaty, but I don't care. I lean my face against his chest.

Wordlessly, he carries me up the stairs and into the bedroom where he strips off his underwear and reaches for me. I'm surprised, but I fold into his arms. If this is the way he needs comforted, then so be it. I'll do anything to take the hurt off of his face.

His lips crush mine, hard. I kiss him back, but I quickly realize that this isn't going to be our normal sex. This is hard and primal. Anguished. He bends me onto the bed, and slides into me from behind with no foreplay. I wince just a bit, but it doesn't take long until I am wet.

He slides in and out; hard, rough, fast.

He grips my ass and thrusts harder.

My hands grip the comforter on the bed and I stare at it. Pax isn't really here with me. This isn't him. This is just him trying to block everything out. I know that, even if he isn't telling me.

It doesn't take long before he shudders against me; straining, pushing.

He falls with me to the bed and when I look at him, for just a second, it is Pax again. His eyes are open and wide.

"I'm sorry," he tells me softly, clutching me. "I'm so sorry. I'm sorry."

I don't know who he is really apologizing to, me or maybe even his mom. I just don't know. But I don't care. I stroke his back as he shakes until he finally is still. He lies there for the longest time before he climbs out of bed and closes the bedroom door behind him.

I don't follow. I know he wants to be alone. And for the life of me, I don't know how to help him.

Chapter 22

Pax

Hours turn into days.

I don't know how many and I don't give a fuck. All I know is that I can't turn the emotions off and I can't un-see the memories that are in my head now.

My father tries to call, but I don't speak with him. Mila answers and turns to me but I look away. I don't want to hear from him. Fuck him.

Dr. Tyler tries to call. But I won't speak with him, either. Mila asks, then she turns away, speaking softly to the doctor. But I don't give a fuck about that, either. They can say what they want.

And Mila.

Fuck.

My stomach clenches at the thought of Mila. I'm causing her pain, too. Because I can't be the person she needs me to be right now. I can't drive back to the doctor's and sit with her while we discuss my *feelings.* Instead, I'm an asshole. Because that's who I am. That's what I do best. There for a while, I tried to pretend that I wasn't, but my true colors are showing now.

I'm a fucking dick.

Nothing I've done so far, though, has caused her to leave. I don't want to talk, I pace instead of sleep, I drink too fucking much and I even angry-fucked her. She didn't leave. She just looked at me, so understanding and soft, and said she wanted to help me however she could.

What the fuck?

My stomach clenches. As angry as I am at life, I don't want to hurt her.

I turn to her now, to where she is curled up on the couch reading.

"Mila, you really should leave," I tell her abruptly. "I'm not fit company. I think it would be best if you went back to your place while I work through this."

She looks at me, wounded. And my gut clenches again. I know I have to do this. I'm only going to hurt her in the long run anyway. I might as well do it in one fell swoop. A clean break. She starts to protest, but I interrupt.

"It's fine to leave me. I'm through the worst of it. You have a life to get back to, a job. Your sister needs you. Please. I need time alone. You can call me tonight."

She looks uncertain and my heart twinges.

Fuck, how I hate this.

But this is what I deserve. I don't deserve someone like her.

She stands up, reaching up to touch my face. I close my eyes for just a minute, but then steel my resolve and open them again.

I stare down at her and remove her hand. That hurts her, I can see it.

It's for the best.

She finally nods.

"Okay. If that's what you need," she says uncertainly. "But call me if you need anything. And I'll come back tonight after I close my shop and check in with my sister."

I nod. I walk away before I stop her from leaving.

I hear her car pulling out of the drive and I throw my glass of water at the wall. It shatters and I replace it with a bottle of Jack.

This is what I deserve.

My chest feels like it is crushing me and I fight to swallow. There is just so much to deal with. I don't know where to start. So fuck it.

I grab the bottle of Xanax from the counter and head to the couch with my whiskey. I drop into a heap and pop the top off the pill bottle, taking several and washing them down with the Jack.

I drink the rest of the bottle.

I close my eyes and for once, there is nothing there but blackness. I breathe a sigh of relief and I finally sleep.

When I wake, it is morning.

I know that because morning sunlight pours through the windows.

I wince and sit up, rubbing my temples.

I slept through the night. With no nightmares, no thoughts of my mother. I smile, my lips stretching tightly. Suddenly, it's clear. I can't handle the issues on my own. I need my old friend, Jack. And my new friend, Xanax.

X marks the spot.

I pick up my phone and glance at it. Three missed calls, three voicemails and twelve texts, all from Mila.

Are you alright?

Pax, answer your phone.

Please answer your phone.

I'm worried about you, Pax. This isn't fair. Answer your phone.

They pretty much all say the same thing. I punch in one answer.

Don't worry. I'm fine.

After I get a fresh bottle of whiskey from the kitchen, I pop more pills in my mouth, three of them. Then I add two more.

It isn't long before the blackness comes back. I welcome it with open arms. I sing to it, I croon to it. I cradle it in my arms. I do whatever the fuck I want to do to it because it's blackness, the darkest of nights, and it doesn't care. If I am alone in the dark, nothing matters. I can't hurt anyone but myself and I fucking deserve it.

I close my eyes and let the darkness cradle me. It can fuck me for all I care.

Mila

I can't think straight. I accidentally didn't charge a customer at the store. So after that, I gave up and turned my sign to Closed.

I sit by the window of my store, staring out at the happy people walking down the sidewalk. They don't know how good they have it. Their lives are so easy.

I try to text Pax again, but like the four days prior, there isn't any answer. I've driven out there, pounded on the door, called him, even cussed into his voicemail.

No answer.

Only once. *Don't worry, I'm fine.*

He's not fine. And no one seems to care but me.

I've thought about calling the police to have them check on him, but I doubt they would. He's not doing anything illegal, so what can they do? It's not illegal to drink yourself into a stupor.

And the only thing he has in the house, to my knowledge, is the prescription Xanax. I once again wonder at the wisdom of prescribing that to Pax.

When I had asked Dr. Tyler about it, he explained that he had prescribed it because Pax isn't an addict.

"He's not addicted to any substance," the doctor had said. "He simply hasn't formed proper coping mechanisms for stress. If he feels like he can't cope, I'd rather him take a Xanax during the short term while we're working on these issues rather than seek out illegal drugs. Plus, you'll be there with him. Everything will be fine, Mila."

But I'm not there anymore. And things aren't fine.

I see an image of Jill's open, dead eyes and shudder.

That could have been Pax. And I'm terrified that if someone doesn't do something, that *will* be Pax.

With shaking fingers, I pick up the phone and do the only thing I can think of to do.

I call his father.

Chapter 23

Pax

I am falling, falling, falling.

It is black and dark and I can't see, I can't think, I can't feel. But that's how I like it. If I can't feel, then nothing hurts. So I keep it that way.

If I wake, I drink myself back to sleep with a Xanax chaser. It isn't long before I'm in the black again, drifting pointlessly along, sleeping without nightmares.

Only blackness.

I sigh. This is where I belong, where the dark is timeless.

Painless.

The light is painful. The light is where I see her face and know how I failed her.

I'll stay far away from the light.

Forever.

It isn't worth it.

I start to close my eyes but realize that they are already closed, so I smile.

This is where I belong.

Chapter 24

I open my eyes blearily, trying to focus. I look around at the room. I'm in the living room and I seem to be wearing the same clothes that I've been wearing for a while. What woke me? It's dark outside, so it wasn't the sun.

I reach for my whiskey, but find that the bottle is empty.

Fuck.

That means I'm out. I'll have to make a trip to town.

And then I hear what woke me. Pounding on the door.

My heart twinges. I know it's probably Mila. She's been here a hundred times this week, trying to get me to open the door, but I never get off the couch to do it. She doesn't need to see me this way. She doesn't deserve to be here like this.

The pounding gets louder, very loud.

Fuck. She's pissed now. I'm impressed with the strength she's using on that door.

And then, there's a loud crack and something breaks.

What the fuck?

I stand up and the room spins. I haven't been on my feet in a couple of days. I steady myself and re-open my eyes. When I do,

I find my father standing in front of me. He is clean and shaven and dressed in jeans.

"What are you doing here?" I ask him. "Did you just break down my fucking door?"

My father's jaw clenches. "That's what happens when you don't answer it for a week. Your girlfriend called me because she was worried. Get in the shower. We're going to talk."

I glare at him. "Fuck you. The time to talk was years ago. In fact, you've had any number of chances over the years to *talk*. But you didn't. And now I don't want to talk. Get over it."

I try to shove past him, to walk through to the kitchen, but he grabs my arm.

His grip is strong and determined.

"Take a shower," he says slowly and deliberately. "You smell like piss. Get clean clothes on and come back out here. We're going to talk. Now. Today."

I stare at him and he stares back. He's not backing down. And I do smell like piss. Finally, I look away.

"Whatever. I do need a shower."

I leave the room without looking back. I step into my shower and let the water run over me while my fucking head pounds. I can't remember if I drank any water this week at all. I actually don't remember much at all about this week. Every time I woke up, I simply took more pills and drank more whiskey.

I wash, shave and get dressed.

Then I make my way to the kitchen, where I chug two bottles of water. Even after that, my mouth is still dry so I must be pretty dehydrated. I take another bottle of water with me to the living room, where my father is waiting for me.

He's cleaned the place up while he waited, picking up the

empty bottles of whiskey from the floor. He's sitting in a chair now.

He stares at me as I enter.

He's grim and sober and I find that I suddenly don't want to have this conversation.

"Fuck this," I tell my dad. "We haven't talked about this in years. I don't see the reason to talk about it now. The damage is done."

My father looks at me.

"The damage has been done," he agrees. "But there's no reason to make it worse. Let's talk."

I sit down and take a swig of water.

"Fine. Why didn't you force me to talk about what happened?"

If we're going to talk, we might as well cut to the chase.

My father stares at me, then his gaze drops to the floor.

"Because it was easier that way. I took you to a therapist and you wouldn't talk. I tried to get you to talk about it myself, you refused. And then I decided that maybe I really didn't want to know what happened. If it had scarred you so badly, then I wasn't sure that I could deal with it either. So I stopped trying. And then the therapist told me that he thought you had actually suppressed the memories, so it seemed to be for the best."

I take another drink. My tongue feels thick from dehydration.

"Did they ever catch him?"

I cringe when my dad shakes his head. "No. They didn't have a description to go on. None of the neighbors saw anything, they didn't see anyone coming or going. The police didn't have anything to work with."

Fuck. Yet another reason to feel guilty. I could have given them a description.

"What happened that day?" my dad asks. "I need to know.

There was gun residue on your hands. And you had that cut. But the police couldn't determine what happened, except your mother wasn't sexually violated. She had epithelial cells in her mouth, but no trace of semen. There was no match to the DNA sample in the police database. I know this is hard to think about or talk about. But what did you see?"

I close my eyes, squeezing them hard before I open them again. My dad is still staring at me, still waiting for answers.

"I heard mom crying. I found the guy in your room with a gun held to mom's side. The guy forced her to give him a blowjob. I tried to help, but when I did, I bumped the gun and it went off. She's dead because I tried to help. If I hadn't, she would still be here today."

My father chokes a little and I try to swallow the fucking lump that keeps forming in my throat. He looks at me.

"Do you really think he would have left her alive?" Dad finally says. "Think about that, Pax. She knew what he looked like. If he told you that he wouldn't have killed her, he was lying."

"He left *me* alive," I tell him limply. "Maybe he would have left her, too."

My dad shakes his head, his cheeks flushed. "No. He wouldn't have. He probably couldn't bring himself to kill a kid in cold blood and he felt confident enough that he'd scared you into silence. Your mom never stood a chance, Pax. There wasn't anything you could've done about it."

He turns away now, staring out the window.

"But there's something you can do now. Now that you remember, come with me. Let's fly to Connecticut right now and sit down with the detective who handled the case. You can give him the description. What did the guy look like, anyway?"

I feel a chill run through me as I picture the guy's sneering face. "He was skinny, with a gray ponytail and yellow teeth. Really yellow teeth. He was wearing a blue striped shirt."

My father is frozen.

"I know who you are talking about. That was our mailman. I'd never forget that gray ponytail or those horrible teeth. Pax, go pack a bag. We're going to Connecticut."

"The mailman?" I am incredulous. "I don't remember the mail man at all."

"You wouldn't, would you?" my dad answers. "You were only seven. I used to tease your mother that he would find silly reasons to bring the mail to the door instead of leaving it in the box. I used to *joke* with her that he had a thing for her. We laughed about it. We thought he was just a little strange and lonely. I had no idea..."

Dad's voice chokes off and he looks away for a minute and pulls himself together before he looks back at me.

"Get your things, Pax. That sick bastard deserves to pay."

The idea that I might find just a bit of redemption spurs me and I do get off the couch and go pack a bag. As I'm cramming my toothbrush into my overnight case, I see a ring laying on the counter. I pick it up. Mila must've left it. Her mother's wedding ring. I slide it onto my pinkie and finish packing.

In my haste, I leave my cellphone in the house and don't realize it until we are speeding away toward Chicago.

"Don't worry," my dad says. "If you need a phone, you can use mine. We won't be gone that long anyway. Maybe a couple of days. This is huge, Pax. That fucking guy will finally get what he deserves. All they'll need to do is match his DNA. This is huge."

My dad is more animated now than I've ever seen him. There is life in his eyes. I look at him.

"Dad, why did you think it might be best if I never remembered? What did you mean? Best for me? Or best for you?"

My dad glances at me with a sober look before returning his eyes to the road.

"Maybe for both of us. I knew the memories would shatter you. And after they found the gunpowder residue on your hands, I didn't think I wanted to know what happened. I couldn't begin to imagine, but I wasn't in a good place. And if I'd found out that you had a hand in her death, even accidentally, I didn't know if I could get past it."

"But I was a kid," I choke out. "I was trying to help her."

"Yes," my dad says, leveling a gaze at me. "You were. I'm glad you realize that. But I was in a bad way then. Grief does that to a person. And so I coped in the only way I knew how. I threw myself into work. And when that didn't stop the pain, I packed us up and moved us across the country."

"Did that stop the pain?" I ask him.

He looks at me. "No."

I glance down at my hands and stare at the ring on my finger. I take it off, spinning it round and round in my hands. The inside has words inscribed. I peer closer to read them. *Love Never Fails.*

I gulp.

Sometimes, love does fail. I've certainly proven that. I've failed everyone. I failed my mother. I failed my father when I repressed the memories and couldn't tell anyone what the killer looked like. And I've certainly failed Mila. I know I've ripped her heart out and I doubt I can ever put it back together again.

I close my eyes to soothe the stinging in them.

I nap in the airport until our plane takes off, then I nap on the plane. I think about trying to call Mila, but decide that I'd better not. Our conversation isn't one for the phone. I'll need to see her, face-to-face. In the meantime, I have something important to do.

When we touch down in Hartford, we check into a hotel. Our dinner in the posh hotel restaurant is fairly silent.

I watch my father swirling his scotch absently in his glass for a long time before I finally speak up.

"It wasn't your fault, either, dad."

He looks up at me.

"No? Pax, we joked about that guy. The fucking mailman. I thought he was a joke. But he took my life away. Or he might as well have. Some joke. I guess he got the last laugh."

The bitter agony on my father's face is apparent and as pissed as I am at him, I can't help but feel terrible for him at the same time. I can't imagine what he must feel like.

"Dad," I attempt again. But he interrupts.

"Pax, you don't understand. You can't imagine how many times over the years I've wondered…what if I had left work early that day? What if I'd not stopped for gas? What if I'd hit one less red light? If any of those things had happened, maybe I could have stopped it. The constant not-knowing was terrible. But now, to find out that the fucking mailman took her life…my guilt is ten thousand times worse than it ever was. Because if I'd taken him seriously- if I'd recognized him for the perverted fuck that he was, your mother would be alive today. That's an unarguable fact."

I gulp down the rest of my water before I answer.

"Dad, mom must not have realized how fucked up he was, either. You said you both joked about it. That means that he hid it pretty well. You can't feel guilty for someone else's mental illness. There's no way that you could have known."

I can tell my father doesn't believe me, though and we finish our meal in silence. To be honest, I think we both are happy to be alone with our thoughts.

After a fairly sleepless night, we go the police station first thing in the morning. The detective is more than happy to hear from us.

"This case has haunted me for years," he admits to me, his mouth tight. "I'd never seen anything like it. I've never forgotten it, or the sight of your little face. Your eyes were so big and sad. You'd seen the unimaginable. I'm glad to see you've grown up so well."

So well. Huh. That's debatable.

He takes my official statement and assures us that they will be pursuing a warrant to collect DNA evidence from our old mailman as soon as they can get a name from Post Office records. I feel a feeling of intense satisfaction as we walk down the steps of the station and out into the brisk, fresh air.

Justice might finally be served. My mom might finally be vindicated. It's only taken seventeen years.

"Where is she buried?" I ask my father as we climb into the car. He looks at me.

"Let's stop and get some flowers, and I'll show you."

So we do exactly that. We stop and get two dozen roses apiece and we drive to a beautiful, silent cemetery. It is lined with trees and the ice hangs on the branches, sparkling in the winter sun. It's serene. I decide that if you must be buried, it might as well be here in this tranquil place.

As we walk among the graves, I feel as though I've been here before and I know that I have. I have fleeting glimpses of her funeral, of the casket being lowered into the ground. I remember the intense feeling of sadness that I had felt watching it.

I swallow hard.

Ahead of us, I see a statue of an angel and I recognize it. It is lying across a slab, weeping into its hands and I know that it sits next to my mother's grave. I remember it.

"Your grandfather had the statue brought in," my father says, nodding toward it.

"It seems fitting," I answer. And it does.

My mother's headstone sits next to the angel, made from white marble. It's gleaming and bright. I turn to my dad. "Someone's been taking care of it."

He nods. "Of course. I pay someone."

Of course.

I stare down.

> *Susanna Alexander Tate*
> *Beloved wife and mother*
> *She walked in beauty,*
> *She sleeps in peace.*

The cold wind blows gently against my face and once again, a knot forms in my throat. I am flooded with guilt that I haven't been here to visit her in years. I kneel to place my flowers by her name and for the first time in as long as I can remember; I feel a tear streaking my cheek. I wipe it away.

"Do you think she is? At peace?"

My father looks at me.

"Son, *you* were your mother's peace. You brought her so much peace and joy from the very first time she held you, that she knew she had to name you Pax. Your mother loved you more than anything in the world. She would have gladly given her life a hundred times over to keep you safe. Whatever you do, just live a good life for her. She had so many hopes for you. But when it boils down to it, all she would want is for you to be happy."

The tears flow freely now and my father wraps his arms around me. And just like that, two grown men stand embracing in front of a lonely headstone.

It is a few minutes before he pulls away and I see that he is crying too.

"I love you, too, Pax. I hope you know that."

I nod, too choked up to speak. I feel as though someone has twisted my guts in their hands and shoved them back down my throat into all the wrong places. Everything hurts. But for the first time, the pain is okay. The pain feels normal, like it's the kind I should feel. It doesn't feel like the shameful pain that I felt as a kid, back when I couldn't save my mom.

The old void in my heart is gone. It has been replaced with a quiet sort of acceptance. My life is what it is. My mom died a violent death and I watched it happen. I've got to get past it and move forward. It's what she would want me to do.

Standing here, in front of her grave in this serene place, I know now that I couldn't have saved her. I was seven years old. My father was right. The intruder would've killed her regardless. It was his plan all along or he wouldn't have even brought the gun.

We ride back to the airport in silence.

Finally, my father speaks. "You should call Mila. She's been very worried about you."

I look at him in surprise. "She said that to you?"

He nods. "She's the reason I came to your house, remember? She called me or I wouldn't have known that things were so bad. She loves you, Pax. And if there's anything that you should take away from this is that you need to live for today. Tomorrow is not promised to you."

"I don't deserve her," I tell him honestly. "I've been an asshole. All I've done is hurt her."

My father looks at me doubtfully. "If that were true, then she wouldn't love you so much. She's waiting for you. She's checked on you a hundred times and has asked me a million questions that I don't know the answers to. Only you do. You need to answer them for her."

"Such as?"

"Such as, are you coming back? Are you going to be okay? How are you handling things now? Things that you don't talk about so I don't know. You're going to have to get some help figuring out how to deal with uncomfortable things. You can't keep burying things in drugs and whiskey. You know that."

I nod. And it's painful because it's true.

"I've fucked up," I say simply.

"Yes," my father agrees. "But haven't we all?"

I don't answer. I slip away into my thoughts and continue to twirl Mila's ring on my finger. As we make our way through the airport, dad turns to me.

"I'm going to tell your grandfather that you remember. It's one of the reasons that he stopped talking to us. He didn't agree with me not forcing you to think about it because he wanted your mother's killer found. When I refused to try and force you, he couldn't bring himself to go along with the lies that I told you, that your mother died in a car-crash. His absence isn't his fault, it's mine. The blame rests on my shoulders. And I'm sorry."

I nod. To be honest, I'll worry about that later. It's the last thing I'm worried about right now. There's only one face in my mind and it is beautiful and soft and has wide, green eyes.

Our plane touches down in Chicago and my father drives me home.

"I hope things will get better for us now, Pax," he tells me in my driveway and I can see that he is sincere. I nod.

"I hope so too," I answer. I find that I mean it. It will take a while, I'm sure. We can't fix years of damage to our relationship in a minute. But at least it's a start. If we keep at it, maybe someday we'll be okay again.

He backs out and I watch until I can no longer see his red taillights before I drop into Danger and speed for town. I can only think of one thing.

Her.

I burst into the door of her shop and she looks up in surprise from the counter. She is alone and seems to be studying a portfolio. As I walk in and she recognizes me, at first her expression leaps. In joy.

But it quickly becomes guarded and I feel the sting of that all the way into the center of my heart. I did that to her. I taught her to be guarded and protective around me because I might crush her. That knowledge kills me.

I stride across the store, not stopping, not hesitating. I step around the counter and smash her to me tightly.

"Please," I tell her. "Please forgive me. I'm so sorry that I hurt you. I'm so sorry that I've been an asshole and that I shut you out. I didn't know how to handle things without being self-destructive. Self-destruction is all I've ever known. Deep down, it's what I felt like I deserved."

I pause and look down. She's staring up at me with her gorgeous, clear eyes and my gut clenches.

"Give me another chance," I ask urgently. "I will do anything that you want me to do if you just tell me that we can start again. I know I don't deserve it, but I'm asking anyway. I honestly don't know if I can breathe without you. Please. I love you, Mila. Please tell me we can work it out."

I stare into her eyes and she seems uncertain and I feel a moment of panic.

"I don't want to start over again," she says slowly. "I like what we had. I don't want to re-do it. I love you, Pax. But I don't know if I can handle it if you leave me like that again. You shut me out and I couldn't help you. That's not what people do when they love someone. You ripped my heart out and stomped on it."

"I know," I agree. "I know that. You have no idea how sorry I am. I'm just not that good at relationships. I haven't had any practice. But if you stay with me, if you stay... I promise that I will never leave you again. I will never shut you out again. I'll put in the work and I'll fix what is broken. I promise."

"I want to believe you," she says slowly, her eyes still frozen on mine. "But I'm too afraid, Pax. You scared me. A lot. How do I know that you won't shut me out like that again? How do I know that the next difficult thing we come across won't send you into another tailspin and I'll find you on the back yard, like we found Jill?"

She pauses, her eyes pleading, wanting me to say something, wanting me to argue that she's wrong. But I don't know that she is. So I can't say anything.

"Jill's two babies are in foster care now, Pax. Their whole lives have been shattered. I don't know that I can trust you not to do that to me. I haven't slept in days and when I do sleep, I have horrible nightmares. I'm a wreck, Pax. And I don't want to go through this again. I just don't think I can."

Her words terrify me and I pull off the ring, holding it out with a shaking hand.

"Love never fails, Mila. That's what your parents believed. And because of you, it's what I believe now, too. You stuck by me and loved me when I didn't deserve it. All I want is a chance to prove that I can be worthy of it. Your parents were sort of fucked up in their own way, like me, and they never got the help that they needed. But I will. I promise. I *will* put the work in. I will learn how to cope with painful things and I will never leave you again. Just tell me that you'll stay with me."

I stare at her, waiting, holding my breath.

"Please," I whisper.

Finally, finally, she takes the ring from my hand and leans on her tiptoes, pressing her lips to mine, ever so softly.

"I love you so much," she whispers. "I love you so much. But I can't. Not right now."

A vice-grip crushes my heart as I stare at her; at the face that is so beautiful and delicate, at the woman who has seen me at my worst but is still standing in front of me today without judgment or derision. My chest tightens and my eyes burn. I feel utterly empty.

"I know," I tell her, honestly. "I understand."

And I do.

It is a truth so raw and honest that it hurts. But I haven't given her a reason to stay so there is no way that she should. There's only one thing that I can do… give her one.

I swallow hard, willing the lump in my throat to dissipate.

"I'll give you a reason," I tell her, my voice raw. "I promise. If you give me the chance, I will give you a reason to be with me."

She kisses me again and I fight the urge to inhale her, to crush her to my chest and never let go, to force her to stay.

"I'm counting on that," Mila murmurs as she steps away. "I just need some time Pax; time for you to show that you are serious about this, about putting the work in. That's all I need."

I know this is as hard for her as it is for me and I hate that I did this to her. I hate that I put that hurt on her face.

I nod slowly and the movement seems painful.

"You can have all the time that you need, Mila. I'll wait forever if I have to."

A tear slips down her cheek and she looks away. My gut feels like a cement block as I use my thumb to wipe her tear, then to pull her chin up.

I kiss her cheek. "I love you," I murmur into her ear.

And then I gather every ounce of my strength, because that's what it takes to walk away from her.

Chapter 25

Mila

Nights seem very long now, very dark and cold.

I roll over in my lonely bed again, pulling my quilt up to my chin, trying to force my mind away from thoughts of Pax. As if that will happen. My heart constricts at the memory of what Pax has been through.

Ever since he walked away from me last week, ever since I watched the rejection ripple over his face, the hurt and angst, I have played that moment over and over in my mind. Regretting it, beating myself up over it. But there's nothing else I could have done.

He has to know that every action has a consequence. And even though he says he will change, that he realizes he needs to change, I'm pretty sure he needs a reason to *actually* change. If I take him back like he didn't hurt me, he won't have a very good reason.

Except for the one where his entire life has imploded around him, you idiot, I tell myself. Pax has every reason in the world to change, reasons that don't even include me. If only he is strong enough to see it.

Against my better judgment, I reach for my phone. It has been a week since I have seen him or spoken with him. My heart just wants to hear from him, to know that he's okay. Maybe then I can sleep.

I'm thinking about you. I hope you're okay.

I send the text and wait with the phone in my fingers. There is no answer. Although I probably deserve that.

I waver back and forth in my conviction. Maddy agrees that I had no other choice but to send him away when he came to my shop. But part of me, an increasingly more insistent part, doubts it. I love him. I love him more than anything. And isn't part of love standing next to him through thick and thin?

Love never fails. I gulp.

But then again, sometimes love has to put boxing gloves on and be tough in order to survive. Sometimes, you have to do the harder thing—the thing where you let someone grow on their own.

I fall asleep with tears on my cheek and my phone in my hands. When I wake up, there is a text waiting for me.

I'm thinking about you, too. And I'm getting there.

His words make my heart smile. And it is somehow easier to get up and face my day.

* * *

"I think you're losing weight," Maddy announces, as she prances through my shop in her new boots and a take-out sack.

I look up from where I am framing a print of the night sky and roll my eyes.

"First, I thought you said we had to tighten our belts this winter?" I ask with my eyebrow raised as I stare pointedly at her boots.

She looks sheepish. "That was true. But things are perking up now that spring is rolling around."

"February isn't spring," I tell her wryly. She rolls her eyes.

"A mere technicality. It's late February. Almost spring. Now that people aren't snowed in, business is picking up. But you're deflecting. You haven't been eating right. I bet you've lost ten pounds—and you didn't have it to lose, Slim."

I would say something, but I wouldn't have a leg to stand on. She's right. I've lost weight and I didn't have it to lose.

"Did you bring me something to eat?" I ask instead. She nods, plunking the sack unceremoniously down on my picture.

"Grilled cheese and a bowl of minestrone. Tony said to eat it all and you'll get dessert. He also said you're getting chicken legs."

I shake my head, and can't help but smile. Tony loves us in his own gruff way. I wouldn't be surprised if it was his idea that Maddy brought me the food.

"I saw Pax's car parked in front of Dr. Tyler's office," Maddy mentions as she curls herself into a sleek red chair. "He's been there a lot lately. Have you talked to him?"

I chew a bite of my sandwich and swallow hard to get it to go down. "No. Not in a month. Has he been in to The Hill?"

Maddy shakes her head. "No. And I haven't seen his car at the bar, either. He's pretty much been out of sight, except for when he's with Dr. Tyler."

She stares at me.

I ignore it.

"Well?" she finally demands, her ice blue gaze on mine. "He's respecting your space and he's putting in the effort so that he can move forward. Don't you think it's time that you took the initiative to speak with him?"

I almost drop my sandwich. "Who are you and what have

you done with my sister?" I demand. "You don't like Pax. You've never liked Pax. You've told me a hundred times that he's not worth my time, that he'll never be boyfriend material."

I am beyond shocked at her.

Maddy has the grace to look sheepish.

"I don't know," she admits. "I can't explain why I feel differently. I just do. My gut instincts are telling me that he deserves a second chance. I really think he's trying, Mi. To be honest, not only have I not seen his car at the bar, but when I was in there the other day for a drink, I asked Mickey if he's seen him. He hasn't."

She stares at me again, hard and long. I sigh.

"Madison, just because he hasn't been in the Bear's Den doesn't mean that he's stopped drinking. Or doing worse things. For all we know, he's holed up in his house with whiskey and drugs. We don't know what he's doing."

There is a pause while Madison fidgets.

"*You* don't know what he's doing," she finally says hesitantly. "Because you haven't talked with him. But I have."

I do drop my sandwich this time, right into my soup.

"What?" I ask, as my stomach plummets into my feet. "You lied? You said you haven't spoken with him."

For some strange reason, my fingers shake as I wait for her answer, as my heart beats loudly against my ribcage.

Madison looks uncertain now. "I didn't lie. I said he hasn't been in The Hill. And he hasn't. But he called me a couple of weeks ago. Apparently, he's been keeping an eye on you and he noticed that you've still been picking up a lot of shifts for me and he wanted to help."

"He. What?" I ask stiltedly, trying to wrap my mind around this new turn of events. My icy sister has been speaking to Pax behind my back?

"He wanted to help," she repeats. "He told me that he knows how much The Hill means to us since it was our parents' dream and he wanted to make sure that we don't lose it. He paid off our renovation loan and then he sent one of his own business advisors to talk to me. We sat down and wrote out an updated business plan and now The Hill is back on track. It appears that I needed to make a few changes and so I did. And also, apparently, I needed to make a few changes in my personal life, too, like not judging someone that I don't even know. I didn't know Pax. I had no right to tell you stay away from him."

I am stunned beyond words. I feel like something is sitting on my chest, weighing down my lungs as I stare at my sister. I can't breathe.

I grab my water and take a drink, then another.

"Pax did that?" I finally manage to croak. Maddy nods.

"But I was sworn to secrecy. He doesn't want you to know what he did. He was very adamant that when you finally give him another chance, it will be because he earned it on his own merit, not because of this."

"Do you know how he's doing?" I whisper. "Is he okay?"

Madison nods. "I went to his house to meet with his business advisor. He and I chatted for a while. His main concern was you. He wanted to make sure that you're okay. He feels like such an ass for hurting you and he's afraid he's never going to redeem himself for that. But otherwise, he's okay. He looks healthy and he's been seeing Dr. Tyler two times a week. He even said that he and his dad are working things out. I think those are huge strides, Mi."

And they are. She really has no idea. She wasn't there to see the look on Pax's face when he found out that his dad had hidden everything for years. The gut-wrenching betrayal that lived in his eyes. I really wasn't sure that he'd ever be able to forgive his father.

"I don't know what I'm supposed to do," I finally admit to her in a whisper, collapsing onto the chair with my sister. She wraps a slender arm around me.

"Do you love him?" she asks, staring into my eyes. Without hesitation, I nod.

"Is he worth the heartache and the effort?"

Her face is grave and somber as she brushes the hair out of my eyes.

I nod again.

"Pax is worth anything."

Madison smiles. "I thought you would say that. My advice to you then, little sister, is that you go talk to him. He's trying very hard. I admire that. I have to respect it. And I know he loves you."

I am frozen. Utterly frozen. I can practically feel my heart beating in my ears.

"What are you waiting for?" Maddy asks me gently, pushing at my shoulder. "Go."

So I do.

* * *

The drive to Pax's house has never taken so long before. But even still, I sit in my car for a couple of minutes after I pull into his drive. Danger is parked in front of me, so I know he is home. I am filled with both breathless anticipation and utter anxiety as I slosh through the muddy snow to his door.

What if he doesn't want me anymore? What if I took too long to get to this point? *What if it's too late?*

I take a few deep breaths as I stand on Pax's front porch.

Deep breath in, deep breath out.

Repeat.

I ring the doorbell, then knock. I am suddenly overwhelmed by the need to see his face, to see him healthy and strong. I want to see his eyes without pain in them. My stomach clenches again and again as I wait. It seems to take forever and when the door finally opens, I am breathless.

For the first time in a month, Pax is standing in front of me, filling up the doorframe.

He is so beautiful in jeans and a black shirt. No one can carry off casual like he can.

My knees feel weak.

His eyes widen when he sees me, but then he smoothes his expression out. He's casual now, friendly. But cautious. Clearly cautious.

"Hi, Red," he says quietly, watching my face. Waiting for me to say something. I *am* the one who came to see him, after all. I swallow. I have to restrain myself from vaulting into his arms.

"Hi."

Oh my god. I want to say a thousand things and all I say is hi? I'm a lunatic.

"Can I come in?" I quickly add. Pax smiles and gestures with his arm.

"Of course. Anytime. You know that. Can I get you something to drink? A water, maybe?"

Why is he being so formal? My heart twinges a bit. Did I wait too long? Has he moved on?

The thought practically paralyzes me, but I still manage to decline the water and follow him into his living room. I glance around as I sit. He hasn't changed his house any. It is still light and airy, a modern loft, perfectly neat and clean. A part of me deep down is relieved. If he hasn't changed his house, maybe he hasn't changed his feelings for me.

Even I know that thought is irrational as hell. But I think I'm grasping at straws.

"How are you?" I ask, staring at him. "Are you okay?"

He thrums his long fingers against his denim-clad thigh. He's still working out. That much is apparent. I can see the hard muscle through the fabric. I gulp.

He smiles. "I'm doing really well. I won't lie, though. It's been hard as hell to wrap my mind around everything. But it's given me perspective. And this past month, I've sort of isolated myself and just focused on things I need to change. I wanted to make sure that I gave you a reason to want to be with me."

He pauses.

And my heart pauses as he looks at me. His golden eyes are so warm and vibrant. How had I ever thought they were cold?

"I've done a lot of thinking, Mila. And you were right to turn me away a month ago. You really were. I've spent a lot of time worrying that I'd completely fucked up with you, that you'd never forgive me. Or that I'd hurt you so badly that you'd never want to look at me again."

I start to interrupt, but he holds up his hand. "Please. Just let me finish. I've thought about what I would say to you a hundred times. I'm so happy to have the chance to say it."

I close my mouth and nod. He smiles gently.

"Mila, I've said this before, but you are the most beautiful thing I've ever seen. You are beautiful inside and out. I don't deserve to have met you. I don't deserve you in any way. But there's nothing I want more than to be with you. To wake up beside you for the rest of my life. I am so grateful that you stuck by me for as long as you did. And all I want to know now is what

I can do to make you stick with me again? You name it and I'll do it. Anything."

He waits, his eyes glued to mine and I feel overwhelmed by emotion, completely choked up.

"I haven't waited too long?" I finally manage to say. Pax looks surprised.

"What do you mean?" he asks bewilderedly. "Of course not. I said I would wait forever for you. I meant it."

Tears are streaming down my cheeks as I launch myself into his arms. We fold into each other and I bury myself against his chest. He smells the same, like the outdoors and the fresh air. I inhale him and then he tilts my chin up, his lips meeting mine.

As I lose myself in his kiss, I know that I never want to be anywhere but here, wrapped in Pax's arms.

It's where I belong.

Chapter 26

Pax

Mila sleeps curled on my lap. We've been curled up on the couch together all day and now into the evening. Her head is resting against my chest, and so it is with extreme caution that I reach for the phone, careful not to jostle her around and wake her.

Speaking softly, I order an enormous amount of Chinese food for delivery. Looking down at Mila, I quickly add dessert to our order. She needs to eat. She's lost weight. The curves that used to fit perfectly into my hands have become too thin.

As I hang up the phone, I feel guilty about that. She was under stress because of me.

Staring down, I stroke the hair away from her brow, watching her lips puff out with each breath. It's a trait about her that is cute as hell. She seems so innocent, like a child. She chooses this moment to open her eyes. They widen as she realizes that I'm awake.

"Hi," she murmurs, sitting up. I keep my arms wrapped around her.

"Hi," I tell her with a smile. "Did you sleep well?"

She nods guiltily, like she's ashamed of sleeping the day away.

"You needed the sleep," I tell her. "You haven't been taking care of yourself."

She looks sheepish. "I had trouble sleeping," she answers defensively.

"I know," I tell her softly. "I did, too. But we'll sleep better now, I promise."

She stares at me. "Have your nightmares gone away?"

"Surprisingly, yes," I answer. "For the most part. I've had a couple since I was hypnotized, but not many. Even though it's been painful, remembering everything really was cathartic. Once I started talking about it and processing it, I've been able to put some of my issues to bed."

"You must be talented," she tells me, taking my words from a long time ago. "Sometimes issues don't want to sleep."

I smile. "You're right. Sometimes issues are insomniacs from hell. But mine are behaving for now. Let's hope they stay that way."

"I'm sure they will," Mila answers confidently. "Because you're talented. You'll whip them into shape."

She snuggles into my neck and I pull her even closer. "I don't think I'm ever going to let you off my lap," I tell her. "So I hope you're comfortable."

She giggles. "You say that now, until your legs fall asleep."

"You let me worry about that," I tell her. "You weigh five pounds now. And by the way, we have food coming. You're going to eat all of it."

She giggles again. "You let me worry about that."

But after the delivery guy comes and I let Mila get off my lap, she does end up eating everything I put on her plate. I try to make her take seconds, but she refuses. I let it slide. I'll have all the time in the world now to feed her.

"I have something for you," I tell her as we put our dishes into the dishwasher. She straightens up.

"Oh? I don't need anything, though. I have everything I need now."

And by that, she means me. My heart swells.

"I have everything I need now, too," I assure her. "And you're never going anywhere which is why I'm giving this to you."

She stares at me curiously and I lead her to the second floor, positioning her in front of a closed door.

"You're giving me a guest bedroom?" she cocks an eyebrow as she turns to look at me. "You don't want to sleep with me anymore?"

"Just open the door, Sassy Pants."

She smiles and turns the knob, pushing it open. And then she gasps.

I transformed a guest room into a studio for her. An entire wall of windows face the lake, flooding the room with light. Two easels, built-in shelves filled with every possible art supply she could ever need, a sitting area and I even had skylights installed for nights when the moon is overhead.

Mila is frozen.

"Aren't you going to say anything?" I ask. "Cat got your tongue?"

She smiles slowly, mischievously. "I thought we already established that the cat most definitely doesn't have my tongue."

Memories from the night on my kitchen floor stir my groin and I quickly think of other things. *Dead puppies, nuns, cold fish.*

Once my groin is under control, I tug on her hand, leading her from shelf to shelf.

"I wanted you to have everything you would need to paint here," I tell her. "Did I forget anything?"

She spins around, looking at everything.

"This is amazing," she breathes. "You didn't forget a thing. But you must've been working on this for a while. What if…what if we hadn't worked things out?"

I wrap my arms around her from behind.

"That wasn't an option," I answer. "It was never an option. Love never fails, Mila. And I'll never fail you again. That's a promise."

I pull her around so that she is looking at me with her gorgeous green eyes.

"Mila, that day in your shop almost crushed me. When you said no to me, I didn't know if I would survive it, but I knew I had to. I knew that I had to change, for me *and* for you. And I think I have. I'm still working on it…it's going to be a process. But I'm willing to put in the work. Forever, if that's what it takes. So…I'm going to ask you again, babe. Stay with me. Stay with me here in my house. It's only a five minute drive to your shop when it's open. And you can use this studio for your art. I promise to try not to snore. And to put the toilet seat down. Most of the time, anyway. Just stay with me. Please. I never want to be away from you again."

Mila stares at me, her eyes glittering. "On one condition."

I feel the breath freeze on my lips. "Name it."

"I get to paint you nude any time I want."

A chuckle rumbles through my chest and I grab her, crushing my lips to hers.

"Any time," I mumble against her mouth. "You can do anything to me at all, actually. Nude or otherwise."

She laughs and I lift her up. Her legs wrap around my waist… right where they belong as her fingers rake through my hair.

"Yes," she tells me breathlessly. "Yes. I'll stay with you."

We tumble to the floor, grasping at each other, breathing each other in. Mila's tongue slips into my mouth, her breath sweet and warm. Her hands clutch me, pulling me closer and closer.

Her legs are wrapped around me and I moan as she strokes me. Then my lips are on her neck, her collarbone, her breasts. After a few heated minutes, she pulls my face back up to hers.

With her forehead pressed to mine, she whispers, "I love you."

I grin against her lips.

"I know."

I quickly roll over with her in my arms and I hover above her before I slide my hand between her legs. She is panting within a minute and calling my name within two.

I smile again and as she pulls me to her, I enter her slowly and sweetly.

I groan from the sheer, raw pleasure of it.

The amount of love in this room is incredible; it is thick and almost tangible. It is mind-blowing to me. I've never made love to any other woman before. It was always fucking in its most primal. It was never like this…so achingly sweet.

Until now.

With each stroke that I take, warmth swells in my chest until I feel I can't contain it. I clutch Mila to me gently, not wanting to release her even for a moment. And when I am finally throbbing into her, I wrap her in my arms and we stay enmeshed together for what seems like forever, sticky and wet.

"That was perfect," she tells me sleepily, her fingers playing with mine.

"*You're* perfect," I answer, closing my eyes. I don't even worry about the fact that it's a pussy thing to say. It's the truth.

Mila snuggles into my side and lays her head on my chest. Eventually her breathing grows rhythmic as she slips into sleep and I hover on the edge of drifting off myself.

My last conscious thought is that Mila did what she promised. She chased my nightmares away. It's because of her that I even went to see Dr. Tyler. If I hadn't, I never would have remembered what happened to my mother. And if I hadn't remembered that, I never would have fixed the hole in my heart.

I never would have been whole.

Mila did that.

I'll never tell her because she would just wave her hand and tell me that I'm the one who fixed things, that I put in the work. She never takes enough credit. So I'll just have to love her every day of her life as a thank you. It's enough that I know the truth.

And I'll never hide from the truth again.

It can't hurt me anymore.

Epilogue

Twelve Months Later

Mila

The letter that I hold in my hands is old and yellowed and precious. Tears blur my vision as I read it and I slowly wipe them away, careful not to smudge my makeup. I set it aside and look up at my sister.

"So much has happened this year," I say softly. Maddy nods in agreement.

"Yeah," she agrees with a laugh. "Who would have thought that I'd actually grow to love Pax?"

I roll my eyes. "How could you not? He's amazing. He's done everything that he promised he would."

And he did. True to his word, Pax continued to see Dr. Tyler. He put in so much work on changing the way he handles things and communicates that I couldn't be prouder of him, and our relationship couldn't be more healthy or whole. He's beautiful, inside and out. He completely gave up whiskey and drugs. The only thing he touches now is wine at dinner, with me.

"I can't believe he gave up Jack Daniels," Madison says wryly, shaking her head. "That blew me away. Especially when all of that legal stuff was going on with his mother's killer. It was so stressful. But he never even blinked. He didn't mess up once. I have to say, I'm impressed with him, Sis. Truly."

I nod absently, thinking about how hard that 'legal stuff' had been for Pax to deal with.

Leroy Ellison is the name of the mail man who violated Susanna Tate. DNA evidence proved it within a 99.900% level of accuracy and Pax identified him in a line-up, in addition to describing the snake tattoo on Leroy's hip.

Leroy is in jail now, awaiting trial. The Tate family attorneys don't expect the trial to last long, since the evidence is conclusive.

"And then, for his grandpa to turn up and try to make amends...Pax had so much pressure from every direction. I thought for sure he'd slip up. But he didn't," Madison says, staring at me.

I have to admit, I had been a little nervous too. When William Alexander had showed up at Pax's lake house and wanted to talk, I thought all kinds of shit was going to hit the fan. But he and Pax had taken a walk and talked through things.

And over the course of the past year, as Pax's head became clearer and less clouded by his past hurt, he had decided to take an interest in the family company. He will someday take it over when his grandfather dies.

In the meantime, he is working from a home-office at the lake. He is learning the business and has met with his grandfather several times.

In one of those meetings, his grandfather gave him an old box of letters, written from his mother to Pax, beginning with the day he was born.

Maddy nods toward the letter sitting beside me.

"What's the deal with that letter, anyway?"

"Apparently," I explain, "When Paul moved Pax to Chicago,

he left a bunch of Susanna's stuff in their old house. He just couldn't bring himself to throw it out. Pax's grandfather sorted through it for him and when he did, he found a box of letters in Susanna's closet.

"I guess, when she was pregnant, she got emotional and hormonal and had decided to start writing Pax letters for special occasions in his life, in case anything ever happened to her. Paul said he teased her about it, but she did it anyway. It turned out, her foresight was a good idea."

"Oh my god," Maddy breathes. "That gives me goose bumps. It's amazing."

I nod. "I know. William kept them for Pax all of these years."

"Why did Pax want me to bring you that one this morning?" Maddy asks curiously.

I flip it over and hold it up for her to see. She obviously hadn't looked at it when she carried it in to me.

The envelope is labeled, *For Pax on his wedding day.*

His wedding day is today.

Maddy's eyes widen. "Oh, wow. What does it say?"

My fingers shake as I read through the elegant writing once again, this time aloud for Madison. I struggle not to cry, because the words are just so beautiful.

To my beautiful son,

Looking at you now, as you toddle about my garden collecting caterpillars, I can't imagine a day when you will be grown, when you will be a man. I can't imagine a day when your tiny chubby hands will grow into big, slender ones like your father's and that you will be one day be big enough to find a woman that you love.

But I know that day will come, because days like that always do. You will be big and strong and beautiful and your wife will be lucky to have you. And you will be lucky to have her, too. Because anyone who captures your heart will be beautiful and amazing, as well. You will suit each other in every way. That is my hope for you.

If you're reading this, then I am not there with you. But I want you to know that my heart is there. My love is there. My love will always live on in you. And when you hold your children and your grandchildren, my love will pass through you to them, because love is never-ending. It goes on and on and on.

My beautiful son, I love you. I hope that your married life is full of wonder and laughter and love. You deserve all of that and more. Please know that I am very proud of the man you have become. I know that even now, even as you are still a boy. I know it because of the potential that I already see in your eyes.

Pax, don't be upset that I'm gone. I believe in heaven, in a wonderful place full of forgiveness and love, and because of that, I know that I will see you again someday. Until that day, may your wife keep you happy and safe and loved.

All my love,
Forever,
Your mother

My tears drip onto the fragile paper and I yank it away. I can't ruin this letter. It has to be put away and saved, so that our children can read it someday.

Love never fails.

It is a sentiment that has become a pledge for Pax and me. In fact, it is inscribed in our weddings rings that we will exchange today. And in this most perfect of letters, his mom has echoed that thought. His mother, the woman who gave her life to protect her son because she loved him that much.

And I do too.

I recognize that truth as I put the letter away and adjust my veil in the mirror. I love Pax more than life itself. Like his mother, I would protect him with my life. Wherever Susanna Tate is, I hope she knows that.

"Are you okay?" Madison asks quietly as I wipe away the little smudge under my eye. I nod.

"I'm fine. It's just beautiful. I hope that I live up to her expectations of me."

Madison smiles and adjusts my dress. "Of course you will. You're amazing, just like she said you would be."

Warmth wells up in me and as I'm hugging my sister, Tony sticks his head in the door. He's wearing a tux…to walk me down the aisle in lieu of my dad.

"Are you ready?" he asks as he holds out his elbow.

I nod and Madison kneels to gather my long, white train.

Of course I'm ready.

I've never been more ready.

As we position ourselves in the back of the church, the church that I have seen so many times in my dreams, I am filled with hope and boundless joy. This church that housed my parents' funeral is also hosting my wedding, illustrating once again that life is full of all kinds of good and bad. Pax and I have been through it all and we'll continue to go through it, because that's how life works.

I stare at Pax and suddenly, I am filled with peace. Like his mother before me, he *is* my peace now.

His eyes meet mine and he smiles, beautiful and radiant in the morning sunshine as he waits for me at the front. He's so handsome, so tall and strong, that it takes my breath away.

I take a breath.

The music starts.

Each step that I take brings me closer to him.

And when I finally get there, his fingers entwine with mine.

I look up into his eyes, eager to become his.

I repeat my vows after the minister and end with, "I will love you all of the days of my life."

And I know that I will.

Because true love never fails.

It never dies.

It just goes on and on and on.

Forever.

A Note from the Author

I wrote this book for a couple of reasons.

First, someone I love was using drugs to cope with life. He wasn't an addict, but like Pax, he was teetering on the edge. If he hadn't chosen to get help and learn to deal with stress in healthy ways, he would have continued on a dark, self-destructive path that would have ended in a very tragic way. I will be forever grateful that he chose to get help, that he recognized the need and put in the work to fix it.

Second, there was a news story years ago that has haunted me ever since I heard it. It was about a young mother, a child and an intruder. They were in the same position as Pax and his mother found themselves in this book, but somehow, the real-life mother and son managed to get away. I've thought about that story off and on over the years and recently, when my mind was wandering in the absent way a writer's does, I wondered what would have become of the boy if the intruder had killed his mom. I decided that he would have wanted to live in oblivion, where it was safe and warm. And Pax's story was born.

This story is really about a man teetering on the edge. He could have fallen either way, into the dark or into the light. And he chose to land on his feet in the light, even though the light is harder and it takes more work. My message through this book is for anyone who is in that same place, balancing on that precarious ledge. The light is always worth it, even though it's hard. Stay strong and live in the light.

The use of the verse, *Love never fails*, is something personal to me, as well. It is engraved on my wedding band, just as it is engraved on Pax's and Mila's.

My grandparents were married for sixty years. They were two of the wisest, gentlest, most amazing people I have ever been honored to know. And one of the things my grandma always told me was *Love never fails, honey. It never does.*

And you know what? She was right. True love never fails. It really does go on and on and on. The person might be gone, but the love remains.

Love is stronger than anything else. It can get you through things that nothing else can. So rely on it, lean on it. Embrace it. Count on it.

"Love is patient, love is kind. It does not envy or boast, it is not arrogant or rude. It does not insist on its own way, it is not irritable or resentful; it does not rejoice at wrongdoing, but rejoices in the truth. Love bears all things, believes all things, hopes all things, endures all things. Love never fails."

—1 Corinthians 13:4-8a

—Madison and Gabriel, *If You Leave*

Lastly, if you enjoyed this book, please stay tuned for book two in The Beautifully Broken series, *If You Leave*. It will follow

Madison Hill. As the older sister, she saw more of her parents' abusive relationship and it gave her trust issues that she carries even still.

* * *

"Is everyone in the world broken?" And even to my own ears, my whisper itself sounds broken in the velvety night. Gabriel stares at me thoughtfully.

"I think so," he finally answers. "In their own way."

Pax

I can barely keep my hands off of her. I don't care how tired we are or how long of a day today has been. I still want her. I know I should get used to that. I will always want her. That's a good thing, though, since we're married now.

"You're beautiful," I mumble tiredly into Mila's hair. She smells like lavender and vanilla and I breathe her in. She reaches up from where she is slumped against my chest and sleepily strokes my cheek, keeping her eyes closed.

"You just want in my pants," she answers, her voice soft and husky.

Even as beautiful as she is, the strains of the day are evident on her face. Exhaustion has set in and I wonder how long she has been up. I reach down and pull off her high heels, tossing them onto the floorboard of the limo.

"You're not wearing pants, Mrs. Tate," I point out. As I do, I run my hand up under the long skirt of her wedding gown and let it linger on the top of her thigh-high stocking. She snuggles into me, curling up like a kitten on my lap.

"I know," she answers. "It would have looked weird getting married in jeans. Although don't think I didn't consider it."

I chuckle and brush a loose strand of her hair away from her face.

Mila really is beautiful. Her dark hair is wound into a loose chignon at her neck, but the hectic pace of the day, particularly the dancing at the reception, has pulled some of it down. Her eye makeup is a bit smeared, her pink lipstick long gone... kissed away by me. But even as tired as she is, she is still lovely.

And mine.

"Do you want to take a nap on the way to Chicago?" I ask, tightening my arms around her. She turns in my arms, her wedding dress rustling as she opens her green eyes to look at me.

"No. I want you to tell me where we're going. It's not fair that the bride doesn't know where she's going for her honeymoon."

I laugh, a quiet sound in the dark. At the same time, I hit the button that closes the partition between us and the limo driver. The driver's eyes knowingly meet mine in the rearview mirror before the partition closes him off.

"You already know that we're staying the night in Chicago and then getting up early to fly out tomorrow," I remind her. "And you know what kind of clothing you needed to pack. What else is there to know?"

"Everything," she grumbles, sticking her bottom lip out. I resist the urge to laugh. Mila is hilarious when she tries to dramatically pout. She is the most laid-back girl I know which is one of the things I love about her.

Her eyes suddenly light up, which puts me instantly on edge.

"What?" I ask, eyeing her warily.

"I just had a fabulous idea," she answers, running her hand over my tuxedo shirt. "Fab-u-lous."

"Do tell," I roll my eyes. "I'm pretty sure I won't find it as fab-u-lous as you do."

She giggles, but lets her hand fall to my inner thigh, her fingers lightly stroking my leg. A surge of lust shoots through me, flooding my groin and instantly clouding my thoughts. It's pretty pathetic that her mere touch has that effect on me.

"Okay. I'm listening," I tell her, enjoying the way her fingers grasp at me.

"I thought you would," she answers smugly. "I have a deal for you. I want to try and guess where we're going. If I correctly guess something, you have to tell me. But as your reward, I'll do something *nice* for you."

As the word *nice* passes her lips, Mila runs her hand over my crotch, which of course makes my dick spring to life. Fuck. She's got me in the palm of her hand now.

Literally.

And she knows it.

"Fine," I answer between clenched teeth. "If you're sure you want to spoil your surprise. For such a sleepy girl, you certainly seemed to have woken up in a hurry."

"So did you," she answers laughingly. "Or part of you at least."

She squeezes my dick from outside of my pants, then drops her hand away.

I instantly want to feel her touch again. I lean into her, but she pulls her hand even further away, staring at me pointedly, waiting for me to agree to her terms.

"You're a mean little thing," I announce. "But fine. I'll play. Ask your first question."

She sits up in triumph, staring into my eyes.

"Is it cold there?"

"No," I answer immediately. "Now reward me for my honesty."

She giggles, but complies. She strips away my tuxedo jacket and unbuttons my shirt, shoving up my undershirt.

"I can never understand how you men wear so many shirts," she ponders as she traces a trail with her tongue from my waistband to my nipples. She runs a circle around one, then looks up at me as she pauses.

"Do I need my passport, or did you just ask me to bring it to throw me off?"

I smile. This one's easy.

"You need it."

She promptly pulls my nipple into her mouth, scraping it with her teeth as she rubs it to and fro in her mouth, working it with her tongue.

Sweet Hell.

The crotch of my pants instantly shrinks.

"You're a little vixen," I tell her as I stroke her back. Her skin is soft beneath my fingers. "Next question."

"Impatient, much?" she asks innocently as she pulls away from my chest. I shake my head.

"I can't believe I married such a mean-spirited wife," I tell her and she laughs.

"Fine. Next question. Is it London?"

"No," I answer immediately. "And since it's a wrong answer, I get to do something to *you*."

"Fine," she shrugs. "My married life is such a hardship." She giggles and I bend her backward, kissing the arch of her neck.

"Just give up," I whisper along her skin. "Keep it a surprise. I promise...you will like it."

I nibble at her ear and then envelop her lips with my own, plunging my tongue into her mouth. She kisses me back hotly, pulling me closer to her. I can feel her heartbeat, pounding hard against my chest. I immediately wish that we were skin to skin and I push my shirt off, reaching around Mila to unbutton the many buttons to her dress.

She pulls out of my grasp, her eyes slightly unfocused.

"Not happening, Tate," she tells me breathlessly. "First, there are far too many buttons on this dress. And second, I want to know where we're going. At least tell me one thing. And if you do…" her voice trails off, but her hand picks up where her words left off.

Her fingers deftly flick open the button of my pants and she buries her hand inside my underwear. "If you do, you'll be rewarded," she finishes.

Her fingers close around me, stroking lightly upward, hesitating at the top while she circles my tip, then stroking back down.

I can't breathe.

"Tell me," she whispers in my ear. "You know you want to."

She circles the tip of my dick again and I grit my teeth, my breath hung up in my throat.

"Tell me," she prompts.

Her fingers prompt me too and I can't take it. I want to rip off my pants and bury myself inside of her.

"France," I blurt out. "We're going to Paris."

She pauses and stares at me, her eyes widening and her fingers frozen.

"You're taking me to the Louvre," she says slowly as it dawns on her.

As an artist, Mila has always wanted to tour the Louvre. And when I was thinking of honeymoon destinations, places that would make her happiest, I knew there was no other place we could begin our honeymoon.

I nod. "Yes. That's where we're starting our trip. But I'm not telling you the second half."

She stares at me for a minute more before she throws her arms around my neck and squeezes the life out of me, squealing like a kid.

"Ohmygosh! You don't need to tell me anymore. Holy crap! I'm so excited. You know I've always wanted to go there. You are the. Best. Husband. Ever."

She kisses me and I kiss her back for just a moment, before I pull away.

"So, show me how good of a husband I am," I tell her with a wicked grin. "A deal is a deal, Mrs. Tate."

She grins back. "You're so right. My word is my bond."

Mila giggles as shoves me backward onto the seat and tugs my pants down to my knees before she grasps me within her fingers once again. I practically sigh aloud. The weight of her hand is a welcome relief to the throbbing in my dick.

She strokes me, all the while kissing the side of my neck. I grip her shoulders, enjoying the way she fits perfectly into my hands.

"I want some champagne," she whispers into my ear. I glance at her, surprised that she would take a break right now in the heat of things for a drink. But being the obedient husband that I am, I reach behind me for the open bottle, pouring a glass for my sexy new wife.

She takes it from my hand and gulps it, handing the glass back to me.

What she does next blows my mind.

She bends and takes me into her mouth before she swallows the champagne.

I gasp and clutch at the limo seat as the bubbles in her mouth erupt around the head of my dick.

"Holy shit," I gasp again. Mila looks up at me, her eyes gleaming as she holds the icy liquid in her mouth, keeping it in a pool around my penis. "Where did you learn to do that?" I finally manage to say.

Mila swallows the champagne, then grins…all the while keeping me in her mouth.

"It was just a hunch," she tells me impishly. "Did you like it?"

"Loved it," I tell her, but it's incredibly hard to speak because her warm mouth is heating my dick back up as she slides it in and out. "Although I might have married the devil. Did I sell my soul for you and not even realize it?"

She giggles. "No, your soul is safe and sound."

I yank her up and over me so that she is straddling my hips, her wedding dress billowing around us in a cascade of silky fabric.

"Kiss me," I tell her. "I want to taste myself in your mouth."

She obediently kisses me, her tongue plundering my own.

"You're the sexiest woman in the world," I tell her honestly, as I reach around under her dress and cup her bare ass.

I look at her in surprise. "You're not wearing panties."

She laughs, throwing her head back. I am completely dumbfounded by my sweet, yet wicked little wife.

"You got married with no panties on?"

Mila stares at me again, her gaze impish. "I was going to tell you when you kissed me at the altar, but you distracted me so I forgot."

I remember the deep kiss I had given her with satisfaction now. "You deserved that," I tell her. "Especially now. Holy shit. If Tony knew how much I have apparently rubbed off on you, he would break my kneecaps. And I like my kneecaps the way they are."

Mila laughs again, unconcerned.

"Tony likes you now," she tells me calmly as she once again buries her head in my neck. "But let's not talk about him now.

I'm sitting on you and I'm not wearing panties. Can't you think of something better to do than talk? We've got a marriage to consummate."

I feel like swallowing my tongue.

"You want to consummate our marriage in the back of a limo?" I ask her dubiously. "This is the way you want to remember our first time as a married couple?"

"You're still talking," she answers, staring at me. "And this is so *us*. Roaring down the open road with the moonroof open in the back of a limo. Come make me your wife, Pax."

She doesn't have to ask me twice.

My fingers find her most sensitive spot and discover that she is already wet. Very, very wet. I swallow hard, then lift her up, settling her back onto me, sliding her down my stiff shaft.

I groan and she mutes the sound by covering my lips with her own. She rocks to and fro on top of me, amid the sea of lace and white silk. I don't notice anything but the ungodly amount of pleasure.

"You feel so good," I moan against her neck. I tug the strapless top of her dress down and pull her breast into my mouth, enjoying the softness against my tongue, enjoying the way she stiffens in response.

"Pax," she murmurs. "I love you. Please…please…"

"What are you begging for, love?" I ask. Although I already know. I suck on her other nipple for a moment before I reach under her and rub her with my thumb as she moves, causing her eyes to squeeze shut and her breath to form in pants.

"That," she sighs. "That's what I want."

"I know," I tell her softly.

Within mere minutes, she comes on my fingers with a soft shudder. I close my eyes and enjoy the moment before I follow her with my own release. I throb into her, marveling at the thought that I am coming inside my wife. *My wife.* She is mine for the rest of our lives.

I hold her trembling body upright for just a moment before she collapses onto my chest, her dress still shoved down to her waist.

"I love you," she whispers, her lips pressed against my heart beat.

My gut clenches and I inhale sharply. This woman is too good to be true and every day of our lives, I'm going to remember how blessed I am.

"I love you too," I answer thickly, trying to swallow the hard lump that is suddenly lodged in my throat.

"We're officially husband and wife now," she points out, her eyes fluttering closed.

"Yep," I nod. "You can't get rid of me."

"Mmmhmm," Mila agrees as she drifts off to sleep. I hold her there, suspended against my chest until we cross the bridge into Chicago and the lights and noise from the city wake her.

"We're here already?" she asks as she sits up and tugs her dress back into place. I smile at her.

"You slept for most of the way."

"But not *all* the way," she adds, waggling her eyebrows. I grin again and hand her the high heels that I'd tossed onto the floor. "And I just needed a powernap. It's our wedding night, you know. There isn't going to be much sleeping."

"I certainly hope not," I tell her as the limo glides to the curb in front of our hotel. A valet opens our door and I help Mila from the car. She trips on the hem of her gown and I neatly catch her, then scoop her up into my arms.

"This will just be easier," I roll my eyes as she protests to put her down. "Trust me."

So, I carry her through the marbled hotel foyer, hold her while I check in and then in the elevator as we ride up thirty floors. We ignore the amused gazes of everyone around us as Mila buries her head in my neck.

"I think I'll let you carry me everywhere…for the rest of our lives," she tells me as I fumble to unlock our room.

"I think that will be good for my upper body strength," I chuckle. She swats at me as I put her down. "Kidding. You weigh like, five pounds."

Mila turns in a circle and stares at our suite. Champagne is on ice next to the lavish bed, roses fill every possible space and candlelight flickers from fifty white candles. There are rose petals on the bed which trail in a thick path to the bathtub. The red petals also float atop the steaming water.

"Holy shit," she breathes as she turns to me. "You arranged all of this?"

I grab her and pull her to me. "You sound surprised," I laugh. "I can be romantic. It's our wedding night. You should have flowers and candles. And I know you've got to be exhausted, so I arranged for a bath to be ready. The limo driver let them know when we were close."

She shakes her head. "You're amazing," she whispers as she stands on tiptoes to kiss me. "Seriously."

As she kisses me, she notices the little white box sitting next to her pillow. She pulls away mid-kiss to investigate.

"What's this?" she asks curiously as she picks it up. Without waiting for an answer, she opens it to find a silver necklace that I'd had designed especially for her. Two silver disks hang from a delicate chain. The top one reads LOVE and the larger bottom reads NEVER FAILS. A perfect pearl hangs just above. A tear slips from the corner of Mila's eye as she turns back to me.

"You're perfect. Do you realize that?"

"So I've been told," I answer drily as I lift the necklace from the box and fasten it around her neck. "I know you don't like gaudy jewelry. So I thought you might like this. It's simple and—"

"It's us," she interrupts. "It's exactly us. I love you, Pax. This is all so…perfect."

She wraps her arms around my neck again and I pull her to me. We stand entwined together in front of the balcony as the city lights shine in on us and Lake Michigan crashes against the shore below us.

Finally, I pull away and kiss her on the forehead. "Why don't you go take a bath before your water gets cold. I know you're tired."

She nods. "I am. But not *too* tired. When I get out, you'd better be ready, Mr. Tate."

I smirk. "I'm always ready."

She grins, wicked and sexy as hell. "And pop the cork on that champagne. I've got some ideas for it."

The breath catches in my throat as Mila turns on her heel and heads for the bathroom. I practically break my neck sprinting for the champagne. I pour her a glass and ponder what she could possibly have in mind now.

And that's one of the things I love most about my new wife. She never ceases to surprise me. Our life together is going to be amazing.

About the Author

Courtney Cole is a novelist who lives near Lake Michigan with her family and her pet iPad. Her favorite place in the world is on the shore with her toes in the water. If she's not there, you can find her wearing cashmere socks and staring dreamily out her office window. To learn more about her, visit her website: www .courtneycolewrites.com

See the Next Page for a Preview of

If You Leave,

Book 2 in the Beautifully Broken Series.

Chapter 1

The night air slaps me across the face as I step onto the wet asphalt of the alley behind the thumping club. Inside, wasted women mindlessly mash together in time to the pounding bass, waiting for guys like me to hit on them. But I don't care. I have to get some fresh air, something free from the claustrophobic smoke and sweat, before I fucking explode.

I inhale a long cleansing breath as I glance around. The narrow backstreet is littered by trash and graffiti, by shadows and inky blackness. If I was a normal person, I'd be nervous in a dark Chicago alley by myself. But the shit I saw in Afghanistan has rendered my ability to feel fear impotent.

But not the rest of me.

I shift my weight and adjust the boys and my semi-hard dick. I'd have to be inhuman to not be horny after watching the half-dressed drunk girls rub themselves on anyone who might buy them a drink. Normally, I wouldn't be caught dead with any of them. They're drunk and slutty, nothing I would usually mess with. But after being overseas for three years, my penis isn't listening to reason anymore.

I sigh against the constraining crotch of my jeans, before taking another deep breath, then another. My dick starts to calm down and my claustrophobic feelings begin to fade. Thank God. One of the strangest things I brought back from my tour abroad was claustrophobia, and it's not even the normal kind. It's the weird kind that can strike at the strangest times, like in the middle of a crowd.

Fuck it.

I pull out a cigarette and light up, yet another bad habit I brought back with me, along with a couple tattoos and the tendency to have nightmares.

"You know those will kill you, right?"

I startle to attention, my head snapping around to find the soft voice in the dark.

A woman steps closer and I can't believe that I didn't see her approach. Fucking hell. We're the only two people in an isolated alley. How could I have missed her? She's a tall, willowy bombshell. She's the kind of woman who stands out in a crowd, much less an abandoned street.

Blonde hair falls halfway down her back and wide eyes stare at me. Her full lips are pursed, as though she's trying to decide if it's safe to be out here. And it's not, especially for a woman who looks like she does.

"Don't you know walking alone in a dark Chicago alley is more dangerous than a cigarette?"

I gaze at her levelly as I take another drag on my smoke.

She doesn't look afraid at all as she shrugs.

"Either of those things has to be better than being crushed to death in there."

She gestures toward the closed club door in disdain as if she dislikes the entire atmosphere. I look at her again. She's wearing the right clothes to be here...tight pink leather pants, a cream-colored halter top, equally tight, and a pair of extremely high glittery heels. As I examine her, I notice that she's not wearing a bra under her light-colored shirt. Somehow that looks out of place on her, as though she doesn't fit the slutty clothes.

The problem is, the slutty clothes definitely fit *her*, in all the right places. My dick lurches back to life as my gaze skims over her curved hips and tight ass.

"In that case, want one?" I offer her the pack.

She looks surprised, then chuckles, shaking her head.

"No, thanks. I'm already in the alley alone. I think that's enough of a risk tonight."

I grin back as I tuck the smokes into my pocket. "But you're not alone now. I'm here."

She eyes me and I can see now that her eyes are blue.

"Somehow," she says thoughtfully, "I doubt I'm any safer."

I smile. "Somehow, I think you're right."

The funny thing is, she doesn't look worried. In fact, she steps closer and leans against the filthy brick wall beside me. Even under the yellowed dingy streetlight, she looks flawless.

"You're going to get dirty," I point out. She looks up at me innocently, her blue eyes wide.

"I like getting dirty sometimes."

And then she grins a wicked grin.

I feel like I've been sucker punched as all of the air whooshes out of my body. It's been far too long for me and a suggestive grin like that on this runway model is too much for my logical thought process to overcome. My good sense is apparently being hijacked by my hormones.

Tossing the smoke down on the sidewalk, I grind the heel of

my boot into it. I don't know what the fuck I'm doing, but I don't much care at this point. I'm horny and she's gorgeous. That's a perfect arrangement if I ever saw one. The air between us practically crackles with sexual attraction.

I look down at her and as I do, I let myself lean into her just a bit. She's soft and she smells even softer.

"I'm Gabriel."

"I'm Madison," she answers. She hasn't looked away from me even once. She's definitely into me, although God knows why. I'm as different from her as I can be.

"Why are you here, Madison?" I ask. "You seem a little out of place."

She actually looks self-conscious. "A friend talked me into coming. She thought I needed a night in the big city. But I really wish I was home instead. I'm tired and these heels hurt."

I smile. Her shoes do look painful as hell. I've never understood why women wear that shit.

"So you don't live here?"

She shakes her head and as she does, her scent seems to envelop us, blocking out the dirty city smells. Her nearness is intoxicating and I brace myself against it so that I don't get sucked into it too far.

"No. I'm from Angel Bay. It's on the coast, just an hour or so from here. But it seems like a world away. I'm not much of a big-city girl."

I actually wouldn't have guessed that. She's got that perfectly put together look that big city girls have, that perfectly confident attitude.

She nudges me, her slender shoulder bumping mine. "Why are you here? You don't look like you fit here, either. Not here at this club, anyway."

I cock an eyebrow. "Oh?"

The Underground is a trendy Chicago hotspot. And she's right. I don't fit in here. I fit in a HUMVEE in the hills of Afghanistan. Except, I don't. Not anymore.

Madison notices my expression and flushes.

"No offense. But you're not wearing skinny jeans and hipster glasses. You seem more like...the football playing type. Or the outdoors type, maybe."

I smile down at her. "No offense taken. And I *am* more of the outdoors type."

The gun-toting soldier type, to be exact, but I don't say that.

Madison looks relieved. "I thought so. So why have you come into the city? Or here to this club, for that matter?"

"What makes you think I don't live here? Can't I enjoy the outdoors but still live in the city? Or am I too uncool for that?" I raise my eyebrow again.

She flushes yet again. "I'm sorry. I guess I just assumed. Where do you live?"

I grin. "Here. I just wanted to see you blush."

She shakes her head and swats at me, but I easily catch her wrist and pull her to me instead. It's a ballsy move, but I'm feeling cocky. She doesn't resist, which both pleases me and surprises me.

She presses against me, looking into my eyes. She looks expectant and nervous; confident, yet hesitant. Her tits are smashed against me, making it hard to form cohesive thought, hard to examine our differences or even her motives. Her softness is the perfect contrast to my hardness. That's all I can think about. My gut clenches a bit.

"To answer your question, I'm here at the club because

my baby sister thought I should come out and meet someone. To quote her, I'm 'getting mean as hell and need a piece of
ass.'"

Madison laughs, a low and husky sound in the night.

"Do you? Need a piece of ass?"

She sounds anxious. And interested.

I hold her gaze.

"More than you can imagine."

I slide my hands from her back down to her ass, cupping it,
squeezing it.

"And I like yours," I add. I'm being cocky again, but she seems
to like it.

She practically purrs as she leans into me even closer, her nose
almost touching mine. Her lips hover so close that I can feel
them.

She slides her hands down to my ass, grabbing it with both
hands.

"Yours will do."

The air hangs heavy between us, charged and electric. Our
eyes are locked and we each pause, waiting for the other to make
a move.

The anticipation is killing me.

I take a breath.

Then she takes one.

Her lips graze mine and her mouth smells like mint. And
then before I can think another agonizing thought, she covers
my mouth with her own.

Finally.

Her tongue slips into my mouth and she tastes like Heaven,
like cotton candy at the end of a long day at the state fair or
crème brulee at a fancy restaurant. Our tongues tangle together

and her lips consume mine. My dick lurches back to life, shoving rigidly against her thighs.

She smiles against my lips.

"I think you liked that."

"What gave me away?" I ask with a grin, wedging myself even tighter against her.

Madison grins back and kisses me again. The second kiss is just as consuming as the first. She seems a little bit desperate, a little bit vulnerable. And a whole lot sexy.

She slides her hands back up my spine, wrapping her arms around my neck. As she does, I run my palms along her sides, feeling the skin of her back beneath my fingers.

"Remember when I told you that my feet hurt? I'd like to take my shoes off."

I stare down at her. "So take them off."

"At your place," she adds.

I inhale sharply as I grip her hips even tighter.

"You don't have to say that twice."

And she doesn't. . And even though Madison doesn't seem like the kind of girl who normally does this kind of thing, who am I to second-guess her?

I grab her hand and practically drag her toward the street, hailing a taxi.

In less than a minute, we have tumbled into a smelly backseat and are speeding toward my apartment.

Madison kisses my neck, nibbling at my ear as her hands skim my chest. "How far away do you live?"

"Not very," I manage to say. I'm actually proud of myself for being able to speak at this point, since her hand has made its way down to my throbbing crotch. I arch my hips so that I am planted more firmly in her hand.

She licks my neck.

"You smell good," she whispers.

I can't take it. I wish she was wearing a skirt, but she's not. So instead, I cup my hand between her legs, moving my thumb in circles on the outside of her pants. She thrusts against me, moaning a bit.

"Are you drunk?" I ask her. I don't know why, but it feels like the right thing to do, to make sure that she's not.

"No."

I don't ask twice. Instead, I lift her onto my lap and rock her against my body. The friction is both delicious and frustrating.

"When we get to my house, I'm going to fuck you," I tell her in her ear. "And you're going to like it."

She nibbles at my lip, her hips firmly planted against mine. "You're pretty sure of yourself, aren't you?"

I smile against her throat before I kiss it.

"Very sure. In fact, let's make a deal. If you end up screaming my name within the hour, I'll buy you breakfast in the morning."

She pauses, looking into my eyes. "Sounds like I win either way."

"You do," I manage to say before consuming her mouth again.

In between panting kisses, Madison manages to ask a question.

"How do I know you're not a crazy person?" She says on a near whisper.

"You don't," I answer, as I pull up her shirt and suck at her bare nipple. She arches against me and gasps. "But I won't hurt you... unless you're into that shit." I pause and look up at her. "We're just two people who are attracted to each other. And somehow, I get the feeling that you need this as much as I do. Am I right?"

Madison catches her breath and nods.

"I do."

I don't answer. I just wrap my arms around her slender shoulders and kiss her again. I am inhaling her scent, sucking it down, when I am startled by a squeal of tires from outside. Before I can even see where it's coming from, instinct raises the hair on the back of my neck. I shove Madison onto the floor of the taxi and duck down on top of her.

The impact is shockingly violent.

There is a crunch of shrieking metal as the door next to me is bashed in and our taxi is flung in a spin across the narrow city street, slamming to a stop against the wall of a nearby building. The car rocks to and fro for a moment, then it is still.

We are stunned as we sit for a scant second, trying to wrap our minds around what just happened. Steam and smoke begin to pour out from under the hood of the taxi and the driver stumbles from his seat, opening the door next to Madison.

"Quick, get out," he says in a heavy Indian accent. "Hurry."

I all but shove Madison out ahead of me and then pull her away from the crumpled car. There is a hissing sound coming from the engine, then a strange crackle. But I know what it means. I know from the acrid scent of gasoline that is stinging my nose.

"Move," I snap to Madison, and her heels click loudly on the pavement as we rush to the curb. We turn as we reach the sidewalk; just in time to see the front end of the cab burst into flames.

"Oh, my god," Madison breathes, leaning into my arm, shielding her face from the waves of heat that roll over us even from this distance.

As I watch the flames, as the heated breeze brushes across my face, I feel the now familiar anxiety coming on and my gut clenches tighter than a vice grip. I can feel my throat begin to close up as it prevents me from getting a full breath.

Fuck.

"I've got to get out of here," I mutter as my chest tightens. Sweat pours down my temples and I wipe at it, squinting as the salt stings my eyes. Madison stares up at me, her eyes filled with concern.

"Are you okay?" she asks, her fingers curled tightly around my arm. "I'm sure we have to stay. The police will want to talk to us."

She gestures toward the crowd forming, to where cop cars have already begun to congregate. I can see uniformed officers milling about, a couple of them headed our way. Heat from the fire and from my own anxiety begins to overwhelm me.

"I've got to get out of here," I mutter again. Her fingers are too tight now, along with everything else...my shirt, my waistband, my shoes. Everything bears down on me in blurs and smells and sounds. I can't take it. I'm going to fucking explode. Or implode. I yank my arm from her grasp and stalk away.

The last thing I remember seeing is the astonished look on Madison's face backlit by the red and orange glow of the taxi fire.

I wake up in a cold sweat four hours later.

I'm not sure where I am.

This isn't unusual, so I force my breathing to slow, to regulate, to gain my bearings.

I glance around, at the gray walls of my stark bedroom, at the white ceiling, at the familiar ceiling fan with the blades that look like large leaves.

I'm in my apartment. In my bed.

I just don't know how I fucking got here.

My hands are shaky as I reach for the glass of water on my bed-stand, swirling the water inside the glass as I force myself to calm, as I remember more about where I am, as I try *not* to remember the nightmare that woke me. I take a gulp and force the blurs of reds and blacks out of my head, even though I know from experience they are unwilling to go.

Darkness and blood.

These are two things that will apparently always haunt me. I doubt I will ever get a full night's rest, or that I will ever feel comfortable in the dark again.

I slump against the pillows, then startle as I remember Madison.

The beautiful girl from the club.

We were on our way here when we were in a car accident. I hold up my hands and look at them, barely able to see them in the dim light streaming through the window. I seem to be fine, nothing on my body hurts. We weren't injured.

But I had left her standing there at the scene of the accident. I have no idea how I got here, no idea how I made it home. Everything in between the accident and the stricken shocked look on Madison's face, and the present moment is a black voidAll I know for sure is that I am alone now.

I had left Madison there, standing next to the twisted, burning wreck of our taxi.

I'm not sure if I'm ashamed of myself or relieved. She was pretty fucking amazing. And pretty fucking hot. But there's no way she should get mixed up with someone like me, even for only one night. If I even *can* be with a woman for a night. I've tried and failed a couple of times since I've come home, even though there's nothing physically wrong with me. So it's for the best that I left her on the street. I'm not ready to meet anyone. I might look normal, but I'm far from it.

I think back to Madison's question in the cab.

How do I know you're not crazy?

I almost smile grimly in the dark.

I'm not crazy...exactly. The Army doctors say I just need time. They call it PTSD. Post traumatic stress disorder. I call it something else entirely: Fucked up.